As Hammers Fall

As Hammers Fall

Mark Svendsen

Published by Tablo

Brisbane 1917

I need not fear my enemies, the most they can do is attack me.
I need not fear my friends, the most they can do is betray me.
But I have much to fear from people who are indifferent.

Russian proverb

Our Joseph Hill

Australia Will Be There
The Commonwealth of Australia,
Is a link in the Empire chain,
Which has been sorely tested,
And stoutly stood the strain,
Its wide open spaces,
Will give a welcome true,
To all who come and settle,
With friends both old and new.
Rally round the banner of your country,
Take the field with brothers o'er the foam
On land or sea, where-ever you be,
Keep your eye on Liberty,
But England, home and beauty
Have no cause to fear;
Should auld acquaintance be forgot?
No! No! No! No! No! Australia will be there,
Australia will be there.
"Skipper" W. W. Francis

Extract from the diary of Joseph Hill
Somewhere in Brisbane (not France. Ha ha!)
March 1917

Dear Comrade,
'Some days change the world,' Segeyev says. He is right. Today was one
of those days. You should have seen us, Comrade. You should have heard my
speech! Let's just say that today is a new beginning for Yours Truly. What's

changed you ask … I have … because I did something. Something they'll write about in the papers tomorrow with me right up in the headlines:

JOSEPH HILL SPREADS SOCIALIST CONTAGION!

Yes, you're right Comrade, I need to stop my self-congratulations and draw the picture properly for you don't I?

Molly, Mick and I, and some other Peace Army kids, spent the morning at Trades Hall – cutting, stitching and painting a big banner and making ribbon rosettes – red for Socialist, green for Sinn Fein and white for Peace. All good fun. The afternoon was hot.

Mother suggested we join Miss Thorpe, Mrs Griffiths and the other Women's Peace Army ladies for lunch in the Botanical Gardens – they had corned beef sandwiches, scones and pineapple cordial. The little ones were keen as mustard! I admit, the scones were very tasty.

After a quick lunch we pulled up stumps ready to head off to the march. Miss Thorpe had suggested we take our banner along with us, just to be sure, and sure enough, by the time the young'uns had finished eating, and we'd dodged a downpour, the march had begun without us. We did get to give our banner a showing though, when we met up with the parade at the end of Queen Street. Dad scowled at me for having missed the start – mainly because the Children's Peace Army banner was supposed to be leading. You know how cranky he gets when his best-laid plans go awry. We did manage to be at the front most of the way down to the Domain.

You should have seen us, Comrade! What a rowdy commitment we made. A milling ocean of red-raggers and pacifists and conscientious objectors all demanding an end to any talk of Conscription. What a noise we made too from under our sea of parasols and hats and flags, placards and banners. We raised the city from its Sunday slumbers, to be sure – as dear Molly would say. Leading that march made me so proud. It was right that I should lead because I was right to demand peace for all the children, in all the nations of the world. I was right to … but I do get carried away. Back to the story, Joe Hill!

I was shaking like a leaf inside as we marched.

I looked back up the street for reassurance. You should have seen them, Comrade. Being with them gives me goosebumps every time. One commitment of free men and women, with scarlet flags floating blood-red above them. They looked like the flags of a galleon from my old "Boy's Own" adventure stories. A peace armada in full sail, streaming past the purple and red bougainvillea on the fences, and all singing, singing, singing. We sang The Red Flag. Everybody cheered so loudly when we finished. Then Dad called up to the onlookers on the verandahs of the Bellevue Hotel,

'Join the Socialist March to Peace!'

One old squatter from a top floor balcony yelled down,

'You Socialists believe in Karl Marx? That's a bloody German name!' Before the squatter's smirk had a chance to fade, Dad responded,

'Marx is a German? Crikey, you had me worried, cobber! Thank Christ he's not the Kaiser's cousin or we'd call him the bloody King!'

The Russian, Segeyev, catcalled,

'King! Kaiser! Csar! We know who your cousins are!' Everyone took up the cry. The squatter retired, with a final dig,

'To hell with you and your Russian kikes, Kamerade!'

But Dad just laughed at him, like he does.

'Don't worry about that bloke,' he said to the Russians, 'his nose is too close to his arse. Everything smells like shit to him!' Segeyev laughed but Madorsky growled. That Madorsky's always looking for a stoush, Comrade.

Mick took the mick out of the Government agents in the crowd by mimicking them. He held an imaginary notebook out at arm's length and bunged on a weaselly voice like Prime Minister, Billy Hughes'.

'These notes will be assessed for "seditious content, or intent" under the War Precautions Act. Anyone found guilty will be sent to Canberra for a term of three years – to be served locked in a sheep paddock.' The faces he pulled along with it were the very picture. Molly was laughing and laughing and the "black devils" all went red as the flag. I wish I could think of funny things to say to make her laugh but I must stop thinking such thoughts. She's Mick's girl and that's that.

Comrade, you should have seen the placards and signs and banners. Ours had "Children's Peace Army" on a huge bit of calico Mrs Griffiths said she'd been keeping just for us. The words were surrounded by fabric flowers and peace doves the young 'uns made. We'd stuck a couple of Trades Hall broom handles in either end. Molly held one and I held the other. She looked so proud.

Then the Women's Peace Army women showed their placards.

"Death to Conscription",

"Don't Fight This Filthy Bosses' War"

"Thou Shalt Not Kill"

And an old one from the first Anti-Conscription rally,

"I Won't Support The Blood Vote".

Miss Thorpe reckons that they, the ladies, have marched together so many times they're better at it than the soldiers. I told her she had to be good at marching to be in the Peace "Army". She thought that was funny and pulled my hat down over my nose.

The ladies' ankle-boots tapped the hard road like a Morse code warning – We … Vote … Vote … Vote! I tell you what, Comrade, I'd think twice if I saw that lot coming down the street at me!

I was still nervous but it felt good to be among my people – some of them especially. You know exactly who I mean by that, Comrade.

Chapter 1

The Red Flag
The people's flag is deepest red,
It shrouded oft our martyred dead;
And ere their limbs grew stiff or cold,
Their heart's blood dyed its every fold.
Then raise the scarlet banner high!
Within its shade we'll live and die.
Though cowards flinch and traitors sneer,
We'll keep the red flag flying here.
Ralph Chaplin

The marchers swam through humidity after days of rain. The last shower passed away only the minute before they began and now it steamed back up from the mud-churned footpath. Before them to the east, the khaki river crawled away, mud-swollen with storm rain, away from Brisbane, away from politics and war. For a sliver of a moment, Joe Hill wished he was going with it, or that he could evaporate with the steamy vapour and vanish. Unsure, he felt. Uncertain, unsteady.

'A penny for your thoughts, Joe.' Molly called from the other end of the Children's Peace Army banner.

'A penny?' Mick Doyle laughed sarcastically, thumping Joe in the arm. 'You'd be paying double what any of them are worth!'

Joe Hill was startled from his reverie and thumped Mick back. Mick bristled, like he always did when someone gave him a touch-up, even in fun, then laughed because they were mates.

Joe winked at Molly and answered,

'Just dunno how I'm going to go, that's all.' He coughed nervously. Mick answered for both Molly and himself,

'Cobber, you got a gob full of the biggest words in the dictionary,' he added, 'you'll go as good as a cold beer on a hot day.' Mick grinned his encouragement.

Joe wasn't sure but he knew this much was true – Peace and Universal Brotherhood through non-violent action were the two greatest goals Mankind strove to achieve. Joe gripped tighter to the broom handle in his hands, hoisting it unintentionally. He dropped it down again just as quickly when somebody hit him in the exposed side of his ribcage,

'Help! I've been robbed!' A wild, wide-eyed face appeared no more than a hand's width away from his.

'You bloody galah!' Joe burst out.

Tomfool recoiled like a frightened pup, unsure of what he'd done wrong. Joe felt ashamed at his temper.

'Let's save it for later hey, Tomas?' he suggested. Taking no notice of Tomfool's plea for help, Joe patted him reassuringly on the shoulder.

'Besides, you'll get nowhere with this lot, cobber,' Mick agreed, adding a second calming voice to quell the young man's agitation. He nodded back over his shoulder to the marchers behind them.

'They all know what your game is, mate.' The Peace Army children were bumping into them. It was Molly who started them again.

'We'll be playing the game later for sure, Tomas,' she said taking Tomfool's hand and leading him and the marchers onwards.

'I promise we'll play, directly Joe has made his speech and shown the world.'

Molly Pearce gave Joe a look of pride and hope that would shine until the end of time.

'We'll see if Joe Hill makes a seditious speech!' Tomfool said, hunching his shoulders like a murderer in a music hall melodrama. 'Then we'll lock the damn-fool red-ragger up and throw away the key!' They all turned straight to Tom.

'Who said that to you, Tomas?' Mick asked, almost nonchalant, so Tomfool didn't guess it was important and act the ninny.

'The man with the broken tooth,' Tomfool answered. No one bothered to look around, half the men in the crowd had been in street fights, or at war, or kicked by horses, or played cricket or hockey or boxed. It was unbroken teeth that were at a premium.

'Can you see him?' Mick prodded. Tomas looked above the crowd.

'Yes. I can see him. I can, but you can't.'

Molly recognised Tomfool's tone.

'Now, Tomas,' she said. 'Don't you be letting those other boys see where he is!' She tilted her head coquettishly and a tress of hair fell across her face. Joe knew he would remember that tress forever, draped across her eye as she spoke sidelong.

'But you'll tell me. Won't you, Tomas Madorsky? It'll be our secret.' They all loved Molly better than breathing with that look in her eyes.

'Whisper to me, Tomas.'

Which he did, of course. Molly passed the description to Mick. He craned his neck until he could see.

'Never seen him before,' Mick said. 'The bloke loafing by the streetlight with a head like a boarding house puddin'.' He nodded without pointing.

Joe took a look.

'Don't know him either.'

Molly shook her head.

'You go on,' Mick said, 'I'll tell Ted.' He handed the banner to Molly and darted back to look for Joe's old man.

'We'll see if Joe Hill makes a seditious speech!' Tomfool repeated, voice conspiratorial.

'And we won't be surprised if that bloke gets a kicking soon,' Joe muttered, oblivious to the irony of such a thought from the leader of the Children's Peace Army.

'What are you all whispering about?' one of the Army children asked them.

'Look! We'll almost be there next, so someone has to go and prepare things for Joe's speech. We're just deciding who,' Molly fibbed. Then she began to sing, waving like a conductor to the crowd behind her, 'The people's flag is deepest red.'

'Molly, dear!' a quiet voice broke through the singing. Molly glanced down to the edge of the cobbled gutter. Obviously affected by the heat, Miss Thorpe sat with her head hung down between her skirts looking for all the world like a pile of dirty washing. Kathleen O'Donahue sat beside her fanning her hard with a folding lace fan as she mopped Miss Thorpe's brow with a handkerchief.

'Be a dear, Molly and run over to the pub and ask the barmaid for some cold melt water for Miss Thorpe. It's hotter than the inside of a hospital laundry.' Molly handed her banner pole to another marcher and ran, calling over her shoulder to Joe.

'I'll catch you up soon!' holding her hat in her haste. Tomfool made to follow but Joe held him back.

'Strike, Mum! Your revolution'll be spent making sure there's no stragglers and everyone's fed and feeling all right,' he said, even though he knew he sounded just like his father.

'That is the *all* of the Revolution, Joseph Hill and don't you forget it,' Kathleen answered hotly, forgetting momentarily that her son was not his father.

'Joe!' her voice came again, gentler now, but still loud enough to carry above the motley of voices up and down the street.

'Yes, Mother,' he replied.

'Don't worry. Molly and I'll be along directly. We wouldn't miss your speech for quids. I'll be right in the front row.' Then she smiled at him and, for just a moment, Joe thought he might be able to get through the next hour – Joe Hill's finest – he hoped. He smiled back at her and the crowd cheered. He knew the cheer wasn't for him but he was happy to let himself feel as though it was.

'Get on with you, then! You're holding everyone up,' Kathleen called. Joe attached Tomas to one end of the banner and together they marched back to the front of the Children's Peace Army contingent.

'Go on yourself,' a partially revived Miss Thorpe half-smiled, pale with heatstroke, though warm with gratitude for Kathleen O'Donahue's care.

'And leave my Sister in the gutter? Never,' she answered. 'Look, here's Molly with the water. Thank you, dear,' she said.

Dousing a handkerchief in the enamel pannikin, she applied the ice-cold water expertly to the back of Miss Thorpe's neck.

'I'll be off then?' Molly half-asked with an anxious look.

'Yes, dear, you go,' Kathleen answered, squeezing Molly's hand in thanks. 'I'll return the mug and, Molly, thanks already from my son. You're a good friend.' Molly could feel the redness invade her neck at the look on the face of Mrs O'Donahue. The older woman saw straight into her. Molly turned away quickly from those all-knowing eyes and hurried back to meet the boys under their banner. As she went she sang that old coquette's song beneath her breath,

'I know where I'm goin',

And I know who's goin' with me.

I know who my love is …

But I don't know who I'll marry!'

Chapter 2

Go To The War, Toiler
War is in Europe toiler, blasting the land;
Workers facing workers, rifles in hand;
Masters have quarrelled, toiler: hear their cannons roar,
Slaying slaves in millions, toiler; go to the war!
Chorus: Go to the war toiler, go to the war;
Heed not the Socialists, but wallow in gore.
Save not your helpless children, care for them no more;
Leave your wife and family and go to the war!
Heed not the sixth commandment, 'Thou shall not kill',
Flout Christ like jingo parsons do, say, 'Yes I will!'
Kill starving children's fathers; fill them with lead.
Cheer up, lad; don't be downhearted, you'll soon be dead!
William Robert Winspear. To tune of 'Click Go The Shears'.

A walloping big red flag and the flags of Australia and the Irish Republic hung from opposite sides of the rotunda, limp as warm lettuce leaves in the stifling air. Artem Segeyev glanced down at the upturned faces gathered around the Domain rotunda.

'In conclusion, Comrades,' he shouted across the assembled hundreds. 'Governments serve one class and one class only – Capitalists.'

'We need to stop Conscription!' an interjector called. The crowd murmured agreement but Segeyev was not to be deterred.

'As soon as any politician, Tory or Socialist, comes into power they become an honorary member of the Capitalist class and an enemy of the people. The working class must take the reins of power. Only then will we have a true dictatorship of the proletariat.'

Ted Hill had had enough of Segeyev too.

'Put the kid on!' he called from the centre of the crowd. 'We've heard you on Socialism a thousand times. Today's about the next Conscription vote.'

Sitting in the rotunda behind the Russian, Joe Hill studied the faces in the crowd. They looked ready to crucify him! Joe worked his tongue in his mouth trying to keep it moist. The palms of his hands were sweating. He rubbed them on his pant legs.

But Segeyev returned to his theme.

'As Socialists we have won some concessions here at home. The eight hour day, meal breaks, a basic living wage, an industrial commission to hear our disputes, one week's holiday a year. We win the battles, Comrades, but we do not win this war!' he bellowed. Passion filled his voice until the air vibrated with it. Segeyev's revolution-black hair fell across his eyes.

'We will not beg like whining dogs for crumbs from the table of our masters. We must rise up and take power – by force if necessary! Only then will we stop this war!' he bellowed, his voice like a pile-driver ramming the point home. At last the crowd cheered.

'Soldiers of the world unite!' Segeyev thundered. 'You have nothing to lose but your chains!'

The crowd went wild. Scuffles broke out. The Peace Army Children huddled close to Molly and Mick and Miss Thorpe at the back of the rotunda.

Mrs Griffiths walked forward to stand beside Segeyev and raised her hand for silence. The fraças died down, though several angry voices could still be heard.

'Ladies and Gentleman,' she said loudly. 'Please join me in thanking Mr Segeyev of the Union of Russian Workers for his stirring speech.'

'Go home, Bolshevik!' was the loudest response amongst more general applause. Segeyev waved a clenched fist to the crowd, before retreating to sit beside Joe.

'Ready, Comrade?' he asked. His dark eyes still smouldered with righteous zeal. Joe nodded and again tried to swallow as he rearranged his notes. At least the crowd had turned a bit more positive.

Joe jumped at the unexpected touch of Molly's hand on his forearm. It was cool, her hand, cool and soft and calming. He turned, she smiled and …

Oh Gawd and little fishes!

Over her shoulder Joe caught sight of Mick, who nodded coldly at him. Joe jumped to his feet. Whatever composure he had mustered dissolved at her smile and Mick's jealous look. He had to steady himself. This was no soapbox on some street corner. This was the proper business.

Mrs Griffiths was already introducing him. Joe could sense them both behind him. He couldn't speak with them there. She'd hit him for six and he knew Mick was angry with him because of it. What could he do with the two of them? Joe gnawed his bottom lip so hard the blood almost came. Sweat dribbled down the back of his neck. Some of the Comrades, including his father, were already talking about him as a future leader. Joe Hill, Light-horseman to the Socialist cause, sweeping all before him to claim the Republic of the Australian Proletariat! He winced at the pressure the thought produced. If only they knew, Joe Hill only wanted peace: politics, Socialism, everyday fairness, were merely means to that end. Peace … and that'd do for now.

Mrs Griffiths finished her introduction. The crowd clapped. Joseph Hill stood alone.

'Tell them what we stand for!' Molly whispered at his back.

Joe gazed out, transfixed for a moment by the expectant faces that gazed back.

'Tell them like you tell us! Make them understand,' Molly urged.

Joe swallowed. He clenched his notes hard. Saying anything would be a start! He swayed like a flagpole in a stiff breeze. Joe opened his mouth, but no words came. A hand pushed him in the back causing his mouth to snap shut.

'Tell them, Joey, or by the devil, I will!' Molly hissed. The crowd's sympathy waned.

'Can he talk at all, Missus Chairman? Or is he mute on the subject of Conscription?' a heckler called. The Comrades in the crowd growled him down. But even the most supportive of them was growing restless. Joe could see his father and mother frowning up from the front ranks.

'Come on, son!' Ted Hill said. 'Give 'em curry!'

Molly took a step forward, twisting free of Mick, who gave up trying to hold her back.

'He's got something to say for sure you stupid man,' she shouted, 'about Kaiser Wilhelm and all his kind! Those shameful parasites in the royal families of Europe and their family squabbles! Millions dead because of them!'

A few weak cries,

'Disloyal!' and

'Saboteur!' greeted her remark amid 'Hurrah's' from the Socialists. But Molly wasn't finished,

'Disloyal am I? So you support the English murdering the Irish Martyrs for declaring a free Republic in their own land? That's loyalty to your own is it? That's …' But Mick would have no more. He stepped up and dragged her back. She glared, shaking her open hands, first at the hecklers, then at Joe. He shot her a despairing look.

Then, high above the crowd's head, a hat was hoisted on a walking stick. Everyone knew it was Monty Miller's, around it the red pugaree he'd first worn on the Eureka Stockade. His voice followed it on high,

'I'm with you, lad! Give us Peace and be blowed with politicians!'

The crowd gave him a loud,

'Hooray!' Calls of, 'That's the spirit!' echoed around the Domain.

Kathleen O'Donahue saw the uncertainty on the face of her son. So, while the crowd were still at sixes and sevens, she burst into the song they'd sung so often to beat the last Conscription Referendum. She gave them *Go to The War, Toiler* – full bore. The crowd joined her, ringing closer around the podium. The rowdies and detractors were drowned out when they tried to start up their own *Rule Britannia* and *God Save the King*.

'Decide now, Joseph Hill, if we have something worth saying!' Segeyev urged from behind him.

Oh to be Segeyev – to have his passionate eyes, his revolutionary hair and his mesmerizing, stentorian voice.

Before the last note died in the throats of the singers Joseph Hill turned to them, his face afire with savage indignation. Clenching his fist around his notes, he punched the sky,

'Comrades!' he bellowed, his voice cracking with the strain. The crowd cheered once more. 'Comrades!' he cried again, egging them on. 'We want Peace! We demand Peace, now! And an end to any more talk of Conscription!'

At last his voice had come.

'Comrades! We, the Executive of the Children's Peace Army want two things,' Joe continued, half-turning to acknowledge Mick and Molly and the children behind. 'We add our voices to the tumult of dissent from around the world – Socialists, churchmen, Pacifists, people of good conscience all – to demand an end to this bloody Capitalist war! And we, the Children's Peace Army, demand the Commonwealth Government repeal its legislation to hold this second Referendum on Conscription. It is immoral. It is unnecessary. And-it-is-wrong!'

From the corner of his eye Joe saw the black devils scribbling away in their notebooks to send off to their Commonwealth masters in Melbourne. He had just the thing for them.

'Fellow-workers, the ruling classes must be held to account. War is when governments coerce us into believing that murder is right and to commit it is to do good. To compel more young men to die, beyond those brave souls who have already volunteered to do so, is a tax on our Nation conjured by the very Devil himself. Conscription is a blood tax. A blood tax, nothing more!'

Joe looked down to the field of faces shining like ploughed soil waiting to receive the grain. The reporters scribbled on.

'Billy Hughes, the Prime Minister of this great nation of ours, already has blood on his hands! The blood of our brother-workers! Not content with that, he now wants to be able to conscript young men to send to Europe to fight for the Empire.' He stared defiantly down at the nearest government agent.

'But he has been directed! He has been told! No! He has been commanded by the first referendum of the people on this matter – we said NO then, we say NO now to conscripting the youth of our nation to his war!'

The crowd cascaded his vitriol.

'Hughes the rat!'

'Turncoat!'

'Down with Hughes!'

'Even after he lost the referendum, or should I say,' Joe corrected himself, 'even after we won it.' He saw his father smile broadly up at that, smiled and tapped his finger down hard on the notebook of the reporter standing beside him, dislodging his pencil into the mud.

'This misbegotten politician still bathes in the blood of your children, your sons, fathers, uncles and brothers.' Joe lowered his voice to a stage whisper and pointed at the youngest Peace Army children for the effect.

'This government must be stopped! Let's conscript all politicians to go to the war!'

The audience broke into factions at this final remark, some baying for Hughes' blood and some for Joseph Hill's.

'How much more of this slaughter? Will we all simply fall silent? We will never be so timid a people! Never! Speak, Comrades! We must speak or we acquiesce! Damn the talk of another Conscription Referendum! Damn William Morris Hughes! We will redouble our voices and – Vote No!'

The crowd cheered anew. Joe shuffled his notes.

A tomato, rotten by the stench of it, careened past Joe's nose. Tomfool stretched out a huge hand to catch it in a spray of splattered juice. Joe glanced around quickly, reading the surprise on Molly's face and the grin from Tomfool, he turned back to his crowd. Zuzenko and Madorsky, began to shoulder their way through the mob to the point from which the projectile seemed to come. Tomfool took aim and hurled the remaining mush in the Peace Army children's direction. They giggled, skittering out of the way. Mrs Griffiths stood to move forward and take control of the meeting.

'It's bleeding!' Tomfool laughed with joy. 'Billy Hughes has blood on his hands!'

Segeyev's hand clapped down on Joe's shoulder,

'You have alarmed the Capitalist lapdogs. You must be saying something right, Comrade!' Joe thought quick.

'Tomatoes remind us all of the life-blood that is spilled daily!' he ad libbed weakly, raising his voice and arms above his head. A bit of movement often worked.

'We will agitate until this madness is done!' Joe continued. 'We will educate, agitate and organise!' he thundered, enunciating his words, 'And-we-will-win!'

But the crowd's attention was gone.

Joe turned to Mrs Griffiths.

'A song maybe?' he asked, lost.

'Go on, Joe!' Molly urged. His father looked at his feet.

Segeyev pulled out a pea-whistle and blew – hard and long. At its ghoulish shriek, the crowd cast about to see if the coppers were coming.

'Comrades!' Joe leapt to the moment. 'Young men, some no older than myself, are daily being sent home from the front maimed in body and mind. They should be here beside us, living in peace and prospering by their honest toil. Bring the living home. Bring them home … right now!'

'This is sedition!' screamed one of the agitators. 'Treason!'

'Mrs Chairwoman, does this rabble hold a permit for this assembly?' a voice demanded.

Before she could answer, a hail of heavy road gravel peppered the stage and the roof of the rotunda. Joe and the official party all winced away. Some of the children behind the rotunda screamed. The gravel was jagged and hit hard. Molly threw up her hands to cover her face. In one movement Mrs Griffiths turned her back, lowered her hat for cover and grabbed Molly.

It was too late for talking, but this was Joe Hill's crowd.

'Peace!' he yelled, his elbow thrown up before his face. 'Comrades! Only peace will endure!' Then he turned, running after Molly and Mick as another shower of rocks stung their backs and legs.

'Quick!' Segeyev commanded. 'Out the fence!' They ran down the wooden rotunda stairs, gravel rattling around them, biting where it hit.

Only Tomfool stood still, amazed, howling like a dog.

'I've been robbed!' he yelled.

'Joe! Mick!' Molly screamed as she ran back into the hail of stones to bring him with them. Tomfool stood bewildered, shoulders hunched, hands protecting his head. Joe dashed to Molly's side.

'Not now, Tom!' he yelled urgently dragging at his friend's arms. But Tomfool stood firm. He took his hand down, gazing at it. His fingers were stained from both the tomato and a gash to his head.

'Billy Hughes has blood on his hands,' he said staring first at his hand then at Molly and Joe, pleading for meaning. Real blood began to drip down his face. Molly produced a handkerchief from somewhere and held it to his wound.

Over his shoulder Joe could see Madorsky leading a mob of unionists, all bellowing like enraged bulls, as they surged through the crowd towards the offenders. Although he couldn't see his father, Joe could hear him screaming,

'Don't hit 'em! Wait till it matters! Pick a fight we need to win!'

'I've been robbed,' Tomfool repeated over and again. They dragged on his shirt sleeves.

'Come on, you idiot,' Joe yelled. Molly darted a fierce glance at Joe, but spoke urgently to Tomfool.

'We'll play later, Tomas,' she whispered. 'Come on,' she cajoled. 'Let's be getting home now. Cake for afternoon tea.'

Tomfool followed her then, the idea of cake convincing him. He scowled at Joe for his trouble.

Segeyev urged them from behind, herding them forward like a cattle dog at their heels,

'Go! Quick!'

'Molly!' Joe called as they reached the bottom. 'I didn't mean … about Tom.'

'I know,' she said, forgiving him in a breath.

'Are you all right?' Joe asked her. But there was no response as Kathleen and Mrs Griffiths and Miss Thorpe and a whole gaggle of women swarmed around her and the children.

'The stupidity of violent men!' his mother raged as she wiped at Joe's face, her hands efficient with the handkerchief she'd whipped from his pocket.

'As if there isn't enough violence in the world.' He took the cloth from his mother with a press to her hand. She nodded at him, so intense a look of fierce pride as he'd never seen shining from her eyes.

'You're all right. Nothing serious. Now you go straight home and stay there. Your father and I'll be back for tea before tonight's meeting. You get Molly and Tommy home safe.' Joe nodded.

He caught sight of Molly held between Mrs Griffiths and Miss Thorpe. Mick was there too. Joe pushed his way over to her.

'Are you hurt?' he asked, expecting maybe blood or, imagining the worst, a cut on her perfect face. Before he could look Segeyev's voice brought him back to the present.

'You must go!' he commanded. They could hear the Loyalists thumping up the front stairs of the wooden rotunda. The Socialist crowd surged behind them, forcing them to follow the Peace Army kids.

Segeyev stood beside him. His finger traced the faint blood track down Joe's cheek,

'"Their heart's blood dyed its every fold!"' he said nodding his head almost imperceptibly. Then he turned towards the Loyalists who were heading down the back stairs.

'Halt!' he bellowed. The sound of his voice stopped them for a moment, but even Segeyev couldn't hold them for long. At last Joe could hear real police whistles in the street.

'We'd best leg it or they'll arrest us!' Joe grasped Molly's arm dragging her with him. Her touch was electric. 'Hurry or we'll have to swim the river!'

'Between the devil's and the deep blue sea,' Molly laughed, unrestrained and loud.

'Go home!' Kathleen's voice counselled good sense above the tumult. 'The little ones will be safe with us once you've made yourselves scarce.' Joe nodded.

'Mick, Tomas! Run!' he screamed.

They ran like billy-oh. Not looking back. Out of the Domain and down into George Street. Shriek of whistles and din of voices in their ears. Bedlam in their wake.

Chapter 3

That's the wrong way to tickle Mary,
That's the wrong way to kiss.
Don't you know that over here, lad
They like it best like this.
Hooray pour Les Français
Farewell Angleterre.
We didn't know how to tickle Mary,
But we learnt how over here.
Anon. To the tune of 'It's A Long Way To Tipperary'.

A few slow buggies sagged up George Street after their turns around the Botanical Gardens, the occupants and their sweat-bathed horses all as limp as eucalypt leaves in the afternoon's heat. Too hot to show any sign they heard the sounds of agitation echoing up from the Domain, or they were so used to the Socialists' meetings they simply paid no mind. It was a slow Sunday afternoon in need of a storm. Verandah beds with mosquito nets would give only small comfort in the city's houses that stood high on their spindly wooden crab's legs, craning to catch the cool.

Running footsteps and relieved whoops echoed along the dull city street.

'They were going to kill us for sure!' Mick yelled as he ran.

'No, it's only our Joe they'll be wanting dead! They'll just be wanting to hurt you a lot!' Molly laughed.

'Heeeya!' Mick yelled. 'Let's go back again! There's a stoush on!' He was serious but the others laughed at him as he headed back down the street towards the Domain. Relief and excitement flooded them, hearts booming like cannon on the front line.

Tomfool whooped in excitement, for no other reason than to hear his own voice louder than the sound of four pairs of Sunday best boots clattering on the roadway.

'I've been robbed!' Tomfool called. They laughed louder, sillier, at him. 'I've been robbed!' he sang out again and again as he dashed along the footpath behind Molly.

'Tomas! No!' Joe puffed as sternly as he could. Tomfool stopped cavorting to turn with a devastated look.

'Maybe later,' Joe recanted. Tomfool beamed, pushing his tomato and blood-smeared, turned-out pockets back into his trouser legs.

Molly stopped dead.

'Come back here, Micky Doyle!' she called, without looking.

Tomfool ran on.

As Molly turned to look for Mick, Tomfool crashed into her, knocking her sideways. Molly ended-up sitting on her rear end in the middle of the footpath in a very unladylike fashion – laughing loudly. Tomas and Joe stopped beside her, bent over and panting. Mick paused, torn, drawn towards the donnybrook but wanting to be with his friends, before he ran, decided, to rejoin them. No pursuers could be seen or heard, only snatches of song wafting up the street. *God Save the King* and *The Red Flag* mixed with other lively tunes in a musical duel.

They laughed again.

'That'll be your mother for sure,' Molly said. They all pictured Kathleen O'Donghue, hands on hips, singing it at them like every note was a Mills bomb.

'It's like she says,' Molly panted. 'The right wing are such blockheads because they don't have any decent songs. When she starts the *Internationale* the Loyalists won't have a hope!'

They laughed even more.

Joe Hill smiled wider than a cracked watermelon, with elation and with … just being alive.

'There hasn't been a reaction like that since after the last Referendum vote,' he puffed. 'Dad should be pleased. Segeyev was, and Mum too.'

'Shame we couldn't have a crack at 'em, though,' Mick added, almost ruefully. 'You wind 'em up Joe and I'll knock 'em over!'

Molly still sat akimbo on the footpath.

'No, they'll only be wanting Joe Hill dead!' Tomas grinned at her.

'Tomas, you're a fool,' Molly said. Her green eyes glinted up at him. 'A lovely fool but a fool for sure!' She laughed, her red hair bouncing as she shook her head like a mop with a straight-cut.

Joe couldn't help but laugh with her, especially now he could see there were only a few red scratches on her cheeks and no deeper gravel wounds.

'Thought you'd have a bit of a sit-down on the way home, Moll?' Mick panted.

Molly smiled *that* smile at him.

'By the sweet loving Jesus,' Joe groaned, covering his unbidden utterance with a catch of breath.

'I was looking at that fellow at the pub,' she said, nodding towards a blonde-haired soldier at the window. 'He's Babushka's new lodger.'

Mick and Joe gave the bloke a furtive once over. Mick didn't like what he saw.

'He'll fit right in,' he said, 'he's got a head like a boarding house pudding.'

'I've been robbed?' a voice whined. Tomfool pulled at Joe's sleeve and pointed across the street to the crowd of men milling around the doors of the pub for the six o'clock swill.

'I've been robbed?' Tomfool asked again.

'Why not play it? For divilment!' Molly suggested, her eyes aglitter.

'Tweak a few noses,' Mick agreed. They both still simmered like a kettle just off the boil. Only Joe was reluctant.

'Come on, cobber,' Mick remonstrated. 'You've had your say today, but we haven't. I'll do it if you don't want to!'

Joe glanced around their eager faces.

'All right, then,' he agreed, though he knew it would detract from his triumph.

But that look in her eyes. Her hair. Her dress. Her smile.

'As long as you three play it. I'm tired.'

All of them nodded.

'Right-oh,' Mick ordered. Get on with you, Tomas!'

Tomfool jumped like a scalded cat, flying across the road, he ran helter-skelter, pulling his trouser pockets out as he fled.

'Help!' he yelled. 'Help, I've been robbed!' he wailed. His voice was truly desperate, close to tears. Pedestrians stopped to gawk. A woman, out for an afternoon stroll with her bloke, crossed the street. The crowd from near the pub followed. Tomfool ran on until he stood on the footpath in front of the building beyond the pub. He pulled at his turned out pockets like they were rabbits' ears, all the while wailing at the top of his lungs,

'I've been robbed!' Tears of real distress stained his cheeks.

'Righto!' Mick nodded. They all ran across the street to join the crowd, tut-tutting and fretting over Tomas. Mick jumped up onto the stairs of the building.

'That's right ladies and gentlemen, he's been robbed,' Mick yelled. Tomfool smiled slyly. With all the crowd's attention drawn to the new speaker he slowly withdrew to stand at the back with Molly and Joe.

'But so have I!' Mick turned out his own pockets. 'And so have you. We've all been robbed, my friends. We've been robbed by the Capitalist system that turns us into slaves.' The faces in the crowd turned from concern, to puzzlement, to laughter or, in a couple of cases, anger, as they twigged to what was going on. Mick hustled them along.

'The Capitalists take our toil and turn it into huge profit and what do we get in return? A pittance. Ladies and Gentleman as the fat pigs …'

A burly bloke in a navvie's singlet, the sort who at first glance you would expect to be a member of the Movement, stood unsteadily.

'What would you know, you white-anting whelp? You're still wet behind the ears. Join the Army and fight for your bloody King. That'll make a man out of you!'

But Mick was not to be undone.

'That's just what the bosses want you to think,' he began, but again the burly bloke interjected.

'You know buggar-all about nothing! My brother…' he yelled at Mick, his words slurred, spittle flying like shrapnel. But he was too much for Molly.

'Well, you know buggar-all about anything so that makes you even,' she retorted.

The bear of a man turned, focussing all his attention on her. Joe reached for Molly's hand and they quick-stepped together back down the street. Mick jumped down the stairs to place himself between the bear and Molly. But Mick was backpedalling too.

The crowd had seen it all before and mostly started thinking of dinner, all except one fellow who walked up to the big bloke and clapped a hand on his shoulder. The bear whirled around, unsteady, stopping as he recognised the uniform and the voice.

'Sarge?' he said.

'Show's over, eh, Jack. Time to go home.' The big bloke cast an uncertain glance at his tormentors.

'They don't know, Sarge. They got no bloody idea how Caleb copped it.'

'No.' The sergeant spoke softly. 'But these jokers are going home right now, aren't you?' he asked.

Joe, Molly and Mick nodded in unison. Surreptitiously Joe let go of Molly's hand.

'I reckon you should too.'

The sergeant waved them away, steering the big bloke up the street.

'Maureen'll have a nice stew for tea, I'll bet,' he encouraged.

The singletted bear cast them one final glare before, sheep-like, he followed. They all breathed easier. Not quite what they'd hoped. Took the edge off the fun, though secretly, Joe was glad.

'I'd have gone a round with him!' Mick skited.

'Wouldn't have lasted a half,' Joe answered. 'One belt from that bloke would knock you to the other side of Christmas.'

'Well,' Molly breathed. She turned, tripped on her heel and, for the second time in a quarter of an hour, landed with a surprised yelp, flat on her bottom.

'You all right, Miss?' called a soldier from an open window at the front of the Land's Office Hotel. It was the lodger. His enquiring face pale, yet friendly. He seemed older than his looks belied, in his early twenties, but his dark hair was beginning to grey, as was his well-groomed moustache. Molly guessed he had honest eyes, though she hadn't fully decided yet.

'I'll be for takin' a quick sit down's all, thanking you,' she replied curtly. Molly took Mick's hands as he helped her up. She patted down her dress while Joe scooped up her fallen floppy cotton hat.

'Can't help a maiden in distress? Pity!' the soldier winked and raised a half-empty beer glass in salute. Mick scowled as the fellow drained it and picked up another from the three on the table in front of him.

'Sounds like we're in for a bit of fun tonight, Miss?' the soldier continued amiably, nodding down the street towards the sounds still issuing from the Domain.

'Bloody red-raggers! Ought to be ashamed.'

'Ashamed of what?' Mick demanded as he strode between Molly and the Digger at the window.

'Ignore it, Mick,' Joe whispered. But his mate was stoked-up hotter than the boiler on the Ipswich Express.

'Ashamed for their disloyalty to King and Country, that's what,' the soldier continued. 'There's thousands of us Loyalists fighting in Europe while at home these damned Socialists white-ant the war effort.' He stopped a moment to drink.

'And what would you know about Socialism?'

Joe tried to divert the fire away from Mick. The soldier finally noticed the rosettes fluttering on each of the three chests stuck out before him.

'Pah!' He spat dismissively, not wanting to ruin his last drinks arguing with hardheads. He took a long swig of beer and ventured nothing further.

But Mick was primed to go on with it whether Joe, or this bloke, wanted to or not.

'You're such a slave you think getting killed for the bloody bosses is striking a blow for freedom! What's freedom if you're dead? You'd be better taking a leaf out of the Irish book. The bosses won't give you freedom any more than the English'll give freedom to the Irish – we have to take it!'

'The Irish!' The soldier spluttered beer froth over the table.

'They deserve the same we give all traitors! The firing squad's too good for 'em!'

Mick puffed out his chest like a rooster about to crow.

'I'll be Patrick Doyle,' he enunciated every word clearly. 'That is an Irish name. And this,' he said pointing over his shoulder at Molly. 'Is my sweetheart, Molly Pearce. That'll be another Irish name. And these colours,' he continued pointing at the rosette on his chest, 'are the colours of the Irish. And you,' he yelled in the Loyalist's face, 'can bloody well take that back right now or by the sweet lovin' Jesus … !'

Mick raised his fists.

It was for Molly's sake the Digger backed down. He'd faced death enough times to know if a threat was worth the effort. This half-smart guttersnipe didn't worry him one iota. But there was a lady present, one he recognized from the boarding house, and he didn't need any trouble there. He composed himself.

'Now look, son, I didn't …' he began.

'Don't you "son" me, mate.'

Mick advanced, fists still raised before him. Warily the soldier watched him. Joe knew the look on Mick's face all too well: this wasn't about his mother, or the Irish Martyrs, it was about Molly – he was sick of extricating Mick from jealousies of Mick's own imagining – the fellow had only enquired, innocently enough, about Molly's welfare and now look where they were headed.

'If you had the choice between pulling your head in right now or finding out if we know how to fight, what would it be?' Joe asked the soldier. Mick relaxed knowing Joe was still there. The soldier gazed at Joe, trying to figure out what his game was.

But Joe focussed on Mick. He knew his face would be tightened into that ready scowl, three furrows deep above his pugilist's nose. His cleft chin thrust forward, eyes glittering with that unnatural blue that seemed poached from another body and fixed in the face of someone old before his time. Joe had seen it in a hundred bloody blues they'd been in together. He placed a hand on Mick's shoulder.

'Pick a fight you know you'll win,' he murmured.

'So we just leave this Loyalist dog off his chain?' Mick sneered. 'He doesn't scare me!'

'He'll have ten mates if he's got one, all full of last drinks and primed to go,' Joe soothed. 'We'll see him soon enough up some dark alley. Besides,' he added, 'you told Babushka you'd bring Molly home before dark, didn't you.' Mick softened at that.

'When we meet him again, we'll make sure we're ready,' Joe whispered.

'Just watch your mouth, son!' Mick growled at the soldier, spitting out the word "son". He lowered his fists as Joe pushed him towards Molly on the opposite footpath.

'Feisty little Fenian aren't we?' the soldier dismissed the bit of unpleasantness and turned back into the bar to laugh with his mates.

'Come on, Moll,' Mick said, holding out his hand. 'I hate the smell of spit and bad company!'

Joe nodded in agreement. He hated pubs too. He'd spent too many days waiting with Mick outside some bar for his father or, after Mick's mother first died, playing on the bar room floor in the sawdust, full of spit and beer spills, with him. Everyone up and down the whole length of the South Brisbane wharves knew them both by name. Every tapster, shyster, sailor, lady of loose virtue, Unionist, copper, criminal, as well as all the Russians, tried to keep Micky Doyle on the straight and narrow. Which was just as well as Joe Hill had nearly had enough.

Molly led Mick off hand in hand. Joe followed close behind, but Tomfool had crept along the footpath under the bar windows until he was close to where the soldier sat.

Tomas jumped up suddenly, thrusting his head and shoulders in through the window. Eyes bulging like an angry monkey he screamed in the unsuspecting serviceman's face,

'They'll be wanting to hurt you a lot!'

The Digger jumped back, knocking the table over. His two remaining beers smashed on the tiled floor. Tom grinned like a madman.

'What the blazes!' the soldier swore. He tried to save the beer in his hand and whack Tomfool at the same time.

'You bloody galoot!'

Tomas backed out as quick as he'd entered, banging the back of his head hard on the bottom of the hopper window as he scarpered.

'Hoy, you!' the Digger bellowed, wiping froth from his uniform. 'You owe me two beers!'

But Tomas ran down the street, dodging the hansom cabs and buggies that had begun to appear just on closing time, he babbled loudly,

'They'll be wanting to hurt you a lot!' as he rubbed hard at the back of his head.

But the soldier hadn't finished with Tomfool. Downing his remaining beer he hobbled up the street. Joe turned at the kerfuffle.

'Damn it, Tom!' he swore loudly. 'Why can't we just walk home for once without you annoying someone!' Molly and Mick turned too.

'What's he done now?' Mick asked. He wasn't in the mood for any tomfoolery.

'Stop that idiot!' the soldier yelled. His voice rang clear above the sudden six o'clock busyness.

'Quick, Tomas,' Molly called. 'Quick! Time for tea!' Not that Tomfool needed any encouragement, either to escape the trouble he was in or to get to his spot at the table. They were nearly at the tram. But the soldier was a stayer.

'Stop that miserable … Socialist!' He yelled his best insult as he hobbled across the uneven road. Only now could they see he carried a cane and dragged his left leg. Joe felt bad. Mick's shame at his earlier outburst was written across his face. But being in the wrong never stopped Mick and as for feeling guilty about it? Hah!

'Hop-a-long!' he laughed at the Digger. The three of them were ready to jump the tram the moment Tomas caught up. Mick grabbed Tomfool's arm and turned face to face with …

'A copper!' Mick moaned. 'Of all the miserable!'

'So, what do we have here?' asked the policeman, his gaze roving over them, noting with interest the red rosette, the white, and the green.

'Sergeant O'Hagen, what a happy surprise,' Molly said, smiling her best smile, her eyes all aglitter, eyelashes aflutter. 'How is Mrs Kerensky?' Not waiting for a reply regarding the Sergeant's landlady, she was interrupted by the arrival of Hop-a-long.

'That runt there owes me two beers!' he said, perforating the air with his cane. 'I demand … remedy!' he panted. Tomas moved behind Molly, a grin still flickering around his lips. Mick and Joe prepared for battle, fists clenched.

'If it isn't enough that these red-flaggers be allowed harangue decent people in the street but they drag along their tame monkey to attack them too,' Hop-a-long began, but was interrupted by O'Hagen.

'Attack people you say?'

'Yes, attack!' Hop-a-long repeated. 'I was sitting in the public bar minding my own affairs when this, this … idiot,' he said jabbing his stick at the hapless Tomfool, 'jumped through the window and startled me.'

'I thought you said he attacked you, sir!' O'Hagen interrupted as Hop-a-long tried to stare Tomfool down. Tomas shadowed Molly's every move. His ruse was more or less successful and Hop-a-long found himself glaring balefully at Molly instead of his hidden adversary. His ire could not outlast her smile.

'Well, I was startled by this … this … fellow!' Hop-a-long continued, but his heart was no longer in it. They all relaxed a little.

'This … monkey, as you so kindly put it, is a little simple, Mister … Mister …?' Molly asked for a name but continued without. 'And as such he's under the guardianship of my family. At the moment that means me.'

She smiled as she finished.

'No,' O'Hagen continued. ' I don't think I caught your name either, sir?' he finished, all very proper, taking the final wind from Hop-a-long's sails.

'Name, sir?' he asked again.

Hop-a-long glanced to Tomfool but saw only Molly.

Polite and belligerent in the one look, Joe thought. *Isn't she better than breathing.*

'Winterson,' Hop-a-long replied. 'Harold Charles Winterson,' he continued. 'Everyone calls me Harry. But look,' he said. 'I don't want to make a formal complaint, just a good telling off from you, or a swift kick in the seat of his pants.' Harry Winterson's voice trailed off.

'Then you'll not be making a complaint regarding the alleged attack?' O'Hagen pressed. Winterson was beaten.

'No,' he said. 'But I would like you to caution this buffoon. If I catch him spilling people's beer like that again I'll …'

'Now, let me caution you, sir, against making threats,' O'Hagen interjected. 'You leave the policing to the police and we'll all be sweet.' Sergeant O'Hagen was finished with Winterson, but turned his gaze firmly to Tomfool.

'As for you, Tomas Madorsky, it's my very strong advice that you refrain from such reckless acts. If not I'll be forced to talk to Mrs Kerensky about your wayward behaviour. You know she'll not be liking that. No pudding for a week!' he scowled at Tomfool, who winced obligingly at the thought. Molly took Tom's hand. Winterson looked askance at the mention of Babushka's name.

'Be warned, Tommy. If I catch you doing the like of this again,' O'Hagen lowered his voice, then yelled for effect,

'I'll boot your backside from here to blithering breakfast!'

Tomfool jumped like a shot rabbit.

'We'll take care of him,' Joe said to O'Hagen. 'We always do.'

'Just make sure of it this time,' O'Hagen answered, before adding brusquely for effect, 'or else!' Then he waved them away with a dismissive hand.

'Time to be getting home with the lot of you, before that mob from the Domain get among the drinkers and we have a real to do. And to you, sir,' he added, doffing his cap to Harold Winterson. 'Enjoy the cool of the evening.'

'You too, Sergeant,' Winterson replied, meek as a lamb. Tomfool lurched off quicker than a West End tram, with Molly and Mick in tow.

'Give my best to Mrs Kerensky – if you just happen to see her before I do.' O'Hagen winked at Winterson, as he strode off down George Street.

Turning to chase them to the tram, Joe almost collided with a small contingent of police.

It never rains but it bloody pours!

He tried to get Mick's attention but Molly had linked hands with him and they were all lovey-dovey and oblivious.

Tomfool ran back to circle the coppers, cutting a caper about their flanks like a hungry horse fly. Joe was curious. He wondered if they were going to the Domain, but surely it was all done there now … unless something serious had happened? Joe called Tomas and they ran to catch up with the others.

'What was all that about with Hopalong?' Mick asked. 'What does Babushka have to do with him?'

'I'm sure he's a bloody nark,' Joe answered. Molly smiled an easy smile.

'He's Babushka's other new lodger,' she said. 'I saw him moving his things on Friday afternoon.'

'It's my lucky day!' Mick shook his head in mock despair. 'First I get stoned on my best mate's behalf then, to add insult to me burden of iniquitous injuries, a copper and the bloke I just had a blue with both move into me sweetheart's grandmother's boarding house! And me not the jealous sort,' he finished with the slightest menace.

Molly laughed. Everyone did except Tomfool who was too far ahead, muttering to himself as he skittered along.

'What's the story with all the coppers?' Joe asked. Molly looked blank, as though she hadn't seen them. Mick shrugged. The afternoon's high emotion had worn away and they were tired. A tram lumbered up Queen Street.

'Quick!' Mick said, grabbing Tomas' shirt. 'That's Uncle Vanya driving. He'll give us a lift home for free!'

They ran to catch the tram, Molly holding hands with Mick and laughing. Joe watched. He remembered then that he'd been bleeding and his face hurt. He held the handkerchief his mother had used to his cheek and, on his day of triumph, the world grew small once more.

Chapter 4

Freedom on the Wallaby
Our parents toiled to make a home, hard grubbing 'twas and clearing,
They wasn't troubled much by lords when they was pioneering
But now that we have made the land a garden full of promise
Old Greed must crook his dirty hand and come and take it from us.
So we must fly a rebel flag as others did before us
And we must sing a rebel song and join in rebel chorus
We'll make the tyrants feel the sting of those that they would throttle
They needn't say the fault is ours if blood should stain the wattle.
Henry Lawson

But no one rode Uncle Vanya's running board across the bridge to South Brisbane. It was Tomfool's fault again. It was his babbling.

'We should just leave them alone to sabotage the presses!' he panted. 'Hughes'd be happy and so would we!' That stopped them all. It was Molly who asked.

'Who said that, Tomas?' Tomfool almost stopped in his headlong rush to the tram to answer,

'Cake for tea!' before he hurried on.

'You'll be telling me this very instant, Tomas Madorsky!' Molly stamped her foot. 'Or there won't be any cake, ever at all!' Joe wasn't the only one the afternoon had turned sour on. But Tom knew which side his bread was buttered. He dawdled back to Molly's side. They heard the tram rattle onto the bridge and Joe resigned himself to walking home.

'It was the coppers!' Tomfool begrudged any longer answer.

'What presses … and who's sabotaging them?' Mick asked, looking with sudden interest down the street after the coppers. But he turned to look quickly up the street again when he heard the tramp of another contingent, properly marching this time, not like the policemen's lackadaisical stroll. They were AIF men, in uniform, the proper army, bearing sloped arms, maybe a hundred strong.

'That mob don't look like they're out for a mooch around the city,' Joe muttered. 'C'mon Molly, let's take Tomas home.' They could see the wallopers taking up position on the footpath in front of the Government Printing Works, lined up in ranks three deep – freeing their batons, ominously, from their belts.

'Whacko!' Mick whooped. He legged it down the street, yelling back at the others when they hesitated,

'There's gonna be a proper ding-dong donnybrook, or I'm a scab's bum! I'll save yez a seat!' In this new excitement Tomfool forgot his dinner and was raring to get after Mick.

'I said I'd get you home by dinner time,' Joe urged.

But Molly nodded to Tom and he was off after Mick like a dog from a chain. Reluctantly, Joe followed.

'We'll just take the littlest of peeks,' Molly said. 'But if it seems like trouble, we'll go. I promised Babushka too you know.'

Joe's tiredness left him as he stepped out beside her and his curiosity was piqued once more.

The army was quick-marching and they found themselves hard-pressed to keep ahead. By the time they got to the Government Printers quite a crowd was gathered, especially from the pub. Somebody must have organised runners to get the word out, as more blokes were arriving by the minute.

'They reckon Billy Hughes is sending the Army against Premier Ryan!' Mick called as he reached down to help Molly climb the side of the sandstone building footings at the entrance to the lane.

'Apparently he read the No case against Conscription into Hansard so they have to print it!' Mick laughed gleefully. 'Ryan sent the coppers to see it done … but the army isn't happy. Roll up, roll up and play the game!'

Tomfool hung shrieking like a drunk parrot perched as high as he could get up the wall,

'The army isn't happy! The army isn't happy!'

O'Hagen wasn't amused,

'This is the second time I've had to speak to you this afternoon. My patience is wearing thin. Down! Now! And out of here!'

'No bloody fear, sport!' Mick taunted. 'We wouldn't miss this for quids!' He knew that O'Hagen would have to force him and besides it was too late, the army had arrived. The contingent halted in the street and, still in their ranks, wheeled to face the footpath. Their Captain, a youngish man still in his twenties, ordered them to stand easy before he approached the police commander. O'Hagen stood before the door, his constables close-ranked beside him. It was like watching two opposing kings in a game of chess, except the coppers were outnumbered four to one.

'Horatio on the bridge!' Molly tittered. Joe assessed the crowd and the two opposing sides for trouble. It felt knife-blade tense and – important somehow. Joe felt it too but was more worried about Molly. Who knew what might happen? At least as long as Tomfool and Mick stayed up the wall they wouldn't be in a position to start anything. The listening crowd drew tight around the forces of the Commonwealth and the State. The young Captain seemed uncomfortable, twisting his head left and right as though his collar was too tight, but his voice held solid.

'I have orders from the Office of the Prime Minister to investigate whether these premises are being used to produce materials which would stop a citizen from volunteering for the war effort. Such materials are in contra ...' he stumbled over the word.

'Spit it out, son!' Mick yelled. The crowd laughed, even a couple of the coppers, and a lot of the soldiers managed smirks. The officer's face darkened but he did not avert his gaze from O'Hagen. Mick looked pleased with himself.

'Such materials are in contra-vention of Section 4 of the Commonwealth War Precautions Act Amendments of 1916. I am authorised to search for, seize and destroy any such materials.' The crowd growled as the troops began to fidget with their rifles. O'Hagen though, looked unperturbed, steadily meeting the younger man's gaze.

'You'll find nothing in there but publications printed by the duly elected Government of the Colony of Queensland,' he explained. Mick sang out,

'State! You mean the State of Queensland!' O'Hagen reddened a little. Of course he did. It'd only become a State sixteen years ago and he'd been a copper close to twenty-five, an easy mistake in the circumstances. Still, he stood firm, confident and calm as all his years' service had taught.

Joe responded to the tension around him, taking the opportunity to move closer. He reached to take Molly's hand, squeezing it gently, leaning to her ear,

'Be ready to bolt if needs be.'

She squeezed back acknowledgement. Joe knew Mick could not see their hands, just them close together, both craning to see.

The eyes and ears of all: the small crowd, his band of coppers and the army coves, followed every movement and every word. It was like watching boxers dance around the ring before the first punch. O'Hagen addressed his adversary as an equal, as though they'd had a spot of unpleasantness at The Queensland Club during an evening of cards.

'I understand what you're saying, sir. But there seems to be a bit of a … problem,' he explained. 'I must be making myself crystal clear here. I've had my orders, from Premier Ryan no less, to ensure that the printing of the proceedings of the Parliament of Queensland, The Hansard, which is taking place inside this building, is protected, and protect it I will, sir,' before he added, perhaps for effect, 'by all means necessary!'

It was the Captain's turn to look perturbed. The tension of this public confrontation, in front of his men, was not what he was trained for. He couldn't very well shoot the Queensland Police!

'But blow it all, man!' he remonstrated. 'We're both on the same side. Let us have a look and we'll be on our way.' O'Hagen stepped towards the Captain until he was close enough to speak quietly. His constables closed ranks behind him.

'You and I both know Ryan's read his "No" case into Hansard and he's going to hand them out on street corners. It's a dirty trick, but this is the proceedings of a duly elected Parliament we're talking about here. Stop them printing it and it will be like the Commonwealth declaring war on the State of Queensland. We can't have it. Hughes'll just have to cop it sweet!'

O'Hagen stepped back.

'I've had my orders, sir,' he repeated.

'Damn it, man, so have I!' the Captain yelled. He removed his cap, ran his fingers through brilliantined hair, and conferred with his sergeant. The performance was all too much for Mick,

'Put in the boot, O'Hagen!' he yelled loudly. 'Put in the boot!'

The Captain swung back to fix Mick with a murderous look. The crowd agreed, catcalling and goading. Some of the soldiers and plods looked perplexed but most seemed ready to go a couple of rounds.

'Let me deal with the public, sir,' O'Hagen suggested above the noise. 'Law and order's my job.'

He nodded to his men. A couple of coppers advanced on Mick and some other rowdies, while a few more strolled meaningfully towards the crowd. Joe stepped back, pulling on Molly's hand. She resisted, pulling back.

'Molly we need to go,' Joe urged.

'I'll be waiting for Mick and Tomas to get down and come with us,' she insisted.

'They'll catch up,' Joe said pulling her hand hard. 'You know Mick'll land us all in hot water again. I'm tired. Come on.'

'You'll be letting me go this instant, Joseph Hill,' she hissed, twisting her hand from his. 'I'll not be told what to do by any man.'

From the corner of his eye Joe caught Mick watching. He released his grip, stepping away, but his temper was frayed by too much argy-bargy and too much lovey-dovey.

The Captain calmed a little at the police action and O'Hagen took the opportunity of the turn of mood and the product of a few moments' unpressured thought.

'Might we consider a compromise, sir?' he suggested.

The Captain, nonplussed, nodded.

'What say I take you and a couple of your men for a guided tour of the Government Printing Offices and we'll see what this is all about?' Adding in a stage whisper,

'Honour will be satisfied. All orders carried out.'

The Captain agreed with a preemptive nod, his voice belying his relief as he issued his orders,

'You two men with me. Corporal stand your men easy.'

The policemen circulated through the crowd.

'Nothing more to see here. Move on now. Home you go.'

'What? So that's it?' Mick shouted at O'Hagen. 'Hopeless! Bloody hopeless!'

O'Hagen smiled back at him.

'I'll know you've done some growing up when you understand the fine art of compromise,' O'Hagen responded. 'Now get, or I'll have you arrested.'

'I'll second that, you mob of smart Alecs!' one of the constables at their feet agreed. 'Hop it like kangaroos!' But before he began to climb down Mick nodded up the street.

'What's he still doing here?' he asked.

Lounging against a lamppost, cane-in-hand and with a fag-end smirking from the corner of his lips, stood Harry Winterson.

'What he does best,' Molly suggested. 'Loitering with intent.'

'Let's go job him one,' Mick said.

'You said you'd have Molly and Tomfool home by dark and so did I,' Joe reminded him. 'He'll keep.'

'Maybe you'd like to take Molly home while I clean up here?' Mick said, his voice an accusation. Joe knew the tone,

'For crying out loud Mick,' he said, feigning exasperation. 'I wanted her away so she wouldn't get hurt, but she wanted to stay … with you … and Tom.' Molly glared at them both and, without speaking, grabbed Tomfool by the arm and marched him off towards the tram. Both knowing they were right, Mick and Joe followed like little dogs.

Up the road Harry Winterson flicked his fag end, spat in the gutter, and wondered.

Chapter 5

Hush! Here Comes A Whizz Bang
Hush! here comes a whizz bang,
Hush! here comes a whizz bang,
Now you soldiers get down those stairs,
Down in your dug-outs and say your prayers.
Hush! here comes a whizz bang,
And it's making straight for you
And you'll see all the wonders of no man's land
If a whizz bang [bump] hits you.
To the tune of 'Hush! Here Comes The Dream Man'.

Joe rested his head against the wooden window frame of the tram and gazed west to Mt Cootha. A fingernail of crescent moon hung just clear of the mountain, shrouded now and again by the bloated summer clouds that drifted, hushed along by the failed breeze. The last remnants of daylight dropped from its purple-dark bulk.

Joe knew how it felt.

He was dog-tired too from the afternoon's shenanigans and so was Molly. Her attraction to violence and therefore Mick always wore her down. The way she insisted on staying with him even though things looked like turning nasty.

Or was it that she was loyal to her friends above all things? He liked that idea better. Even if he and Molly would never be more than friends, to have such a friend was armour against a million woes.

Or perhaps she confused love with compassion? Maybe that's why she'd been so vociferous when he suggested they leave.

Or perhaps he was grasping at straws to explain why she chose Mick instead of him. There was so much he still could not understand about people, about men and women. Ideas were so much easier, neater, manageable. But … how she'd stood up for him when he vacillated in his speech. He leaned in pleasant reverie.

A lamplighter trudged from post to post lighting the gas-lights across the bridge. The khaki river reflected the yellow glow of the lamps, like brass buttons decorating a uniform.

Ships moored at the wharves along the southern bank hoisted their riding lights. Under the lights a river of wheat flowed on the backs of wharfies, up gangplanks, or into slings to be swung aboard. Grain and bully beef and all the foodstuff the country could produce to feed the war's hungry mouth.

From the back seat of the tram, Joe smiled at the bitter irony. He knew so many of the wharfies, Mick's old man to begin with, who were utterly opposed to the war, yet on their backs they carried the food so necessary to keep soldiers alive long enough to kill or be killed for King and Country.

His thoughts drifted to more recent events.

If Hughes sent the army in against Queensland anything could happen, maybe even the break-up of the Commonwealth, or a civil war. Joe shuddered at the thought. As if the current war wasn't bad enough without another one erupting at home. It could happen. Look at America. Only 50 years since they'd been trying to kill each other. He felt sick at the prospect. However bad this war was, it could be far worse.

Kathleen always told him to redirect his imagination when it took a turn too far into the woes of the world, so he wondered instead what Ted Hill would have to say, when he heard what had just happened at the printing works? Maybe Joe could be the bearer of new intelligence for once. Ted's network of informants was renowned as the best in Brisbane. Maybe this time Joe would have a scoop.

But more importantly, what did Ted think about his speech? Not that Ted and Kathleen and Uncle Bill didn't know the content.

They were all up late, night after long night, tossing lines back and forward as Joe scribbled down and crossed out and drew lines from one point to the next – but what about his delivery? He knew it was a bit messy at the end. Did he hit the mark with the Movement? Whether he had or not, he knew from the reaction that he'd sure stirred the possum. Maybe he'd even read about it in the morning paper? That felt good. He looked around for Molly.

She and Mick sat three seats in front of him, billing and cooing like Trades Hall pigeons. He felt sick with hunger. It was strange how, even when the worst things seemed to be happening, when everything stood on the brink, it sometimes seemed that no one cared. Real life seemed to go on unaltered. Workers went to work, housewives paid the grocer and lovers kissed, oblivious.

Molly laughed,

'No!'

Mick turned to him,

'If you had the choice between being in the Army or the Navy, which would you take?' he asked. Molly rolled her eyes.

Joe tried to ignore him, but it was no good.

'Neither,' he answered, hoping to shut him up. 'You wouldn't catch me dead in any Imperial Forces.' Joe smiled. Mick and Molly laughed.

'Caught dead!' Mick chuckled, shaking his head. Joe laughed too, though the joke was unintended.

He don't know if he could be so cruel as to damn soldiers outright, even in jest, with so many dying. He wasn't joking when he'd said his friends were dead. There were a half dozen, some not close, but close enough to have been the furniture of his social day: school and workmates, a bloke from three streets over and the shop boy from the other butcher. The one his mother went to sometimes whose name he always forgot. Weren't they just ignorant slaves, fighting because they didn't know any better? Like Ted always said,

"It's only when a bloke has all the facts that he can make an informed decision." To which he always added.

"And I mean real facts! Not the propaganda the Tory Press and the Government hand out."

Joe had drifted again.

'But what if the Conscription Referendum gets a "Yes" this time?' Mick pressed. 'Then there'll be no choice. You'll have to join up.'

He's more persistent than a bloody March fly, Joe thought and resigned himself to answering, or at least making some comment.

'We'll beat Hughes again and that's it. No Conscription. Never, ever!' Joe tried to make his voice sound final. His heart was not so sure, even after today. It seemed the whole world teetered … in everything. Besides, he knew Mick' was just 'taking the Mick'. Molly and he began to whisper to one other. Tomfool was babbling to himself too, so it was hard to hear.

'Segeyev disagrees,' Molly turned to say. 'He reckons Hughes is mad with power and he'll do anything to make Australians fight.'

'Look, Moll,' Joe answered. 'You know my opinion of Segeyev but he's not always right you know. No one is.'

'But he says if Hughes doesn't win the Referendum then he'll legislate before the year is out.'

'Blow it all, Molly,' Joe exploded. 'We haven't got Conscription yet and it won't happen. Australians have more sense, whatever Segeyev says.'

Molly fell silent before Mick weighed back in.

'For the sake of the argument just imagine you're in a time and a place where there is no choice. You *have* to choose!'

'I'd take the bloody Army then!' Joe said, his voice tight. 'Because,' he added knowing Mick well enough to know there would be a supplementary question about why he'd answered the way he'd answered.

'Because, I'm frightened of being caught underwater in a ship and then slowly drowning.' Mick was silent for a moment, contemplating the answer.

'And you know I get bloody sea-sick!'

That finished Mick off. Molly laughed and Tomas parroted to the whole tram-load.

'Would you be an infantryman or a gunner?' Mick asked.

'I'll knock your bloody block off, Mick!' Joe exploded. 'See that!' He pushed back his hair from the wound on his forehead.

'That's as close as I'll get to warfare. Class warfare,' Joe said. 'And I'll do my fighting here at home. I'll fight to get the war ended and for decent wages and fair conditions for workers. This *is* the real war!'

They both fell silent. Joe knew he'd raised his voice, but Molly's eyes smiled. She loved his passion. But she was the real warrior. Mick had no chance.

'You know, Comrade,' Mick said quietly, emphasising the word comrade unnecessarily. 'For all your brains you're boring. At least with me it's a different answer every time. With you, all the answers end up the same.' He laughed aloud, in Joe's face. Molly joined with him. Her laughter stung like a slap.

Why do they do that? Aren't we all in the Peace Army? Don't we all agree on Socialist principles? So why? Joe smiled weakly back at them, trying not to let his feelings crawl across his face. He was tired and today was his big day and no one would ruin that for him.

Tomfool changed seats so he could pat Molly's hair, as though she were a dog.

'Besides,' Molly continued. 'It's all fine to be having the answer "in theory" but like your mother says we're needing practical solutions to people's problems not just high falutin' talk.'

She was right of course, but the criticism still hurt.

Joe tried not to let it show but it must have, because she added,

'Not that we don't need the speechifying too.' Joe bit his lip.

'Well,' he concluded quietly. 'Maybe that's just the difference between you two and me, you're frightened of ideas. Frightened they might be real and they'll hurt you somehow.' Joe wanted it to be spiteful, but Mick just shrugged his shoulders.

'What? More real than my old man?'

Joe retreated, returning to his own thoughts.

Perhaps that's the truth, ideas don't hurt, not like a thump in the head. Or, at least, no one thinks that's it's the idea that's hurting them when someone is thumping them in the head. But isn't it the idea of love that made Mick's old man the way he is. After his Mum got the typhoid and died the real world changed but the idea of love stayed the same … it's just he couldn't work out how to deal with the real world not matching the world in his head anymore … just like me and Molly.

Or Babushka? Her idea that no one could be as perfect a man as her husband was when he was leading strikes in Russia. The scorn she pours on Old Nik if he so much as opens his mouth about Socialism. No one could live up to her idea of perfection.

Joe thought hard, staring at his friends. Mick and Molly were quiet. What's the idea behind us all?

No more unanswereable questions, Joe, he agreed with himself. The tram clattered on in silent contemplation.

Only Tomfool was bored and started his games again, sticking his head out through the window and squealing in the ear of the person sitting in front.

Joe ignored him.

The tram lumbered off the bridge. The winning shouts from the men playing two-up behind the Terminus Hotel could be heard clearly above its clatter.

'Come in spinner!' a voice called in Irish brogue. Cockatoos were on lookout at both entrances to Fish Lane. *To be sure! To be sure!*

Tomas had stopped frightening people and sat chatting to himself and gesticulating with a shake of his index finger.

'The Doctor's going away! It's not right! It's not right! We need him to look after us!' Tomas turned towards the other passengers,

'You like my story?' A young rowdy told him to pull his head in. Two girls whispered and turned away. The drunks ignored him. Most of them knew him, at least by sight, from around the streets. A child stared hard at him until Tom rolled his eyes back to show the whites. The child began to cry.

Joe glanced up to find Molly also looking at Tomfool.

'Tomas,' she admonished, shaking her head gently and smiling at the kid's mother. She has a smile for every occasion, Joe thought, but always the second best for me.

'My stop,' Mick called. He jumped down from the seat to the running board to trot beside the slowing tram.

'I thought you were coming to the meeting?' Joe protested. Mick shook his head. 'Better make sure the old man makes it to bed,' he said, his voice dispirited, 'or he won't be able to work in the morning.' He turned to Molly.

'But I'll be seeing you at Babushka's after work tomorrow won't I, Molly dolly?' he asked.

'Right you are then,' she answered, waving. 'We'll be expecting you for tea. And be behaving yourself when O'Hagen's at the table. There's the warning!'

'You behave yourself when you're anywhere near that Winterson nark,' he advised, 'and that'll be an order!'

Molly pouted as she waved her red handkerchief, like a damsel from an old fairytale. For a moment she seemed infinitely high and infinitely sad as though she knew the woes of the whole world in that moment. Mick stared hard at her before shifting his gaze to Joe. His face swung shut.

Joe had seen that gate close a thousand times.

'Come to the meeting!' he yelled. 'I'll wait for you!'

'Maybe, all right,' Mick replied and Joe smiled. In spite of all, they were mates.

Mick stood on the corner watching the tram clatter up to the Merivale Street stop where the three of them jumped down. He waved one last time before turning to walk back to the room he shared with his father above the Anchor Inn.

Mick knew it'd be unlikely he'd get to the meeting. The Peace Army sandwiches at lunchtime were good but that was all he'd eaten all day. He knew better than to try and keep his earnings back from his father on a Friday, even if it was only so he could buy something for weekend night's dinners, and he would never ask for charity. But he also knew he wouldn't be able to work a full day without a feed and he'd never hear the end of it if he ran out of steam.

I'll ask for some washing up work then, maybe the meeting, he thought. Old Montague Miller's worth an hour of anybody's time.

Mick sauntered up to the back of the Plough Inn. He loitered there for a few minutes, kicking at rubbish bins and poking aimlessly at anything of interest. It seemed less like he was expecting a handout if he didn't knock. Finally the back door opened and a small bird-sized woman in a starched white apron appeared, an enamel bowl full of potato peelings on her hip.

'Top of the evening to you, Mrs McGinty,' he said to the cook as he pulled the lid off the bin nearest to the back of the pub door. 'Those tired old hands of yours could do with not being up to the elbows in soapy water this fine evening,' he charmed. She knew him well.

'A full hour's work or there'll be nothing for ye!' she growled. But she took his arm as she turned and walked Mick Doyle into the kitchen.

Chapter 6

Nursery Rhyme
One year, two year, three year, four,
Comes a khaki gentleman knocking at the door.
'Any little boys at home, send them out to me
To train them and brain them in battles yet to be.'
When a little boy is born feed him, train him so.
Put him in a cattle pen and wait for him to grow.
When he's nice and plump and dear, and sensible and sweet,
Throw him in the trenches for the great grey rats to eat.
Toss him in the cannon's mouth, cannon's fancy best
Tender little boys' flesh that's easy to digest.
Frank Wilmot

Tomfool was the first to see it.

'Kaiser Bill! Kaiser Bill! Kaiser Bill, come down the hill!' he rhymed as he ran towards the sulky parked in the street.

Joe caught sight of the vehicle.

'Yes, he must be waiting for Mum and Dad to get home.'

'We've not been seeing Uncle Bill around lately,' Molly said, her face alight with new excitement.

'What would you be thinking he'll be wanting?'

'To see me of course,' Joe laughed. He didn't know why Uncle Bill was there either, but Uncle Bill, who wasn't his, or anyone else's uncle, was always great fun. He and Molly began to walk faster.

'Ha, no, he's come to take me on as his indispensable probationary nurse!' Molly proposed in a voice that more than half-sounded as though she would very much like that to happen.

Tomfool scampered ahead of them like a happy pup. They both laughed at him as the dull feeling of the evening dropped away. Besides it was cooler now.

Joe mused that perhaps there was something in what Tomfool said about Bill. He could be a bit of a Kaiser with the nursing staff by all accounts. According to Kathleen O'Donahue he was misunderstood and he was only a stickler for cleanliness and getting everything … just so.

'The sort of bloke who'd wrestle a crocodile in his evening suit, then come up looking like he'd just taken his coat out of the laundry press. A dapper little dandy,' was what Ted Hill said.

But they didn't work for him so they always wanted to see Uncle Bill. He was that sort of bloke. Hail-fellow, well-met. Had an outstanding bedside manner … according to all the society ladies of Brisbane.

Molly walked on ahead, quicker now.

Tomfool ran back to them trying to catch Joe's eye.

'I've been robbed?' he asked plaintively.

'Race you, rather!' Molly cried as she scampered up the street, her face flushed to match the red of her hair. She had Joe's full attention.

Tomfool made a strange, strangled sound in his throat, pleading with Joe, his face alive with anticipation.

'Go on then. Quick!' Joe encouraged him.

Tomfool ran towards Molly, pulling the insides of his trouser pockets out until they hung like white handkerchiefs from his hips. When he was close to her, he stopped dead. His face fell. His lips quivered.

'Help!' he wailed, pulling hopelessly at his pockets. 'I've been robbed!' he cried, his voice a telegraph of shock.

Molly stopped to play her part. She could never resist once the game had started. Her accent changed into that of an actress from a music hall melodrama.

'What? What is it, my child?' she cried, knuckles pressed to her mouth. 'Oh you poor boy! Who could have done such a thing to an innocent young man.'

Molly turned, pulling Joe by the shirt until she'd forced him to stand very close to her. A broad smile flooded his face.

'Well?' she demanded. 'What are you going to do about this outrage?' Joe looked suitably upset.

'I've been robbed,' Tomfool wailed. Joe raised Tomfool's, by now tear-soaked face, and placed a firm hand on his shoulder.

'I can see exactly what has happened here, Ladies and Gentlemen!' Joe said, addressing Molly alone.

'Yes, I can see very clearly! My friend has been robbed. But so have I!' Joe yelled angrily. 'Robbed by the Capitalist bosses, their pet bankers and all their idling class!' Joe performed for an audience of one.

'But most importantly, I've been robbed,' he continued, playing his part to a 't'. Molly waited, enthralled, as Joe turned to her, his face suddenly miserable.

'I've been robbed of a kiss from the most beautiful girl in Brisbane!' Joe finished in a rush, taking his opportunity to kiss Molly full on her unsuspecting lips.

Joe's shenanigans were too much for Tomfool. He began to laugh like a waterfall, great tumbling belly laughs poured down, the tears on his cheeks of pure joy. Molly broke from the kiss and smiled too.

It took all Joe's willpower to drag his attention back to Tomas's game, hoping that somehow he hadn't seen what just happened or, at least, that he wouldn't tell Mick.

'You get them in every time, Big Fellow,' Joe laughed, slapping Tomfool on the back.

Molly smiled her most mysterious smile. Joe thought he knew just what a smile like that meant. They turned together to continue up the street, eyes fixed on the Ted Hill's front door, not so much as mentioning the thing that now lay between them, leaving Tomas to calm himself.

'Come in and we'll all say a quick hello to Bill,' Joe urged as they arrived at the front gate. 'He'll only be reading the paper and spoiling for an argument.'

'As usual,' Molly said quietly, as though preoccupied, but added. 'Not that I don't like to listen, but we really need to get home now, Babushka will be waiting.'

It was Joe's turn to turn on his best winning smile. Even though he knew what he'd done was utterly wrong, he didn't want her to leave. Not yet. There was such deliciousness in this kiss, stolen in front of a witness as part of a charade and, he told himself, she kissed him back.

Molly nodded. Tomfool had stopped giggling like a ninny long enough to pat Bill's horse and line up behind Molly at the gate.

'Girls first,' Joe said, swinging open the unlocked door and bowing for Molly, before jumping in front of Tomfool when he tried to push in second.

'Don't you mean ladies?' Molly asked.

'Maybe,' Joe answered, wondering if that made him a coquette.

He began rehearsing what he'd tell Uncle Bill about the afternoon's exploits. It'd be good with Molly to listen. Maybe he'd even mention what happened with Mick and the smart Alec soldier at the Lands Office. That'd make it sound fair, like Mick was a bit of a hero too.

They traipsed through, boots echoing hollowly on the bare wooden floor of the hall. Entering the house with visitors always made Joe self-conscious, as though he was seeing things for the first time. It made him want to rearrange his life.

He could smell the faintest whiff of her soap, it smelled of lavender. He followed close. From now on the scent of lavender might always make him want to change his life too.

The doors to the bedrooms at the front of the house were closed. A sitting room opened out behind the hall. The room was full of half-finished garments spread across four single tattered lounge chairs in various stages of decrepitude. A treadle sewing machine sat under the only window and piles of books and papers were stacked about the floor in unsteady towers. A brick fireplace on the side wall was topped by a mantelpiece with a framed print of Karl Marx on one end and a clock on the other. Kathleen always had a vase of fresh flowers obscuring the portrait. Ted's reading-of-the-moment was on the mantel too, including the newspapers, so they didn't get lost in the detritus.

Joe felt even more self-conscious. No one else's house looked so … well used. He pushed onward, close behind Molly.

'I always feel at home in your sitting room,' she mused aloud. Joe felt foolish once more, for not guessing that she would think that.

'You never said so before,' Joe murmured. How much more he wanted to hear that he'd never heard before. Through the back of the house was the kitchen. His father's voice greeted them,

'Is that you, Kathleen?'

'No, it's us,' Joe said, stepping from behind Molly as they filed in. Sitting around the bare pine table, with enamel mugs of tea in their hands and a copy of *The Worker* spread out before them, were Ted Hill, Bill Carroll and Artem Segeyev.

'How did you get here so soon?' Joe asked.

Truth to tell, he felt a little dismayed as Ted had probably already entertained Uncle Bill with tales of Joe's speech and the fraças.

'Say hello to our guests and I might tell you,' Ted Hill said. They all chorused their g'days as Bill and Artem stood, Bill almost formally and Artem a little uneasy as he stepped behind his chair, empty mug in hand.

'Cripes, you don't have to come to attention, Bill. You're not in the Army,' his father said. 'Yet!' he added.

'Sit down, man!'

Molly and Joe shared a glance.

'What do you mean, "yet"?' Joe asked for both of them.

'Haven't even got to the first question and he's already onto the second,' Ted laughed. 'He'll make a politician "yet"!'

'You make a good show tonight. A good show,' Artem smiled, nodding.

'How did it feel, Comrade?'

Segeyev was usually frugal with his praise and his question surprised Joe. He glanced at Molly.

'I …' Joe couldn't get another word out. Ted and Artem waited for the second time that evening.

'I felt,' Joe finally managed in a rush of breath. 'Once I got going I felt … exalted!' he ended, happy with a word that sounded as high and as joyous as the moment had been.

'Blimey son, I hope you don't hesitate so much come the Revolution,' his father laughed. 'Or you'll dance for the hangman before we get started.'

He winked at Tomfool and pulled a strangled face as he tugged on an imaginary noose. Joe felt the red creep up his neck. Blushing in front of them all. In front of Molly.

'Mind you, not everyone was happy with him,' Molly offered. 'Look at what the Loyalists did,' she said, lifting Joe's hair so they could all see the wound. Its blood was coagulated now. Her hand was warm, and soft and careful. He blushed a deeper, more thankful red.

'And hello to you too, Miss Molly … Tomas,' Uncle Bill said, nodding to them each in turn.

'You'd make a rose blush for beauty these days, Molly,' he continued, looking with feigned interest to where she showed Joe's injury. Now it was Molly's turn to colour.

Segeyev took his usual blunt action.

'I leave to prepare for lecture,' he said. Molly stepped away from Joe, to make way for him to pass, fumbling to recover her composure.

'Tonight, Montague Miller. He may be old man but he is valiant,' Segeyev continued. 'Though I sometimes think his Socialism is merely a fierce hatred of injustice in disguise. And Mrs Griffiths – a rousing speaker and good to hear a woman-worker. I must ready the rooms,' Segeyev said more to himself than the others.

'You come up after your meal and help me with chairs?'

Joe nodded as Segeyev continued, addressing both Uncle Bill and Ted.

'You are both wrong in the matter we discuss,' he said, staring hard at Uncle Bill. 'I say no more. My regards, fellow-workers.'

Artem walked down the hall to see himself out.

'What's he mean, "wrong"?' Joe burst out. 'Who's wrong?'

'And about what?' added Molly.

'And you still haven't told me what you meant by, "yet"?'

'The doctor's going home,' Tomfool chimed in. Joe turned to Tomfool's voice. He grinned, pleased with the attention.

'Well, is it true?' Joe demanded. 'Is someone going somewhere?'

Uncle Bill glanced down at Ted Hill.

'I suppose I have to tell them sooner or later, Ted,' he half-asked.

'Don't look to me for help,' Ted Hill answered. 'Spit it out!'

Bill gazed at a point out the kitchen window on the other side of Tomfool's head.

'I've decided,' he said, as all their eyes followed the every move of his lips. 'I've decided to go to France.'

'No!' a voice sobbed behind them. It was the sort of voice they'd heard many times before, when the Postmaster delivered those black-bordered telegrams that swirled around the suburbs like leaves from the war's far-off, dying tree.

'Kathleen!' Ted and Uncle Bill said together. They all turned.

Her hat was only half-off, her face pale. She trembled, then swayed. Joe jumped to her side, grabbing her arm.

'Mother?' he asked. He'd never seen her like this before. Was it the shock of Uncle Bill's news, or worse? Joe had his own trouble dealing with what he'd just heard.

'Ouhah!' she answered. Her voice sounded as though she had been struck a blow to the stomach. Her eyes, as she gazed at Uncle Bill in dull surprise, seemed vacant for a moment then, they rolled back in her head.

'Sit her down. Quick!' Molly ordered. She took Kathleen's hat as Joe directed her collapsing body to a chair at the table. Ted stared at her strangely as her head fell to the tabletop. Uncle Bill strode to her side.

'My bag, Joe!' he ordered. 'Under the seat of the buggy!' Joe ran.

Tomfool put his hands to his ears. His mouth moved soundlessly. Uncle Bill lifted the kitchen chair and moved it back from the table. He lifted Kathleen's head, to lower it down, between her knees. She hung, limp as a rag doll. Molly held her on one side, Bill on the other. Joe ran back, thrusting Bill's doctor's bag into his hands.

Joe looked from Kathleen to Ted then to Molly, hoping someone would tell him what was going on. What if she died? But everyone fell silent. The clock ticked insistently on the mantelpiece in the living room. Ted Hill stood up, pushing his chair back from the table. He stared hard at Bill, half-concerned, half-accusing.

'She's fainted is all, man,' Dr Carroll said, his voice sounding quite alone. If the statement was meant to be reassuring it wasn't. Molly stood and put her arm around Tomfool. Joe placed his hands lightly on his mother's shoulders. She felt cold as he crouched down beside her.

'Ma? Are you all right? Kathleen?'

Dr Carroll fumbled with the cork in a bottle of smelling salts waving it under Kathleen's nose. Her head jerked up slightly and she pushed his hand away, but she stayed in the same position.

'Look at me,' she mumbled to herself. 'I can't believe this is me! Like a teenage girl.'

'Ma?' Joe asked again softly.

'Take no notice,' Kathleen said, 'of your silly mother. I'm quite well. I fainted is all. Shock, I expect.'

She turned her head to Joe.

'You made me very proud today,' she whispered. Her eyes were glistening, the pupils still large, but she smiled, almost her old self again, thinking first of others.

'I'm fine, thank you,' she said loudly from below the table. She raised herself upright once more.

Molly managed to pull Tomfool's hands from his ears so he could hear the good news. Uncle Bill packed his smelling salts away. Ted sat back down in his chair.

'I just needed to sit like an ostrich with its head in the sand.' Kathleen uttered a queer laugh before adding,

'I suppose no-one's put the stew on?'

'We were waiting for you, old mate,' Ted tried a lame joke. 'You know I'd burn water if I tried to boil it!'

Tomfool took his hands down, reassured.

Kathleen O'Donahue raised her head slowly, her face still ashen.

'How many for tea then?' she asked.

Molly snapped out of what seemed a daze.

'None of us, Mrs O'Donahue,' she said, indicating Tomfool with a nod.

'Thanks but, if we're for being late, Babushka will turn into Baba Yaga and eat Tom and me for dinner,' she added, glancing out the kitchen window at the light-drained sky.

'Hope she tenderises young Tom, then,' Uncle Bill said, poking Tomfool in the ribs until he backed away, laughing once more. Bill replaced the smelling salts in his bag.

'William,' Kathleen continued. 'You'll stay, of course.' Her tone brooked no contradiction.

'I …' Uncle Bill began. 'Of course!' he agreed. 'If you're up to it.'

'This nurse thinks she's fine,' Kathleen said. Slowly she stood upright. But still held tight to the edge of the table. Her face was white but not pallid, the pupils in her blue eyes almost normal.

'Yes,' she said to Molly. 'You'd better get off home *tout suite*. Your grandmother will be in a blue funk.' Molly stood, unwilling to leave.

'As long as you'll be well enough?' she asked.

'It was a hot afternoon and a shock is all. Besides, if I'm not all right there's a doctor close at hand,' Kathleen answered, nearly in her usual style.

'Get along!' she shushed them all down the hall.

'Joseph will see you home, won't you, Joe,' she continued as she chased a loose hair away from her face.

'Now then,' she turned back to the men in the kitchen, 'that stew needs re-heating.'

'Come on you two,' Joe said.

Kathleen still seemed … disjointed, but he'd promised her twice now that he'd get Molly and Tomfool home safe. Still, for once stew appealed, if only because it sounded like this stew might make a very revealing meal and he still had his own news to tell. Before they'd got down the footpath a house distant, Ted Hill appeared, calling from the front door.

'Joe! Your mother says she was followed home by a half-dozen hooligans. They were a bit vocal, that's all, but still, might pay if you took the doovey-whatsits off,' he said motioning to the rosettes still fluttering, forgotten, on their chests. 'That's the good oil from Mother!'

'Righto then, Mr Hill,' Molly answered for them all. Ted Hill turned to go back inside the house but swung back as Molly called him.

'Mr Hill!' she sang out. 'You didn't answer. You know, inside when Joe asked.'

Ted Hill stood mystified.

'How did you manage to get here before us?'

Ted Hill broke into the knowing smile he had when he thought he'd been caught being clever. He tapped the side of his nose.

'If you're going to cause a nuisance, have a good plan of retreat!' he answered. 'Segeyev had one of the lads tie up his dinghy in the mangroves at the bottom of the Domain,' he explained. 'First they lost you, then they lost us, and then they lost interest! Don't worry,' he finished, 'we gave the black devils enough to write in their reports. You'll be remembered, Mr Joseph Hill!' He laughed and strode back inside the unpainted house.

Joe knew the last comment was just for him. Praise his father would never give man to man, not even father to son. Joe smiled to himself. It was a good feeling.

'Come on!' Tomas called. 'Stew for two and you for stew,' he sang, pointing at Molly. 'And no stew for you, Mr Joseph Hill. And no cake too.'

Laughing, they started off again. Tomfool broke into a trot.

'Come on slow-coaches,' he said trotting along, the thought of food urging him.

Joe knew Babushka would be angry with Molly, but he also knew that he wanted to stay with her as long as he could, even though he was dying to know what was happening at home.

Joe was thinking hard, not believing that, after so many years speechifying about pacifism, Bill had suddenly jumped off the idea. No wonder Kathleen reacted so badly. Still, it hadn't happened, "yet".

They all almost jogged the last two hundred yards to Babushka's. If the light was on in the front room it meant dinner had started and they'd get a dressing down in front of all the boarders. They reached the front gate.

'The light's not on,' Molly breathed thankfully as Tomfool leapt the stairs two at a time. She bounced up the stairs after him, closely followed by Joe.

'Say hello to Babushka,' Joe smiled as they reached the front landing. Molly smiled her beguiling smile.

'As if I'll be getting one word in sideways!' she said, her hand on the door latch.

'Joe,' she continued quietly, her voice barely a murmur as Tomfool yelled his goodbyes and hellos from inside the front door.

'You were an inspiration today. The way you spoke and they listened. All of them. Not just the kids in the Peace Army. All of them. Joseph Hill, you're going to be a somebody one day. And when you are I'll be so proud and say, "I knew him when he was just a strip a nothin'!"' Molly laughed. Joe blushed.

'Tell me about Uncle Bill when you know,' she added.

'I'll keep an eye on both the new lodgers,' she nodded towards the inside of the house, then, she stood on her tiptoes and kissed him quick, light as the breath of a butterfly, right on his lips.

Molly turned and ran into *Erin* to the smell of re-heated leftovers and the rattle of crockery and the wooden door that closed with a click. Joe could smell jasmine mixed with her lavender. He could have stood there all night. He may well have done if it weren't for the voice that rang out,

'Hey! Don't I know you?'

It came from some way down the street. Joe knew who it was.

'Hoy, you!' the voice sang out again. 'It's that bloody Wobblie from the meeting!' Harry Winterson repeated. 'It's the red-flagger! Let's have him!'

But they were too late. This was Joe's home block. He knew it like the back of his hand. He ducked across the street, jumped the front fence of Old Nik's, then the side fence into the yard beyond.

The sound of Old Nik's violin turned the humid evening air bittersweet with nostalgia, mingling disparately with the hoarse yells and curses as the soldiers stumbled into his yard.

Joe shivered with the thrill of the second chase of the afternoon, running like billy-oh, dodging the obstacles that he knew were there. Heart beating loud.

He dodged through the side gates of two more cottages, then over the front fence of the second before sprinting home.

Joe leaned, gasping for breath, against his own outhouse wall, listening to the dogs barking and the cackle of disturbed chooks and the raised voices and his heart.

In the light-the-lamp-time distance, Old Nik changed his tune to a jaunty rendition of the *Internationale* before yelling at the soldiers who were trampling through his garden.

'Who stumbles in darkness, trampling my tomatoes! You are up to mischiefs! I call police!'

Finally, Joe's thoughts caught up with him once more.

She kissed me back!

Guilt caressed his lips where so few moments before *her* honeyed lips had been. Joe could still smell her hair. Her eyes fluttering closed. But she was Mick's girl and Mick was his best mate. It had been a long, long day already. It was all too hard.

Suddenly, Ma's stew smelt so good.

Chapter 7

Hooray!
Hooray for my mate,
Hooray at last.
Hooray for my mate,
For he's a horse's arse!
Anon

His breath back to normal, Joe trudged up the stairs, following the smell of dinner into the kitchen. Ted Hill was sitting at the table reading the newspaper, as usual, but there was something odd, awkward, about the scene. Joe was suddenly assailed by the dread of the Death List. Perhaps someone they knew had their name printed on the page he was reading, there in black and white. He held his breath, not daring to ask, though he felt like exploding with it all.

Uncle Bill sat at the table, his eyes sometimes on Ted Hill, who read aloud from the paper or, more often, on Kathleen O'Donahue, who busied herself, moving the cast iron pot to the cool at the edge of the wood stove, preparing to serve the stew and her famous dumplings, out onto the plates.

As he stood, an observer, unnoticed at the edge of the stifling hot kitchen, Joe thought it odd that his mother didn't look at either of the men, or interrupt as Ted read. That was very strange. It was always Kathleen who interrogated every word that was printed in the Press, worrying at all the writers – Right and Left in equal measure – as if she were debating with them, (if a terrier debates a rat), while his father kept up a rattle of side commentary,

'The writer covers that point later, Kathleen' or, 'I'll get to it momentarily.'

Joe needed to tell them about what had happened at the Printers that afternoon and that he'd outfoxed the hooligans in their street. He knew could never them about Molly though he needed that most of all.

Joe thought he might interrupt but … something had changed. A something that warned him to hold his peace no matter how difficult that was.

'It says here in *The Worker ,*' Ted began to read as Joe leaned against the backdoor jamb, half in the cooler evening air and half in the sweltering kitchen.

'"At the present, the number of men volunteering grows ever smaller, and the number now offering their services is a mere trickle of what it has been in the early years of the war."'

It was as though they were actors trying to remember their lines, as though they had never discussed these ideas before, despite the fact Joe had heard them do it a thousand times.

What had been said? If only he hadn't taken Molly home … but then she wouldn't have … holy of holies! Joe watched and listened, trying to make the pieces fit.

'It says here,' his father continued. '"The reports carried in the daily press of the horrors which take place at the present slaughtering shop we call this war, and especially the long lists of killed or maimed, and the graphical descriptions in connection therewith, all tell us what a hungry worker joining the Expeditionary Force can expect. This acts on the mind of the Australian workman in favour of holding them back from joining up.

'"The Government sees this and, even by browbeating employers to guarantee volunteers their positions when they return from the war, they cannot increase enlistments. In Sydney now, the merchants have hung up notices that all single men able to carry arms will be dismissed from their work."'

Kathleen pushed past him, interrupting his reading as she set the places for the four of them at the table in a silent ritual. She turned away then to the plates and stove. Ted cast her a strange look before straightening the paper to continue his reading,

'"How far a government led by the scab, Hughes, will go, is hard to say. It is likely that this unholy alliance between coercive Government and blood-lusting bosses will push each one of us into the trenches!"'

'We agree with that, don't we?' his father demanded. 'They go and declare war on our behalf and then, when we have the temerity to tell them we think war against our fellow workers is a bad idea, they try and force us to fight! That's what we fought against in the first Conscription Referendum and now it's happening again!'

Ted Hill was growing red-faced with passion, which seemed unnecessary, given the audience. He dropped the paper to the table in disgust. Bill, knowing Ted's comments were entirely for his benefit, crossed his arms in the attitude of a schoolboy being chastised. Ted read the piece as though it were a challenge. As if Bill hadn't said the same things a thousand times himself, but now here he was, denying himself to himself. Denying his own history and his own conscience.

Joe stared in amazement at the performance. Still Kathleen kept mum. Ted leaned across the table towards his friend.

'Why would you go and support those bastards, Bill? You've been a pacifist as long as I've known you.'

Ted's face was a portrait of genuine bewilderment. He looked to Kathleen for support. Her back was turned to the table as she served the meals out onto the five plates spread on the bench. She stiffened, but she did not speak.

'It's not easy,' Bill began, as Ted leaned back and folded his arms in a "this had better be good" manner.

'You don't have to deal with the wounded, day-in, day-out, knowing that better doctoring immediately after their wounds were inflicted would mean so many more would live, or at least, recover so much better. I can do that initial doctoring and save lives. I should do it. I should do it. First do no harm,' he muttered as though trying to convince himself.

Kathleen hit the handle of the enamelled ladle down loudly on the side of the pot then threw it hard towards the sink, not attempting to amend its violence. It clattered like rifle fire around the metal bowl. Neither Bill nor Ted acknowledged the gesture.

'But don't you see, it'll look to everyone like you support them?' Ted said quietly. 'Whether it's true or not that's how it'll look from the outside and that'll damage us. You carry a lot of respect with the rank and file.'

Ted looked to Kathleen for support and found – his wife's back once more. He expected her to burst into a tirade. But she did not, would not, refused point-blank to respond, simply leaned heavily on the edge of the bench and wiped her forehead with the back of her hand.

He turned back to Bill, who also gazed at Kathleen, his face drawn in an almost haggard expression, as though facing her silence was more difficult than deciding to place himself in the firing line in Europe.

Joe was also silent, not understanding how such a turn-around could have ever happened to someone so certain in his views. Surely Uncle Bill didn't mean what he said. He was a great doctor. Everyone in Repatriation said that without him many patients would never have got better, or become so well, or … they would have just died. He was already doing his best work here, at home. Ted was right. If he went to the front it'd look like he deserted the Cause.

'Ours is a bigger goal than fixing the maimed and the wounded,' Ted tried a different tack. 'Ours is to stop men from putting themselves up as cannon fodder in the first place. We've always said if they weren't there they couldn't get hurt. What's changed?' Ted asked again.

At the edge of his voice was a plea. He'd watched Bill all evening and his demeanor had not changed. Ted had to confront the fact that his friend was deadly serious. It seemed as if all their history together fighting against the war and, even before that, for the rights of workers, counted for nothing. His medical logic Ted could understand but he couldn't find the political logic. He needed to find a rational excuse or else Bill's intended actions amounted to a betrayal – pure and indefensible.

'But Uncle Bill!' Joe said, his voice louder than he'd expected. They turned, unaware he'd returned, too absorbed by … whatever it was that was happening.

'If you cure people here you are doing your job too. There will always be those not well looked after over there and they need you even more when they get home and, if you are here, you can make sure they continue to get what they need even after they leave hospital. People respect you. They'll take notice of you. You can stop even more from going. We all see you and Mother with them every day on the streets. Here you can say war is wrong and stop the young fools from signing up. There you are simply a … , a … ,' Joe fought to think of an analogy. 'You're simply a mechanic fixing up the broken parts of the war machine. You go and you've sold your soul.'

Bill slammed both his hands down on the table.

'"The young fools"? Look at yourself, Joe. Still wet behind the ears! It's never so simple!' Bill enunciated his words as he swung to face Joe. His voice stabbed with anger.

'There's more to this than you know. It's not about you and your kindergarten peace group. This is real politics for real adults!' he finished. All his ever-present good grace had abandoned him, his face red as boiled mudcrab.

His words stung Joe like a swarm of wasps. It was his turn to redden. He watched as his father's face turned bitter, sour, ugly, dizzy with disbelief.

Kathleen O'Donahue turned from the bench, a plate of stew in either hand. She gazed at her son.

'So this is the real William Carroll,' she said, her voice like a insult. 'This is how he treats his own?' Bill hung his head, rubbing his hands through his immaculate hair.

'Well!' she demanded. 'You owe our Joe an apology!' The room breathed.

'Bill?' Kathleen repeated almost inaudibly. Bill Carroll kept his head lowered and his voice silent.

'So you'd betray your own as well as the Cause?' Bill eyes were fierce with torment.

'That, from you? Jesus, woman!' He made to stand, but too late. Kathleen turned and in one movement threw a full plate of hot stew straight at his face.

'Judas!' she screamed. Bill jumped, sending the chair flying as the plate smashed to the floor. He scraped the burning gravy from his cheeks and ran the two steps to the kitchen taps to douse his face with water.

'You dirty cow!' he bellowed, rounding on her, finger stabbing, as stew and water still dripped from his face, waistcoat and trousers. But Ted and Joe were beside her in the time it took to utter the threat. Bill did not approach. Kathleen dropped the second plate uselessly onto the table and slumped into a chair like a burnt-out log collapsing in a fire.

Bill wiped himself down as they stared at him. Dumping the excess stew on the floor, he pulled a handkerchief from his pocket to wipe his hands and face. He squared his shoulders, ready now to take them on, one by one, staring each of them down.

'I'm going,' he said, his voice tight with control. 'I'm going home now,' he repeated as he bent to pick up his bag and coat.

'Then I'm going to the front in France to help … as soon as I can. I had hoped,' he continued, his voice black-edged with bitterness, 'that we could have parted differently. But,' he concluded, 'I always hope for too much … especially from those I love,' he added, a smile of sorts twisting the side of his always-happy mouth into a leer. He waited a moment for a word, a look, a gesture. But it was momentary, the pause and, as for response … there was none.

Joe's heart beat hard. Ted anguished, but adamant. Too much of an insult had been given. Joe looked at Kathleen. If he thought she was unwell when she'd taken her turn, now she seemed ready to die.

Bill turned and walked slowly down the hall. They stood in tableaux. Heard the door, then the gate, click, the creak of the buggy, the clip clop of his horse off through the blood-warm air of the street.

It was Kathleen's voice broke the silence,

'Joe, Old Nik will be missing his tea,' she said, her voice without any music, either soft or strong. 'Take it down to him.'

'Are you … ?' Joe began. But she continued, her voice monotone.

'And hurry back for yours or we'll be late for the meeting. I promised Mrs Griffiths I was coming to hear her and Mr Montague, and I will.'

Joe watched as she endured his father's touch to her shoulder. Then he took Old Nik's plate, covered with a second overturned onto it, wrapped in a rabbit-ear-knotted tea towel, and headed out again onto the street.

'Get yourself washed up,' his mother said to his father as she bent to clean the mess from the floor. 'It'll get cold.'

Chapter 8

Eureka Oath, 1854
We swear by the Southern Cross to stand truly by each other and fight to defend our rights and liberties.
Peter Lalor

The evening's humid air was tepid as a lukewarm bath. The odd cigarette or clay pipe on the verandahs glowed with indrawn breath then faded like a firefly into the darkness. The only sound was the rustle of Kathleen's skirt and the murmurs of greeting she and Ted returned to the nearly inaudible salutations drifting out from front verandahs where neighbours sat, trying to catch the cooler evening air.

There wasn't a sign of the hooligans from earlier. Joe hoped they'd cleared off to harass someone else, somewhere else. He hadn't told his parents what had happened with Winterson but, with one thing and another, there wasn't time, and now … definitely not. It could wait. After he got home from Old Nik's they'd said nothing about what had happened in his absence. Kathleen hurried him to wash, eat his meal, and dress. Next, they were on their way to the meeting.

Joe wondered whether Mick would be there. If he got in a blue with his father he wouldn't, even though he'd promised to come. Thoughts jostled for attention.

Joe was glad he was going to the meeting. Being with other people took the pressure off him, being the only child and all.

'The rose between two thorns,' Kathleen called him.

'The meat in the sandwich,' was Ted's more blunt, and more accurate, assessment. But, as they walked closer to *Erin*, the thought of Molly took his mind off nearly everything else. He wished she was allowed out, though he knew she wouldn't be, not at night without a chaperone. 'If wishes were horses, beggars would ride.' Joe sighed – a deep sigh.

There was something about this hush, especially from his mother, that unnerved him. She was the type who liked to talk things through, taking the contrary position, to play the Devil's Advocate (as she called it), but now – this utter silence. Trudge on, trudge on in silence, seemed the best policy.

When they finally arrived at the Russian Workers' Association rooms they were late. The *Internationale* started as they made their way up the stairs. Artem was leading the singing from a makeshift speaking platform at the head of the room. On his right stood Monty Miller, with Mrs Griffiths beside him. Joe craned his neck to search the crowd for Molly or Mick. He wanted to tell Mick about Uncle Bill. Find out what he thought. Mick had a lot more experience dealing with prickly characters than Joe did. Had to deal with his father for a start. Maybe he'd have a few ideas about convincing Bill not to go to the Front. That is if Bill would talk to any of them again. Joe knew what Mick would say,

'Thump the scabby mongrel.' And he'd get that look in his eye that really wasn't helpful in dispute resolution. The Bill Carroll that Joe knew was a vain bloke who'd had his pride dented – by a woman, a nurse no less, who was in the right defending her own, and Bill knew it. Who knew what he might do? Joe needed to talk to someone ... anyone.

Hurry up, Mick, he thought.

Ted and Kathleen made their way to the only seats left, right at the back of the hall. Joe stopped just inside the door, grabbing his mother's forearm.

'I'll stay here,' he said, breaking the evening's silence, 'and keep an eye out for Mick.'

Kathleen nodded and started to sing as she followed her husband.

Joe nodded his 'G'days' to the lads near the door and walked back out onto the landing. From here he could keep one eye on the street and one ear on the proceedings.

The Peace Armyists were sitting together and waved him over but Joe signalled his apologies by hand, pointing out the door and down the street. He joined in singing, finishing the *Internationale* with great gusto. It was a relief, singing like that, gave him an outlet for the emotions that twisted him into a knot.

Molly, Uncle Bill, his speech, Mick, his parents' silence, Winterson, the everyday of the war – it was a big knot.

Vainly he hoped that Molly would appear. After all *Erin* was only two houses away. Maybe she'd sneak out, allowed to, or not? He knew she did sometimes, on moonlight assignations with Mick, when they whispered sweet nothings and kissed behind the tankstand. Mick told him about their lover's trysts whether he wanted to know or not. They were a badge of his daring all for love and a veiled threat directed at him, Joe often thought, to keep his distance from Molly. But most times Mick seemed in awe as he spoke, as though he were in a music hall hypnotist's trance from which he'd soon wake, in the cruel stage light, with the whole audience laughing at him. In awe that Molly should even so much as deign to look at him. She was his girl and his mother rolled into one – a heavy load for any woman to bear.

Joe wanted so much to talk to Molly too, about Uncle Bill and … but Monty was about to begin his speech and besides, it would never happen. Molly was as faithful as the day was long. He could only ever hope to feel the touch of her lips again on his cheek; to smell the waft of her hair from afar. Nothing would happen. And so it should be. I'll meet someone one day soon, he thought, though he couldn't begin to imagine anyone other. But twice today it was different … wasn't it? He touched his lips.

Artem Segeyev rose to his feet. The crowd quietened, scraping their chairs till they were comfortable.

'Fellow workers!' Segeyev began. The crowd applauded. They were certainly raring to go!

'Comrades,' Segeyev continued, 'tonight we will hear from a man who is a warrior for the Eight Hour Day and the Forty-Four Hour Week, votes for women, and the new Industrial Court. A man who has been gaoled for defending the rights of the working class.'

Segeyev's voice grew deeper.

'A man who understands that on our side we stand for Brotherhood. But Capital stands for profit and greed – the lowest animal-form of self-interested humanity. Capital must be redistributed, Brothers. We must take from each according to their means and give to each according to their needs.'

Artem was striding headlong into his usual spiel.

'How about we hear from Miller!' a member of the audience called, not unkindly, but Artem was, for once, put off. He glanced at the crowd, who expected his trademark explosion, but finished instead with the briefest of introductions,

'Comrade Montague Miller!' The crowd applauded.

Monty Miller pushed back his chair and drew himself up to his full six feet four inches. Though time-bent in his red-striped shirt and grey serge trousers, he still bore the cast of a powerful man. His grey hair was neatly cropped, but wayward even so, above a long face with watery blue eyes and a thin walrus moustache that drooped a grey arch about a mouth where yellowed teeth stood awry. A large, red rosette, printed with the number "54", was pinned to his chest. At that moment Joseph Hill thought Monty Miller the very ideal of an Australian revolutionary. He wanted to be Monty Miller almost as much as he wanted to be Artem Segeyev.

'Citizens! Fellow workers! Friends!' Montague began loudly, looking to the ceiling. 'And those paid by Billy Hughes to come out and record the evening's proceedings!' he finished, dropping his piercing gaze full onto the crowd. They guffawed as they tried to pick the disconcerted looks that would give away the narks.

'For those of you who do not know me I will give a short biography which will serve as an introduction to my talk on the nature and practices of coercive government,' he began.

'I was born working class near what is now Ballarat. My parents believed in hard work, education and, above and beyond these, fairness in all things. I was apprenticed at twelve years of age. Twelve hours a day and six days a week. Here's to the eight hour day, Comrades,' he said raising an imaginary glass to toast their future success. The crowd was delighted.

Joe looked anxiously down the street towards the 'Gabba, thinking that Mick was missing the good stuff.

Monty continued,

'During my teenage years, gold was found in Ballarat. Workers from around the world flocked to the Rush.'

Monty stopped, letting his mind drift back through space and time to a world so many years before. The audience waited. Joe did too, but also listened to the street. Mick should be close, if he's coming.

Joe would hear him. He took a step away from the door towards the landing.

'To raise revenue, the government issued paid licences to all the diggers – a flat tax for the lucky and the unlucky miners alike. When Lalor and Carboni and the united miners resisted this unjust tax they were branded criminals and outlaws.'

You could hear a pin drop in the hall. All eyes were turned to Monty. His voice rose and fell like a ballad singer remembering injustice, solidarity and pain.

Joe thought he heard a noise in the street towards the 'Gabba. Breaking from Monty's spell, he stepped out onto the landing.

'When the miners raised the stockade at Eureka,' Monty continued, touching his red rosette unconsciously. 'I was there. I was there when the troops marched up the hill. I was there beneath the flag of the Southern Cross as we defended our rights and, I was there on that field where many of my brothers died. Not in France but here, Comrades, in Australia. From that day forward, I vowed that never again would I be the slave of coercive government. Never again, fellow citizens, would I be told I had no rights!'

A smatter of applause hit the hall like the first splattering rain drops blown before a storm. But from outside there were other sounds. Running feet echoing in empty streets, catcalls and whistles up and down alleys. Joe was torn. Is that Mick out there being hunted … ?

'Citizens of Australia!' Monty called. 'Politicians believe that your power is theirs to exercise as they will. They call it their mandate. The mandate is yours! We must educate ourselves, citizens, about the facts of all the matters facing our nation – no less is enough!'

Montague Miller raised his right hand on its long arm high above his head, as though, Joe thought, he was taking lightning bolts from among the clouds. His voice rose.

'We must think for ourselves, citizens!' he roared, hammering the table down hard before him. 'I will not allow any political party, any prattling paperman, any other person to do my thinking for me. There are,' he said, holding up his hand to silence applause.

'There are those very learned people amongst us who believe they know what freedom is. I am not well-educated but my view is this: to study the facts of a matter as deeply as you can; to consider for yourself what these facts mean; then to act with your brothers who share your conclusions, this, my friends, is freedom.'

Joe watched as his parents jumped to their feet, applauding with many of the crowd.

Monty's right. The best ideas, most passionately put, will surely always win.

'Citizens,' Miller continued. 'We educate, agitate and organise for the common wealth; they accumulate, manipulate and despise us for their private profit. No one looks to government for the truth. No one looks to the marketplace for moral guidance.'

Voices were calling out on the street. One of them, he could hear clearly now, was Mick.

'Hallo, Mick!' he yelled from the landing.

His call distrupted the meeting as Ted and a few others turned in their seats.

Joe took the stairs down three at a stride. He was sure it was Mick's voice. He was certain it was Mick's voice calling,

'Help!'

As he ran Joe tried to think.

How many are there?

What will I do if there's a lot of them?

You're a pacifist, Joe.

But will they listen or will they attack?

How should a pacifist respond if they do?

He'd always run away from them before, or used his tongue to get him out of trouble. This might be different. The only things he knew for sure were: Mick was his mate and his mate needed him!

Joe sprinted down towards the bridge end of Merivale Street – the opposite direction from where he expected. Mick must have led them a chase round the back streets. He saw them on the footpath, only a few houses down from Babushka's, six of them in uniforms. Maybe there were more of them waiting? Babushka's gate opened as he passed. The mongrels had Mick on the ground. His arms flung over his head. Protecting it. One joker had a fence paling in his hand. Mick had stopped calling. Lying silent. They were kicking him and … Joe was on them.

'Bastards!' he yelled, smashing a fist into the face that held the waddy. The head snapped back, staggered, dropped the paling, threw a shocked hand to a now bloodied nose.

Joe pressed his surprise. Flailing like a chaffcutter he landed one in the guts of one and one in the face of another. A piercing whistle shrieked beside him, that close it was in his ear. Joe turned to recognise Sergeant O'Hagen. Then a fist smacked him with the sick thud of a mattock driven deep into damp earth, a clout that caught him flush on the side of the head.

His legs forgot to stand.

Chapter 9

Bread and Roses

As we go marching, marching, in the beauty of the day
A million darkened kitchens, a thousand mill lofts gray
Are touched with all the radiance that a sudden sun discloses
For the people hear us singing, bread and roses, bread and roses.
As we come marching, marching, we battle too, for men,
For they are in the struggle and together we shall win.
Our days shall not be sweated from birth until life closes,
Hearts starve as well as bodies, give us bread, but give us roses.
As we go marching, marching, we're standing proud and tall.
The rising of the women means the rising of us all.
No more the drudge and idler, ten that toil where one reposes,
But a sharing of life's glories, bread and roses, bread and roses.
James Oppenheim

'Get Nikolai! Get the cab, child!'

Babushka's voice quavered with uncertainty. She took Ted Hill's hand and pulled herself up from kneeling beside the moaning Mick. But she was still in command. Kathleen knelt beside Joe, trying to bring him round with smelling salts. Molly glanced anxiously from Babushka, to Mick, to Joe, but didn't need to be told twice. Babushka says run – she runs.

Molly had seen what happened. Joe wouldn't have been hit if O'Hagen hadn't blown that blasted whistle in his ear, and then him pretending to be so concerned for Mick and Joe, so those cowards could get away scott-free. She damned O'Hagen with an accusatory stare as she passed. She wouldn't forget one of those hooligans' faces in particular – the one who shared her roof – though not for long if she knew her grandmother.

Babushka dismissed her with an agitated wave of the hand. Molly elbowed her way through the crowd. It seemed like everybody who'd been at the meeting was now in the street, including Montague Miller.

'Joe is sometimes awake now?' Babushka said to Kathleen who looked up from where she knelt and nodded, flustered but professional.

'Joe's good. He'll be all right, but I just don't know about poor Mick,' Kathleen said as she wiped the blood from the corner of his mouth.

'Bleeding from the mouth is bad. His lungs you know.'

'I'll have to report this incident to the South Brisbane station,' O'Hagen muttered. 'They won't like how this meeting ended.'

He looked around the faces. The crowd members nearest to him were not best pleased with his suggestion that this thuggery had anything to do with their meeting. For once, for O'Hagen, silence seemed golden.

'We all go in Nikolai's cab,' Babushka informed him without looking away from Kathleen and Mick.

'You come with us. We tell them all together what has happened here this night.'

A shout from towards the river sent a group of younger men from the crowd running towards the wharves. Ted glanced around and nodded at a few older fellows who left too. Ted Hill was unable to stop organising, even when his son lay fallen.

Molly ran up Merivale Street. She knew the cobbler's shop at the front of the building was operated by a man called Mayakov. Old Nik had the living quarters at the back and use of the yard and stable for Kaiser and his cab. Her mind scurried. She'd learned to do that since living with Babushka. Why think just one thing when you can worry about three things at once?

If only it was a fair fight, Mick would have sorted them out. He'd have given them all a clout on the ear and a good kicking if they weren't all damn cowards.

Molly wanted to go back but she knew there was nothing more to do than Kathleen was doing already. She realised, and the realisation almost made her stumble, that she was desperate to see Joe with his eyes open.

So she could smile and watch the blush rise up his neck. She wanted to be there for them both. Her mind moved from scurry to polka, and it swirled.

'Whoa!' called a voice. A horse whinnied close to her. She hadn't seen it with her head so dizzy with thoughts. She could almost taste its breath in her mouth it was that close.

'Ted Hill calls for me. What is happening?'

It was Old Nik peering down like a character from Tolstoy – his glance quick and piercing.

'How did you … ?' Molly mumbled as she scrambled up onto the front seat of the cab. One of the Peace Army boys was perched beside Old Nik. She couldn't, in her confusion, remember his name so she squeezed his hand tight in recognition. Ted must have sent him.

'What is to be done?' Nikolai demanded again.

'It's our boys,' she stumbled over the words. 'The hooligans …' Molly fell back beside him as he cracked his whip in the air above the horse's head. Old Kaiser half-reared with fright before he lunged forward and they all careered out into the street, almost colliding with another buggy heading the same way.

'Uncle Bill!' Molly and the Peace Army boy exclaimed together. Another of Ted's runners? Molly wondered at the organisation of the man.

The crowd was filling with all the right people, and it was growing fast. Men and women from surrounding houses were filing out onto the street – curious but cautious. They'd heard it all before, the bandying in the streets leading up to the Conscription Referendum not six months back. It was bad around here then with the violence and vandalism and the vicious arguments for and against, and it had made them cautious. They were coming out now though in force, angry that it was their own who lay in the gutter.

'We ask Ted Hill what is to be done,' Nikolai said in a tone that meant only a silly young girl would not be able to tell him what he needed to know. Molly blushed and felt very un-adult and like she should be crying. Old Nik touched her hand in apology, his glance kind.

'All are upset this evening,' he said.

Bill Carroll pulled up his buggy at the edge of the crowd. Behind them they could hear the new ambulance, klaxon swirling, as it drove down the street, bringing more people out into the road. The hospital was not so far off. But it wasn't the emergency that had set Bill's heartbeat galloping when the message arrived. He was too professional a doctor for that.

Artem Segeyev held his horse as Carroll grabbed his bag and strode into the crowd, calling over his shoulder for someone to bring the stretcher. As he reached the centre of the mob Ted stood up from where he squatted beside Joe. Babushka held Joe upright, though woozy, on the edge of the gutter.

Ted Hill looked hard at Bill, his emotions released now his friend was here.

'Thanks, we need you,' Ted said as he stepped towards the doctor, hand outstretched to shake. Bill hesitated only a trice. They'd both been angry. Ted was protecting his family. Bill took Ted's hand but stared hard into his face.

'Yes. You and others,' he said as he squatted down beside Kathleen. She cradled Mick's head on her lap. Someone's knee rug covered him.

'What's the situation here, Sister?' he began. Kathleen looked at a place near his collar as she replied.

'The boy's been unconscious for close to twenty minutes,' she answered, quiet and deliberate. 'When I arrived at the scene I saw him on the ground being kicked by some men in military uniform. By which I mean,' she said looking at the doctor's face for the first time, 'They wore military boots and they were kicking him hard. The cowards ran off as we approached,' she added before remembering she was delivering a medical report.

'He's breathing weakly and bleeding a little from the mouth. I haven't been able to bring him round with salts,' she finished. Bill returned her gaze until she lowered her eyes. She saw he had changed his clothes.

'Get that stretcher here!' Bill Carroll yelled as he checked the boy's pupils and his pulse.

'We need him at the Mater, quick.' He looked again at Kathleen.

'I'll need you too, Sister,' he said. Kathleen shook her head.

'I'm going with Joe.' Bill nodded immediately.

'Of course, I'll have to make do with the Duty Sister,' he smiled to cover the awkwardness.

The stretcher was laid beside Mick's prone form and Bill supervised as Segeyev and another lifted him on. The stretcher-bearers loaded Mick into the ambulance, Babushka stroking his inert arm as they did. Molly saw him off before returning to stand by Joe. Bill Carroll turned his attention to Kathleen.

'Now a quick look at Joe.'

'He's all right,' she said. 'You go with Mick.'

'I need to look at him,' Bill repeated.

Kathleen walked the few paces to where Joe sat, punch-drunk as a prize fighter, one of Babushka's black shawls draped across his shoulders.

'If you don't trust me,' she countered, tossing her head and waving him down to look at Joe. A huge bruise was beginning to blacken the side of his head and jaw. He stemmed the blood from his lip with a reddened handkerchief held hard to it.

'For God's sake, Kathleen!' Bill began.

'He was hit in the side of the head. I saw him spin around and fall on the same side of his head as he was hit,' she reported in a professional monotone. 'The boy was unconscious for some minutes. He gained consciousness with salts but no further medical aid was administered.'

Ted Hill grabbed his wife by the arm.

'What's the matter, woman? You should be bloody thankful he came back after the way you treated him!'

'Me?' Kathleen hissed under her breath. Her eyes flashed warning. 'He's your best friend. He tells us he's walking out on us and it's *my* fault for telling him what I really think of him! It should have been you told him if you weren't all mouth and no trousers.'

She pulled herself out of his grip. Ted shook his head and muttered, 'The whole bloody world's gone mad tonight.'

'How many fingers?' Bill was asking.

'Who's the Prime Minister of Australia?' Joe smiled out of the good side of his mouth.

'I didn't know it was a general knowledge quiz,' he almost laughed, his pupils large as the end of a pencil.

'You despise the buggar, Uncle Bill!' he answered, slurring the "despise" like a drunkard.

'I'll keep him at the hospital for observation tonight,' Dr Carroll announced as he straightened up. Kathleen stood her ground.

'He's all right, Doctor. I'll care for him. I'm a qualified Medical Sister.' Bill opened his mouth, but she continued,

'We don't need any more civilians taking beds away from our war wounded do we?'

Sister Kathleen smiled, too disingenuously.

'Well, if he's not sick enough for hospital I'll have to ask you to escort me down to the station!'

O'Hagen had waited quietly for the verdict before he spoke. Ted turned to face him.

'Don't be stupid, man!' he yelled. 'You can see the boy's not well!' Then he checked himself. No use in getting the plod offside, especially while he was staying at Babushka's.

'We'll bring him down in the morning.'

O'Hagen held firm.

'If he is well enough, I have orders to take in any miscreants from the meeting,' the crowd tensed palpably at the word "miscreant" and the unfairness, 'down to the station,' O'Hagen finished.

Molly grabbed at Ted Hill as he stepped towards the policeman. He turned back to her.

'You tell your grandmother to get rid of that!' he hissed, his thumb jerking over his shoulder at O'Hagen, 'or we will!'

'What?' asked a voice from close at hand. 'Let Joe go with you and let your wallopers finish the job in the cells!'

It was Montague Miller. The crowd moved closer again.

'I think it would be better all round if I kept him at the hospital tonight,' Bill Carroll said firmly.

'No!' said Kathleen, her voice sounding louder than it should in the menacing silence.

'I'll go with him. I'm his mother. We'll be all right.'

She turned to the crowd.

'Go back to your meeting, Comrades.'

Then directly to Montague Miller.

'I … we,' she began, correcting herself, 'are very thankful for your offer, Mr Miller, and sorry to interrupt your speech, but please, we're all right.'

Monty eyed her closely, looked down to Joe, then slowly nodded his head.

'Come, we go,' Babushka said.

'Nikolai!' she called as though summoning a serf.

Ted went to help Joe up.

Montague Miller stood in the gutter beside Molly, rubbing his long ear distractedly. Finally he looked down at her from his great height.

'Here,' said the old man, as he fished for something in the fob pocket of his waistcoat.

'Molly isn't it?' he continued. Molly nodded as she held out her hand to steady Joe.

'You're a special friend of these lads?' Monty asked. Molly glanced quickly over her shoulder. She began to blush.

'Yes,' she answered quietly.

'Here's a keepsake. Copy it out and give a copy to each of them when they're in their right minds again.' He took her hand and placed a small piece of paper into it before closing her fingers down.

'Keep the original for yourself.'

'But this is yours,' she remonstrated.

'I'm an old man who memorized it long ago,' he smiled. 'Tell them,' he continued. 'What is best is always with you. It's so easy sometimes,' he finished cryptically, 'to be so busy trying to win the game, that you forget what the game's about.'

Babushka was calling. She almost had everyone onto the hansom cab. Joe was squeezed beside his parents on one side, Babushka was waiting impatiently, O'Hagen standing officiously beside.

'Molly!' Babushka called. 'We go now! Oyoyoy! Children!'

Montague Miller turned back to the crowd.

'Comrades!' he called, his voice commanding the entire street. 'What more example do we need of what happens to young men who return from the depravity of war than this? How can this war be fair to them or to any of us? Only socialism will give us a fair go.'

He continued his lecture where he stood.

Molly ran past O'Hagen to hop into the cab beside Babushka. Ted closed the door behind her. O'Hagen looked miffed, his moustache a little awry.

'Well, I'll just ride on the step then,' he began, stepping forward. But Old Nik started without him. Kaiser put in an heroic effort, given the load, leaving O'Hagen to jog beside.

'No room. You walk!' Babushka directed as he hopped like a one-legged kangaroo trying to grab the side of the cab and swing himself up onto the step. She waved him away, swatting at his hand when he tried to grab the door.

Her voice was almost sad, her hair unkempt about her face.

O'Hagen was flabbergasted. His mouth lolled open.

As she watched the look on his face, Babushka began to smile, then giggle like a child until she was rolling in mirth. The rest of them joined her, laughing more in relief, than at O'Hagen, as Kaiser almost made a trot.

Molly opened her hand to see, by the light of the carriage lamp, what it was she held. A small piece of yellowed paper, so old the creases had turned brown. On the outside was written in a spidery, old-fashioned hand, one word.

Freedom

Molly unfolded the paper, careful not to tear it as the cab jolted across the cobbles. At the bottom of the page she read the signature –

Montague Miller

Eureka Stockade, Ballarat

2 nd December, 1854

Chapter 10

Fighting The Kaiser
Fighting the Kaiser,
Fighting the Kaiser,
Who'll come a fighting the Kaiser with me?
And we'll drink all his beer,
And eat up all his sausages,
Who'll come a fighting the Kaiser with me?
To the tune of 'Waltzing Matilda'.

It was all very well for Babushka to tell O'Hagen to walk but it meant they had to wait for him to get to the police station. The night air had the fug of a recently vacated bathroom. It was still hot, an "on top of the sheets but still under the mosquito net" sort of night. They all sweated rivers. Montague Miller must have continued with the meeting because they could hear the crowd occasionally burst with a cheer or applause in the distance. But they hadn't sung the *Internationale* so it wasn't over yet.

Babushka and Old Nik sat together in the cab, the few words that passed between them desultory and weary as the air. Mick had fixed Kaiser's nosebag and the horse munched quietly, tossing the bag occasionally to get at the better bits of chaff. Old Nik stroked his flank with the tip of his long-handled whip.

Ted and Kathleen slumped against the station wall slapping at the mozzies. Until now, this summer, they hadn't yet had a single mosquito, now it seemed they were all married with children. The storm that threatened in the early afternoon could still be seen, lightning striking like a nest of taipans to the north.

Kathleen insisted Joe lie down on the wooden form in front of the station. Despite the heat she also insisted she cover him again with Babushka's shawl.

'Why don't we just go home and be bothered to O'Hagen?' Molly asked.

'If you hadn't noticed, some of you have to live with him,' Kathleen sighed.

'Besides,' Ted answered like a true tactician, 'everyone's seen the state Joe's in. O'Hagen hasn't won himself any friends. If he takes it further with charges or something, all the worse for him.'

'He wouldn't do that?' Kathleen said, the question worrying her voice. 'He wouldn't. Joe's not well.'

'You said he'd be fine?'

It was Ted's turn to interrogate her, his tone urgent with the possibility they might be putting Joe in danger.

'Should we take him up to Bill?' Kathleen's face hardened but she answered softly,

'I said he'd be fine and he will.'

That was enough for Ted. The tightness that had him suddenly standing at attention left his body and he slumped down onto the form beside Joe's feet.

Kathleen began to whisper the names of those she knew who were involved in the beating and descriptions of others. She didn't know why she was reciting this litany of infamy, or why she was whispering. It just seemed that sort of night, nervous and unsettled and … every time they heard a shout, or even a sound, they all jumped. Kaiser stamped and whinnied.

'We'll get the mongrels!' Ted whispered. 'There's a war going on, Kathleen,' he continued. 'And all we can do is sit here like good little boys waiting to be charged for something we didn't do. It's not fair! It's just like Monty Miller says, it's the Government calls the shots. If we don't fight them over there, they force us to fight each other here.'

Right or wrong, Kathleen did not reply. It was too hot to think. Only the occasional mosquito slap disturbed the night.

'Bloody weather!' Ted finally said, breaking the stillness. He wiped the sweat from his forehead.

'He's right too, they will all be like that,' he murmured.

The comment was mostly to himself but Kathleen looked up.

'Who?'

Ted was talking as though she'd been part of the conversation he was having inside his head. Tonight she wasn't in the mood for trying to work it out. She'd had enough of men, violence and stupidity for one day. God only knew what Madorsky and the others were doing right now. They wouldn't be at the meeting any more, but out in the streets looking for a fight. It didn't give the Cause a good name.

'I don't know what you're talking about.' Kathleen was curt, almost brusque.

She moved to sit at Joe's head and softly stroke his hair. Ted was unperturbed.

'Monty Miller,' he continued. 'He said, as we drove off, that this is what we should expect from them when they came back from the war.' Kathleen turned to face him. It was obvious he was going to talk.

'Who?' she asked, caught not really listening.

'The blokes coming home at the end of the war,' Ted repeated. 'He said they'd be violent and unhinged and he's right, they will be, they are already. Just look,' he said nodding his head towards Joe.

'Of course they will be, how could they not?' Kathleen answered as she finally focussed enough to register what Ted was saying.

'If this war ever ends.'

But Ted's mind had run ahead like a lamplighter's apprentice.

'But they needn't be,' he said.

'For the love of Jesus, make some sense if you want to talk to me!' Kathleen hissed. 'I'm not a mind reader.' Babushka and Nikolai both looked down quickly, as Molly too turned at Kathleen's tone. Joe moaned.

'Look what you've done!' Kathleen said, hushing Joe back to sleep or whatever state of consciousness he was in. She glared about. They all looked away, like chastened children, but Ted and Kathleen's conversation seemed to hold far more interest for them all now. Ted held up his hand in submission to his wife, but still full of his own anxiety. The boy wasn't well but Ted trusted his wife's diagnosis. He'd be better in the morning after a sleep – maybe a bad headache – but her? Ted had never seen Kathleen like she was tonight.

'What's the matter with you?' Ted asked, the edge of his voice hard in the violent heat. 'You're giving me and Bill the gyp.'

Kathleen shook her head.

'If you don't know by now,' she breathed heavily, 'you don't know me at all.' But Kathleen calmed herself, forcing herself to be interested in his political conniving, for everybody's sake. She resumed the conversation.

'The soldiers, they needn't be what?' she asked, her voice conciliatory.

'After this war there'll be thousands, tens of thousands of men returned. Even the lucky ones will be broken somewhere inside. Imagine what that will be like, a whole generation of damaged goods.' Ted stopped, satisfied she was understanding this time.

'And what will that mean for us? More violence in the streets? More bullies? More living in fear of opening our mouths?' she asked the obvious, motherly questions. Ted smiled.

'Maybe, if we let them. But if the Socialist movement can harness that hurt into a force for social change?' his voice drifted off.

'Monty's right. Maybe Bill is too.'

Kathleen did not like the direction this conversation was taking.

'What are you thinking? Tell me!' she demanded. Her voice shook. Surely he couldn't be agreeing with Bill? His decision was betrayal. It was that simple.

'The Cause needs to think about how it can benefit from the war,' he explained calmly. 'Imagine even a thousand returned soldiers, men who've spent years being shot at for a living. Do you think they'll give two hoots what the Sergeant O'Hagen's of the world tell them to do?' Ted looked to Kathleen for support, at least for criticism of the idea. But her face trembled, close to tears.

'The Cause needs to plan now if we are ever to take over the means of production,' Ted continued, lowering his voice in appeal.

When Kathleen responded it was with closed eyes, tears squeezed against the eyelashes.

'Tell me what Bill is doing is wrong.' She needed to hear him say it.

'Bill? No!' Ted repeated, staring off into the middle of the street. 'It's obvious we have to patch the boys up over there, but we need a revolution when they come home.'

'But he's wrong!' Kathleen burst out, a sob in her voice.

'No, I think he's got a point,' Ted answered, still oblivious. 'It's too late to use the wounded for anti-war propaganda if you're only just starting to educate them about Socialism when they get home. It's too late. By then they need to believe they got hurt for something good and shiny and unstained like King and Country. No,' he warmed to the idea, 'if he gets to them over there, before we get them here, imagine what we can achieve.'

But Kathleen had stopped listening. He never listened to her. None of them ever listened. It was a game, their game, and they twisted everything to fit their rules. Bill hadn't said that. He'd said he was going because he could give them better care. Not for the love of the Cause, not for propaganda purposes. That's why she'd miss him. That's why they got on so well. Whatever his position on the big issues it all came from the fact he cared what happened to the real people – the man, and woman, and child in the street.

That's why she was a Socialist, for their Joe, for the old, for the sick, to keep the real criminals in gaol and to fight as hard as required, for as long as it took, to make sure that governments gave them all a fair go, kept them safe and took care of those who couldn't take care of themselves. That's who she was, a practical Socialist, no matter how much he might sneer.

She couldn't hold her feelings back any more.

When O'Hagen arrived at the station, he found Babushka and Molly huddled around the hysterically weeping Kathleen, while the men stood together looking concerned.

'She's very worried … for our son,' Ted added.

'He is all right then?' O'Hagen needed to be sure.

'Yes! He's all bloody right!' Kathleen screamed. O'Hagen stepped back. Babushka straightened, holding hard to Kathleen's shoulder and stared him away.

'Come on, dear,' Kathleen whispered quietly in Joe's ear.

'I'll help you get him up,' Molly said, leaning down close.

Joe opened his eyes. His eyes were still wild, his pupils wide.

'Molly,' he slurred through what might have been at any other time a smile.

'You're so beautiful.'

Molly blushed, feeling the eyes of Kathleen and Babushka intent upon her face.

Chapter 11

Solidarity Forever
When the Union's inspiration
Through the worker's blood shall run
There can be no power greater
Anywhere beneath the sun.
Yet what force on earth is weaker
Than the feeble strength of one?
But the Union makes us strong.
Solidarity for ever!
Solidarity for ever!
Solidarity for ever!
For Union makes us strong.
To the tune of 'The Battle Hymn of the Republic'.

Babushka sat like a broody black hen, almost covering a bare wooden chair in the front office of the darkened City Police Station. Her hair was mostly tied in a bun covered with a headscarf, but some still hung around her face, escaped and anxious, as it had been when she first saw Joe out there in the street. Her eyes were closed, but her head was erect and her mind awake.

Ahh, Vanya you must remember when we were parents, then we were the ones who worry. I have enough for worrying about, without this boy. The boarding house. Young Molly and Tomas. That old fool, Nikolai. But he is only a boy. A good boy, bashed in the streets. Oyoyoy! What can I do?

My Vanya, all the boys that you led in the strike were good boys just like this one. Uneducated some of them, but if you'd lived, you would have taught them … No good thinking this way! Vanya, what can I do but what must be done, that and worry? Who knows this better than me I ask you? We all have sons. But why do I tell you what you know? Maybe young Joseph, once burned by the milk, will now blow on cold water? They will be always after him now. Maybe this time will teach him? That would be the good thing.

'Babushka?' Kathleen O'Donahue whispered, leaning forward toward the pile of dishevelled clothes assembled on the seat next to her. Babushka did not move. Kathleen looked at Ted. He leaned over and touched the Gladstone bag she clutched in her hands.

'Irina?' he said quietly. 'Irina, it's almost dawn.'

Babushka opened her eyes with a quick, distrustful glance.

'God might give to them who get up early – but Babushka does not!' she said, grasping the bag tightly to her. 'What is it?'

Ted and Kathleen smiled, each wearily, and separately, but happier now Babushka was performing like her usual self.

'I could steal an egg from under a hen if I wanted to, you know,' Ted laughed, a laugh that drained some of the tension of a night spent on the bone-weary chairs of the police station.

'Any hen that watches her eggs so badly deserves no chicks!' Babushka answered matter-of-factly, like a sharp peck delivered by a hard beak to the offending hand that dared to try. Ted smiled broadly.

'Enough of that you two,' Kathleen said. 'Babushka, you've been so kind to be here with us all night,' she continued quietly so as not to disturb the morning which still slept around them.

'Ted and I were just wondering if it would be possible for you to be here a little longer? Until they release Joe? We would be very grateful.'

'Of course, of course! This is why I come,' Babushka answered.

'Ted needs to have the steam up at the sawmill at six and I have an early shift at the hospital. We'll have to get something to eat too,' Kathleen explained. Not that she needed to explain. Babushka knew the business of everyone in their street,

"How can I help if I do not know their need, and how else can I know of the need except to know of the business?" she'd shrug.

'You will let me know how is our poor Mick?' Babushka asked, her heart torn by wanting to be in two places.

I know what happens, Vanya, the doctor will do his best for Mick and for Joseph Hill if he needs. Of course I know of all that happened, but Vanya, this

is the business of grown men and women. I am not mother to them all. Who knows how is Joe Hill after a night of sleeping with the police? Perhaps he needs to visit Dr Bill even more then.

'Yes, yes, of course,' Kathleen answered.

'Here,' Kathleen continued, fishing in her purse for the tightly folded one pound note which she had taken from where she kept it for just such a contingency, wedged in the back of the frame of the etching of Karl Marx on her mantelpiece

'These clots have the wrong person in gaol as usual,' she continued, momentarily distracted by her search into being more than usually polite about the police. 'And they'll probably invent some trumped up charge. Just because these louts are in uniform the coppers think they can close their eyes to it. They'll charge him just so he has a criminal record, I shouldn't be surprised, or to salve their consciences for arresting the wrong bloke. Well,' she finished, holding out the unfolded bank note towards Babushka, 'if they charge him you pay bail with this,' she concluded. 'We'll pay our way to the system – like we always do.'

Ted looked up to see if the duty constable took any interest. He did not stir from his reading of the *Brisbane Courier* .

Babushka did not move to take the proffered money.

'Tch, tch,' she said, waving a hand dismissively at Kathleen. 'You children go. I wait!'

'But take the money. Take it,' Kathleen insisted.

'Tch, tch,' Babushka clucked again. 'There are no charges last night. There are no charges today. He is attacked in the street. This happens. That's all. There will be no charges. It will be so!' Babushka insisted in return. Ted smiled to himself. Babushka had a way that was at once absolutely certain and, if found not to be right, she was able to immediately change to accommodate a new certainty – all in the space of a breath. He'd never seen her with the wind taken out of her sails. Ted liked the cut of her jib.

'Thank you, Irina,' he said as he took Kathleen's arm. She reluctantly refiled her spare quid for future use.

'But if it does happen that he's charged, send someone to the hospital for Kathleen,' Ted finished.

'Oh and tell him,' Kathleen said, 'we've sent a message to Mr Jones at the joinery that he's …'

'… had an accident and will be in as soon as it is dealt with,' Ted finished for her.

Jones'd take a dim view of his best apprentice French polisher being late for work because he was involved in a public stoush with a mob of unruly servicemen. Ted had asked Old Nik to go around to the factory with a message for Jones first thing in the morning. The wharfies would sign Mick on and cover for him until he was back to work, just like they did when his father belted him and he couldn't work. Ted hoped she'd realise that they'd have to tell a porky pie about what happened to Joe if they wanted him to keep his apprenticeship.

Kathleen did not resist when he took her by the arm and ushered her to the door. It was time they both got to work.

'And tell him we're proud of him!' Kathleen said over her shoulder.

Following her out, Ted almost walked into a policeman coming into the station. Sergeant O'Hagen stared belligerently at both of them, showing no sign of displaying any courtesy, until his eye caught Babushka's gazing at him from inside the station door. He stepped back and held the door ajar for them.

'I trust you will get this matter with Joe sorted out in no time?' Kathleen asked as she walked down the stairs, not bothering to keep a sarcastic tone from her voice.

'No time that is, except the eight hours we've been sitting here waiting!' she finished.

O'Hagen noticed it as he noticed all things. Everything existed, or didn't, only in reference to himself.

'I will write an accurate report of the evening's events and my part in them, if that's what you mean,' he answered more sourly than he intended. He looked quickly from Ted to Kathleen to gauge their response.

'Then we can expect a very short report and our son home for breakfast?' Kathleen insisted. She turned toward him from the bottom step, the question like a challenge on her face.

'Movement of prisoners is a matter for the duty sergeant, Madam,' he answered coolly but with enough concern to seem to have recovered from his earlier lapse. His discipline made him a better man than any riff-raff on the street.

'For my part, rest assured I'll be finishing my report as soon as I can.'

'When the Commissioner's finished dictating it,' Ted muttered almost inaudibly. Almost. O'Hagen opened his mouth, thought, and said,

'Good morning to you both.' Closed the door behind him. If he could afford any better lodgings he wouldn't be in South Brisbane. He'd be in a better part of town, and would be when his moving expenses from the country finally came through. The officer behind the desk had bestirred himself from his reading at some time during their exchange.

Babushka assembled her clothes, straightened her scarf, pushed her hair back under it.

'Did you have good breakfast?' she enquired, smiling as O'Hagen walked towards her. She stood up, hands stretched as though welcoming him to the station.

'Ah, no Mrs Kerensky. I did not eat at all,' O'Hagen apologised. He was awkward at her presence in his place of work. The old cow made him think of a moulting hen, a clump of dishevelled feathers untidying his otherwise regulation anteroom.

'What! She does not feed you? I beat that girl!' Babushka threw her hands to her hips, to O'Hagen's alarm. He knew how these Russians behaved. She probably would hit Molly. He moved quickly to mollify the untidy hen.

'Oh, no, Mrs Kerensky …'

'Babushka … please, little rooster, everybody calls me Babushka.' He opened his mouth to complain at the informality, with him being at his place of work, but she took no notice.

'I am "the" Babushka,' she continued brooking no contradiction, 'and you are all my little chicks,' she clucked, chucking him with her finger under the chin as though flattering a very small boy. He recoiled.

'Here,' she said, unclasping her Gladstone bag and peering inside. She returned with two shillings pinched between gnarled fingers. 'Here. If the girl does not give you breakfast, this is for a cup of tea.'

O'Hagen tried to wave it away, to explain breakfast had been ready for him but he was just in too much of a hurry to eat it.

'No, Mrs Kerensky, I'm quite …' he began.

'Take this! You pay board and keep. I give you breakfast,' she insisted, gentle as a cattle catcher on the front of a train.

'Mrs … ,' he began once more, though he sensed any response would be totally futile. Besides they both knew two shillings was more than four times the price of a cup of tea and he was in the police station. It just didn't look right. She thrust the silver coin at him. He took it. It was the only way to be rid of her. The old fox.

'Thank you,' he said, taking the money and quickly slipping it into the pocket of his uniform trousers. 'I'll be sure to take my breakfast at *Erin*, before I come to work from now on.'

'You must keep your strength up. To work you must eat!' she agreed. 'Now you will soon be finished with Joe Hill?' She smiled. He knew when he was beaten. The old cow knew what she was doing, knew full well that now he was in her debt. He felt his temperature rising.

'As soon as I know what is happening with Josep … the prisoner, Madam,' he answered, only just managing to keep his anger at bay, 'You will know.'

'You get Joe Hill a cup of tea, too,' she suggested as he opened the counter door and walked through to where the duty officer sat smiling to himself.

'Takin' bribes from old ladies now?' the Sergeant winked as O'Hagen walked into the office behind. O'Hagen scowled at him,

'You heard her, Charlie. She's my landlady!' he growled, adding. 'Tidy yourself up you dosey plod. Your uniform looks like you've spent all night in a bawdy house!' It was Charlie's turn to scowl.

Babushka clapped her hands like a small, mischievous child, and laughed aloud.

Chapter 12

The Internationale

Arise ye workers from your slumbers,

Arise ye prisoners of want,

For reason in revolt now thunders

And at last ends the age of cant.

So away with all your superstitions

Servile masses arise – arise,

We'll change forthwith the old conditions,

And spurn the dust to win the prize.

    So comrades come rally,

And the last fight let us face

The Internationale unites the human race.

So comrades come rally,

And the last fight let us face

The Internationale unites the human race.

Joe dragged his eyes open. Even without much light in the cell, the thumping in his head made him cautious about opening them. He needed to know where he was. Was this the police lockup. A quick look assured him. Concrete floor, barred door, the cell bare of almost anything but the fold-out wooden bench on which he lay. Piercing light stabbed in through the high cell window. His head pressed on a kapok pillow and his torso, still dressed in the clothes he'd worn the night previously, lay half under a thin blanket. The only other furnishings of the room were a deep galvanised-iron bucket squatting in the corner. With a grim-lipped smile, Joe pictured how he must look after his first night as the guest of the King. He had a feeling it wouldn't be his last.

Joe rolled his tongue around a dry mouth that tasted like dried blood, his head exploded anew every time he moved it. Only the memory of Molly Pearce hovering above him, so full of tender concern that she could have been a waking dream, made him feel alive: his pulse quickened, his heart raced and his … Joe groaned loudly and rolled quickly onto his front to save himself embarrassment. It felt better lying there on his belly with his full weight on the hard cell bench. As the pain of his rapid movement subsided, half-remembered glimpses of the previous night flashed into his mind. Montague Miller, the fight – or at least moments of it – then the memories became jumbled.

Joe pieced his recollections together. He did remember his parents taking him to the police station in South Brisbane. He was seeing stars, and double, until a telephone rang and he was bundled into a paddy wagon. From the distance of the journey, the horses hoofs' hollow clopping, and the fishermen's murmured voices drifting across the river, he guessed they'd crossed the bridge into the city – and another cell.

Joe felt the side of his face with stiff fingers. It was swollen badly. He could feel the roughness of dried blood at the corner of his mouth, across his chin. He glanced down, careful to move only his eyes. A small blood-stained handkerchief lay crumpled on the bench, the initials K.O. embroidered in the corner. He began to smile, but stopped in pain, smiled inside instead. Ted always said,

'Your mother's a Knock Out.'

Then he remembered the fight. What about Mick!

His head jerked up off the pillow, dropping just as quickly as pain splintered his brain. How is Mick?

Joe felt ashamed that he was lying here feeling sorry for himself when Mick must feel far worse or … the blackest thought crossed Joe's mind. Was he dead?

The memory of his friend lying motionless and silent on the ground, his arms over his head, was sharp in Joe's mind. He needed to know. Joe rolled over again, straightened his legs, and swung them over the edge of the wooden bench. He sat upright, balancing on the bed edge. Blood rushed to his head. Joe put his head in his hands and groaned, opening his eyes only at the sound of a key in the cell door.

'Rise and shine,' a voice, too loud for his head, called.

Joe looked up. Sergeant O'Hagen stood, proffering an enamel mug of tea that whisped a slight steam into an already steamy morning.

Joe considered not taking it. It was O'Hagen arrested him. It all came back now. Even before his parents and Molly and Babushka had arrived on the scene he'd been arrested for causing a public affray. O'Hagen did the honours, reading him his rights while Joe had lay half-conscious on the street, glaze-eyed and stupid as an anvil. Something else came back too, O'Hagen telling the buggars who'd belted Mick that they'd better make themselves scarce or there'd be hell to pay.

Joe smiled grimly to himself – and winced in pain and self-reproach. He hoped Mick was at least in hospital and not, like him, charged in a watch house cell somewhere. Joe needed to know but, for the moment, only a mug wouldn't take that mug of tea.

Joe tottered unsteadily to the cell door. O'Hagen handed it through the bars. He took a swig. It was milky and full of sugar. He felt better almost immediately, except his hand hurt when he opened it – there was no skin on the knuckles – the skinned knuckles of the President of the Children's Peace Army. Joe knew he should have blushed in shame at that but, like any copper will tell you, sometimes maintaining the peace requires reasonable force.

'Where's Mick?' Joe asked as O'Hagen continued to loiter outside the cell door, feigning ignorance.

'You know, Mick Doyle, the bloke they bashed.'

'They kept him at the hospital last night,' O'Hagen answered equably.

'Apparently Doc Carroll wanted to keep an eye on him overnight for some sort of observation.' O'Hagen emphasised the word "observation" as though it was some sign of weakness that a fellow needed to be observed after a minor altercation in the street.

'They give him a good kicking but he's a solid lad. I reckon he'll just be sore for a few days. A few decent bruises on the ribs but nothing to the head the Doc reckons,' O'Hagen said and smiled.

'Doc Carroll was more worried about you,' he said. 'And so was I.'

O'Hagen smiled mysteriously to himself.

But Joe was beginning to understand that O'Hagen was not a man to keep his thoughts to himself. He waited.

'If I lost you to the hospital I would have lost the grand prize wouldn't I? Mr Joseph Hill is quite a collar these days.'

Joe maintained a stony-faced silence, despite wanting to spit at the mongrel.

'You should be pleased to know,' O'Hagen continued, assuming the knowledge would flatter Joe's pride, 'that you've been making quite a name for yourself around the place over the last couple of years. We've been watching you closely.'

O'Hagen smiled again, intimating there was even more good news from O'Hagen that O'Hagen couldn't wait to share.

'The Police Magistrate will be in for a word in a minute. Wants to talk to you, even before he's had a chance to have his breakfast. He's a man who likes his vittels. So he's keen isn't he?' O'Hagen winked.

Joe now knew that, like most men with a little bit of power, O'Hagen's only interest in him, was O'Hagen's self-interest. There was no "Cause" for O'Hagen.

Even groggy as he was with his befuddling headache, Joe stored the information O'Hagen had provided. He was starting to feel better under the influence of the tea.

'So am I charged with something or just here at His Majesty's pleasure?' Joe asked, deciding to get some confirmation about a night that, despite his best efforts to remember it all, was determined to stay in part at least, a blur.

'I could only get you for causing a public affray,' O'Hagen said almost apologetically.

'What!' Joe exploded, spluttering into his tea. 'You charged me with starting that fight?' O'Hagen shrugged. He seemed completely unconcerned at the accuracy of the accusation or the small fact there was no evidence except for what Molly and Babushka and his parents and half the Socialist movement of Brisbane had seen with their own eyes.

'You're joking! We all saw them kicking into Mick! You bloody … !'
Joe swore loudly before mastering himself. Waiting was a game Joe'd
learned from his father and waiting wasn't only good for politics.

'That's a crying shame for you then isn't it?' Joe said, his voice heavy
with sarcasm.

O'Hagen nodded as though in full agreement. Joe couldn't believe
it. The bloke's got more front than MacDonald & East's Department
Store.

'You'll slip up again,' O'Hagen answered, 'and I'll be there to bring
you in.' Joe managed not to laugh and shook his head.

'No more than I'd expect from a bloody Tory set up like this,' he
muttered to himself. Thinking about going to Court reminded him,

'You said something about a Magistrate?'

'Yes,' O'Hagen answered as he leaned against the door jamb, a well-
satisfied look lighting up his face.

'The Magistrate, Mr Urquhart telephoned South Brisbane station last
night asking for an audience with you this morning – in person no less,'
O'Hagen answered in a tone which meant that he thought a visit a mark
of honour. O'Hagen continued blathering,

'That's why we brought you over to this watch house. Closer to
home for the P. M.. He pacifically said he "didn't want to go over the
bridge into that hotbed of dissent, especially on an empty stomach",'
O'Hagen reported, word for word.

Joe smiled at "pacifically" and "dissent".

He almost felt sorry for the poor coot. Almost. He decided to try his
luck further.

'What do you reckon he wants to talk about?' Joe asked, leaning
towards O'Hagen as if to invite him to join in a conspiracy.

O'Hagen smiled a disconcerting smile and tapped the side of his nose
with his index finger.

'Official business, for sure,' he said leaning back from the doorway.
'I'll give you odds that it's not about the charges though,' he finished.

'You run a book too, do you?' Joe asked with a grimace. O'Hagen's
eyes narrowed. It was obvious to Joe he knew nothing about anything.

'I wouldn't forget who's got the keys if I were you,' O'Hagen half-threatened. Joe took the hint muttering,

'Sorry,' half under his breath, just loud enough for O'Hagen to hear and grunt acknowledgement as he slouched back into the open-doored office.

Joe thanked O'Hagen for the tea with a lift of the half-empty mug towards his receding back. He heard the Sergeant greeting someone. It sounded like another copper, but Joe was sure he knew the voice. They conversed for a moment longer before Joe twigged … Harry Winterson.

Joe drained the last of the tea and bent to place the empty mug near the door. Dizzy, he dropped it instead. He ached all over, especially where they'd kicked him in the ribs. It was time to lie down again.

As he lowered himself back onto the bench, Joe wondered what Jones would be doing without him at work.

He wished he was at home having this lie down. His own bed with Molly beside him reading him the political bits from the paper and between times wiping his head and face with a cool, damp cloth. Joe lay back to fall asleep under the gentle hand of his imagined, ministering angel.

Chapter 13

In Hell
Up in the sky, the bomb-birds fly,
Laying their eggs of death.
Women will cry for men who die,
As they face the cannon's breath.
Over the foam, the great ships roam,
Scattering dreadful mines,
Women will moan, and men will groan,
And still the same sun shines
To-day, as in the days long past,
To-night, the same moon gleams,
The same sky over all is cast,
But oh! what vanished dreams!
No peace on earth, goodwill to man,
How sad I am to tell,
The maxim is, Kill all you can,
We're living now in Hell!
Mary Rattenbury. Poem from 'Pen Blossoms'.

When Joe woke the second time, in the full light of Monday morning, he felt much better. Perhaps it was the tea. He could hear voices from the office. One was O'Hagen's, the second, Winterson. He guessed the third was that of the Police Magistrate, Urquhart. Joe knew him by sight, they all did, and even if they didn't know him "officially" Brisbane was a small place. Occasionally Urquhart would trot by, on the bay gelding the government kept for him, to cast his eye over one of their political meetings, like a squatter overseeing his stock. Joe could almost hear his father's vitriol,

'That bloody horse gets treated better than half the workers in Brisbane.'

'And the cost of stabling it could staff a small hospital,' Kathleen would add. Joe decided to keep any mention of the horse under his hat but thought it would be helpful in any future conversation if he knew more about him than that the Government kept him a horse.

The sharp clatter of a riding crop drawn along the bars of the cell door sat him up quickly. Joe wasn't so faint-headed now he'd had some fluid and a little more kip – almost at his best for an interview.

'Ah! So you are awake, lad?' Urquhart asked, his tone one of genuine concern. It unnerved Joe that he couldn't see the mouth that spoke from underneath the walrus moustache that joined an underbrush of sideburns to cover most of his face. It seemed disembodied, as though he was talking to a spirit summonsed at a seance.

Joe searched for signs of sarcasm, but Urquhart's dark eyes gave nothing away. If anything they seemed to reflect the world like a pair of dirty spectacles. Only the silver buttons on his navy tunic shone with confidence.

'Yes … sir,' Joe said softly. Kathleen always maintained that to be polite, even too polite, put one on an equal footing with an opponent.

'Champion!' Urquhart beamed. Joe thought that utterance genuine too, but was still wary. Urquhart drew himself up to his full height outside the door to Joe's cell.

'Time for a talk then!' he commanded, hitting his riding crop down hard against his thigh. Too hard. His moustache twitched with pain. Joe tried very hard not to laugh.

'O'Hagen!' Urquhart yelled, covering up his discomfit.

'Open the door and bring Mr Hill to the office. Then we'll both have a cup of tea, and close the door behind you when you leave,' he continued as he walked back down the short corridor between the cells. O'Hagen hopped to like a good lickspittle.

'You heard him, Hill,' he huffed. 'Don't make the Magistrate wait.' Joe stood up and followed the P.M. to his office. Urquhart motioned him to a chair opposite his, taking great care to lay his riding crop, like a threat, across the desk between them. Then he waved O'Hagen away, mentioning the door again when it looked like it would be left to ventilate his private conversation.

'Now,' Urquhart began, leaning back in his chair. 'Time for a man to man talk, Mr Joseph Hill.' Urquhart stared hard at Joe. He seemed to be measuring him up.

For a suit, or a coffin? Joe wondered but managed not to let his thoughts show. Urquhart was in no hurry. He sat quite still, staring at a Joe-shaped space. He cleared his throat.

'My officers inform me that you are getting quite a reputation for your political speechifying,' he began again, kind and fatherly.

'It is a fine thing to be in service to His Majesty, especially during this endless war.' Urquhart leaned back, stroking his moustache. 'We all have to do our bit, the young and old, as well as our soldiers,' he said.

'I understand Dr Carroll is taking up a Commission at the Front? Good man that, capital,' he nodded his approval.

Joe was beginning to wonder why he was there at all.

'He's very fond of you, you know,' Urquhart said. The personal touch was unexpected. Joe looked confused as Urquhart continued,

'Oh yes, I spoke to him telephonically after he saw to you last night. He was very concerned for your wellbeing. Wanted to take you off to hospital with the other fellow.'

'Mick. Mick Doyle,' Joe obliged.

'Yes, quite. He wanted to take the two of you to be sure you were all well cared for. And here you are, sound as a bell, but for the little knock on the noggin, eh?'

Urquhart sounded more like the kind old gentleman gently reproving a recalcitrant child than a Police Magistrate. Joe wished he were more hateful, it'd make him so much easier to despise.

This warm passing on of Bill Carroll's concern forced Joe to remember the shameful way they had all parted company with him in their kitchen the evening before.

'I … I didn't know that,' Joe stammered, the blush spreading across his entire face. Urquhart smiled – another genuine smile.

'Oh, yes, very concerned for you he was,' he nodded, 'a capital chap, just the sort of fella we need at the front.' Despite his discomfit Joe knew Urquhart was utterly opposed to Bill's politics so why praise him to the skies?

'And you seem to be well on your way to training your character for the bear-pit of Parliament?' he continued. 'Even preparing yourself to serve in His Majesty's government one day, perhaps?' Urquhart nodded. 'We all have to do our bit.'

Joe watched every move and listened closely to every word, the false front along with the flattery. What was he playing at?

'You see, Hill, that's the point, isn't it?' Urquhart continued, thoughtfully stroking his moustache. Joe leaned forward listening attentively.

'It doesn't matter which side of the political fence you are on. When the chips are down, we are all the King's men in the service of the Empire. In times of strife we must forget our petty squabbles, the political classes along with all the others who serve. Don't you agree?'

That's it! Joe thought. He wants me to say I disagree so he can have me for sedition. All Cause members knew the War Precautions Act backwards.

Joe leaned back abruptly and crossed his arms.

But Urquhart continued without waiting for an answer.

'Politics is like tending a field,' Urquhart began again. 'The arguments are all about what to grow and how best to care for the soil,' he continued, sounding for all the world like a gentleman farmer replete with a stock of little paddock homilies.

'But underneath the soil of politics is the bedrock of civilisation – King and Country. The things we all share, that give us such a solid foundation, the things that make us British.'

Joe was confused, growing anxious that there was a game going on that he did not understand. If it wasn't sedition then what? Urquhart ploughed on.

'Now, Dr Carroll knows this and, despite his sincere and strong feelings against the conduct of this war, he's realised that there is something far greater at stake here than mere political quibbles. This is about who we are.'

Yes, dead if we go to your war, Joe thought. He fought to keep himself silent as Urquhart grasped his riding crop by the handle and hit it against the side of his leg as though urging his horse forward.

'But well you know, my boy,' he continued. 'Well you know there are many on your side who would be happy to take to the bedrock of our British civilisation with the sledgehammers of rebellion.'

Urquhart's eyes were shining, his voice loud, one index finger punctuating his point.

'These Bolsheviks are causing real trouble in Russia and the misguided Sinn Feiners, the naïve God-botherers … we're all British, all of us.' Urquhart's voice trailed away. He shook his head, sighing heavily as he slid back into his chair.

Joe smiled an inner smile of secret pride that he must be truly bothering the Tories or they wouldn't be bothered with him.

'What's wrong with trying to make the world a fairer place?' Joe asked after long silence.

Urquhart raised himself, his fingers stroked his moustache, eyes fixed on Joe.

'I would have thought you, of all people,' he emphasised the words, 'would understand the folly of the Irish violence!' the mockery of Joe's ideals in Urquhart's voice belied his demeanour.

'Their bloody-handed actions set their cause back a hundred years,' he said, shaking his head, now world-weary again. Joe tried to think.

He made to reply, but Urquhart preempted him.

'Well,' he said, his voice controlled again, 'enough of war and rebellions. Let's talk about peace.'

He smiled. Joe was lost. Urquhart changed direction more often than a snake in long grass. Its head appeared somewhere for a moment before disappearing to pop up again somewhere else unexpected. He had the upper hand and he knew it.

'I understand you have a keen interest in peace?' Urquhart stated. It wasn't a question. The kindly old gentleman had returned.

'Peace is not easy won in a time of war, nor is she easy to retain,' Urquhart laughed. 'A bit like a wife really, eh Mr Hill?' Joe felt himself begin to blush again as though his senior had some intimate knowledge of Joseph Hill's private affairs.

'I won't beat about the bush any longer, Hill,' he said, so finally that Joe sat up too quickly. Pain shot through his head.

'The fact of the matter is that if we want peace we must all play our part,' Urquhart continued. 'You want peace don't you?' he asked directly. Joe nodded.

'If you want peace, you must be willing to sacrifice something,' Urquhart continued with an Enlisting Sergeant's guile.

Joe was startled. If he thinks for one moment I'll enlist to get off some piddling charge he's got another thing coming! He opened his mouth to say so but was beaten to the punch.

'Others are sacrificing their lives,' Urquhart said. 'But not you … and rightly so, you're no foolish foot-slogging soldier. No,' he went on, 'you are cut out for better things. You will be in politics one day. A career as leader of the greatest Socialist government in the nation?' He looked at Joe, his smile almost convincing.

'Others sacrifice their lives. But what would you sacrifice to save a life?' Urquhart leaned forward, encouraging Joe into his confidence. 'Would you be prepared to give up something worthy? Your livelihood, perhaps?' Joe nodded imperceptibly as Urquhart paused imperceptibly for him to do so.

'What about your freedom?' Urquhart leaned further across the desk as wordlessly Joe agreed again.

'But that isn't enough,' Urquhart said. 'We need information. Who's plotting against us? What are their white-anting schemes? That's the way you can save lives by bringing the war to its earliest conclusion.'

Urquhart nodded at Joe's stunned look, mistaking it for agreement.

'You already know them all,' Urquhart confided. 'It'll be easy for you to tell us what's happening without them ever suspecting a thing. Believe me,' Urquhart repeated, 'such information will certainly save lives.'

Joe's face drained of colour.

Urquhart sat back as though expecting an answer.

Joe tried, but he couldn't force himself to say anything coherent. Again Urquhart misinterpreted, mistaking silence for agreement.

'Of course,' he soothed, stroking his moustache. 'Of course we'll simply forget about the unfortunate bit of business from last night and,' he added as the cherry on top, 'all our informants can expect some monetary reward for their effort.'

Joe jumped to his feet, the blood rushing to his face.

'You want me to spy!' he exploded, yelling the offending word. 'You want me to spy on people I love. You want me to spy on them because they, no, we,' he said leaning across the desk towards a retreating Urquhart. 'We want a fairer life, a life where we won't be killed in old men's wars. Where we get a fair day's work for a fair day's pay. You want me to spy on my friends for that? Bedrock be damned!' Joe yelled. 'You're just frightened of losing control. Everything's all right as long as the little monkeys don't shake you down from the top of your tree! Not this little monkey! People like you want to get things and keep things so you can show them off to other people who care about things. When will you get it through your thick skulls, things don't matter, people do!'

Ted's voice in the back of Joe's mind said,

Great strategy! Abuse the Police Magistrate.

Joe's tirade was too much for Urquhart. He jumped to his feet, whipping out his riding crop and slamming it down onto the desk. Joe stepped backwards slightly but stood his ground. Not backing down. There was nowhere to run. Not like in the streets. But it felt good, maybe even better than performing for an audience, to stand and mean it – man to man.

'You don't seem to understand what sort of trouble you are in!' Urquhart yelled. 'You can go to prison for a nice stretch,' he threatened, his breathing heavy and his eyes suddenly animated with repulsion.

'And you can go to hell in a hand-cart!' Joe yelled. They both stood, chests heaving, glaring at each other. Joe's face flushed red. Urquhart's moustache twitched.

There was a knock on the door.

'What!' Urquhart yelled. The door was already half-open and Joe could have sworn O'Hagen winked at him as he pushed it further open with his back – a battered silver tea tray with a pot, milk, sugar and two cups and saucers clasped in his hands.

Even before he was fully into the room, Babushka was in behind him, looking for all the world like an innocent child. Joe smiled. A relieved smile. The Duty Sergeant barked like a terrier at her heels.

'Oyoyoy! I wonder what it is keeping the boy,' Babushka said to Urquhart as she shuffled over to take Joe's hand.

'I wait all night,' she explained. 'He is ready? We go.' Babushka began to wipe the dried blood from Joe's face with a spittle-dampened handkerchief. Urquhart mastered himself enough to dismiss the hapless Duty Sergeant with a withering stare. He nodded at Babushka.

'I turn my back for a moment and a private conversation turns into a damned three-ring circus,' he growled. He turned back to Joe.

'Think about my proposal,' he said, 'and don't let me see you here again. You can rest assured Mr Hill, I will not be so understanding a second time.' He turned his gaze to the tea tray.

'Well,' Urquhart snapped at O'Hagen. 'Give them tea if they want it and then,' he added, 'if the paperwork's done, get him out of here.' He nodded at Babushka and pushed past a startled O'Hagen, out through the front office.

'That spoiled his breakfast!' Joe smirked, though he couldn't help but wonder what might have happened if Babushka hadn't appeared. He knew now Urquhart's threat about "next time" wasn't idle.

'Thank you, we go now. Thank you,' Babushka said to O'Hagen, her tone brooking no contradiction. She took Joe's elbow under her armpit and, clutching his hand in hers, led him out through the office and onto the street.

O'Hagen blinked twice at the empty room, placed the loaded tray down on the desk and called out in a dazed voice,

'Fancy a cuppa, Charlie?'

Chapter 14

Manifesto

Rouse ye then ye Anzacs, put forth all your strength, your energy and your eloquence.

Organise and carry the flag to fight the Hunnish foe throughout the length and breadth of this great Commonwealth.

Returned Soldiers and Sailors Imperial League of Australia

Early morning traffic was filling the street. Trams clanked, hissed, swayed – a full load inside with hangers-on off the runners – paper sellers touting on their corners – the trot, clop and canter of horses with their carriage-clatter and leather-creak and heavy horse-breath – people walking brisk, or they talked and called – the milkmen, the fish barrow, and the bread and ice men all busying as the night-soil and the rubbish cart men made their ways home.

'We wait here,' Babushka instructed as they walked from the front door of the City Police Station. Years before some civic-minded gardener had planted a tree that now spread its shade across the stairs. Babushka went no further than the third step before lowering herself, with Joe's help, to sit down on it. She arranged her bag on her lap with her full black skirt tucked in, like a bed sheet, all around.

'Here,' Babushka said, patting the step beside her as she surveyed the scene, 'sit with me.'

'I'll stand if that's all the same, thank you Babushka,' Joe said. He was still very sore and the stooping and folding felt too much like pain. Joe was amazed at how cunning she was to get everything to work in her favour – and in his. Urquhart and O'Hagen never stood a chance.

'Thank you for getting me out from there, I …' Joe began, but before he had a chance to finish Babushka raised her hand.

'This I do for my family,' she said finally.

'But, I'm not your family,' Joe stammered, immediately recanting at what he knew sounded both ungrateful and unkind. It seemed the more time he spent with adults the more he found himself utterly bewildered by them – Urquhart and Babushka both in their different ways.

'You know what I mean,' Babushka answered. She waved her hand.

'You sit here, Joseph,' she said. Reluctantly he lowered himself. He grimaced. It hurt most where they'd kicked him. Babushka waited for him to settle before taking his hand again.

'My Vanya, rest his soul, he leads the Union of Mineworkers, in the strike, in Russia.' Joe heaved a deep sigh. He'd heard Vanya's story a hundred times. How he'd led the strike and the Tsarist troops had shot seventy-five men in cold blood for demanding warm bedding and fresh meat, and bread without horse shit in it. And this in winter in Siberia.

'This tires you?' she asked quickly.

'No, Babushka,' he answered, mollifying her a little with a smile. 'I have heard Vanya's story before. But I will listen now.'

Yes, Vanya, he has heard this but he hasn't heard it all. And it is time. He is growing quickly this boy. He is soon to be man. Oyoyoy! So tall. I hear him in the Police Station. He stands to the Magistrate. No back step. He is one of our sons, Vanya, as sure as my blood.

Babushka smiled.

'Yes, you have heard my Vanya's tale. I will not say it now. But Vanya said something to me I did not tell you. I find him in the gutter outside the hospital. The snow almost covers him. I raise him up. He is near death. I hold him close to kiss his dear face. I hear him speak. There are tears in his eyes. He says,

"They are all our boys, Irina. All our boys. I have betrayed them." He dies then, but he is not thinking of himself. Not my Vanya. He is noble soul. He thinks of his boys. All around they are lying in the gutter and the snow is red.

"No," I say to him though his ears are deaf, his heart grows cold, my tears falling. "No, Vanya, you could not betray our boys. They have not betrayed themselves."'

Babushka closed her eyes. A smile fluttered from trembling lips.

She paused, eyes closed.

'Snow does not weep, Joe. You know this? It flutters like the eyelashes of lovers, then, and at the moment of death.' Joe nodded. He understood though he had never so much as seen a flake of snow. Babushka sighed.

'We are family,' she said, and that was that.

The door of the Police Station flew open and O'Hagen ran down the stairs almost tripping over the two of them where they sat.

'Praise the Lord!' he yelled.

'And pass the ammunition!' yelled a wag from the street.

'Go sit on a pineapple!' O'Hagen muttered. Then, remembering himself, he turned his gaze downward.

'Haven't gone yet, then?' he asked pleasantly.

'No, we wait for Nikolai!' Babushka replied.

'How does he know that we're … ?' Joe began.

'You say we organise, Comrade, we organise,' she answered. 'He is here at eight and a half hours.'

'Well, I've struck it lucky then,' O'Hagen said brightly. 'I clean forgot to tell you that the Magistrate has ordered Joe be released only on payment of a fine.'

'This fine is for what thing that he does?' Babushka demanded. Both she and Joe struggled to their feet like old people.

'Causing a public nuisance and not obeying a lawful direction,' O'Hagen intoned. Joe opened his mouth to complain but he was not as quick as Babushka.

'How much?' she snapped.

'Two pounds in total for the two offences,' O'Hagen replied equally as rapidly.

'Two bloody quid!' yelled Joe indignantly. 'I'd rather go to bloody gaol than pay for the privilege of getting my head kicked in.' Babushka interjected again.

'I pay two pounds,' she said. 'Get receipt!' she ordered O'Hagen. He bounded happily up the stairs as though she was the Commissioner himself. Joe was not so easy to convince.

'But, Babushka!' he argued. 'I did nothing wrong! Why should I pay all that money?'

'You do not pay. I pay,' she answered as she struggled to open her bag.

'But …' he began again, taking her arm to steady her.

'Butt is what the foolish goat does. Your father tells you, "Only pick a fight you can win!"'

'I know, but …'

'Your mother was here all night. She says to pay this fine.' Joe shut his mouth like a lizard with a moth in it.

Babushka unlatched the bag she held clasped to her belly. It was difficult to rummage through it while holding it before her. Joe offered and, at her nod, he took the bag in both his hands while she peered in, scratching around like a scrub turkey up a gully. She muttered to herself as she did so. 'Vanya' was the only clear word Joe could make out.

'Ah!' Babushka finally breathed. Joe saw clearly into the depths of her bag. Glancing furtively up and down the busy street she plucked at the end of a heavy woollen sock. It looked like it was one of a pair rolled together into a ball. Babushka peeled it back to display a roll of twenty pound notes.

Joe had never seen so much money in the one place. Not even when his father did the banking for the Union. It was enough to buy any of the cottages in Merivale Street, maybe even more than one. He could see two rolls in that sock with what looked like one hundred notes in each. He gasped. Babushka glared at him and hissed. Joe blushed as she stuffed the loose end of the sock back into the hollow around which the notes were rolled. She pushed it down under a battered cloth hat in her bag. Babushka pulled out a second sock. This one was full of five and two pound notes. Smiling aloud she peeled one from the inside of the roll. Joe goggled in disbelief.

'Shut your mouth,' Babushka said, as she closed the bag. 'You eat flies.'

Just then, as if summonsed by her, O'Hagen appeared, blowing on the still wet ink of an official receipt.

'I'm sorry,' he huffed. 'I was in a hurry and it ran a little.'

'It is good,' Babushka said quickly, proffering the note. O'Hagen went to take it but to hand the receipt to Joe. Babushka held firm to her money. O'Hagen blinked dully.

'Receipt to the hand that gives the money!' she demanded. 'This is our business.'

'But,' O'Hagen stammered, his brow furrowed with consternation. 'I'm sorry Mrs Kerensky. I made the receipt out to Joe. It's … it's his fine,' he finished in a bluster of justification. Babushka stared at him for a moment then drew the money from his hand and handed it to Joe. At her insistence Joe handed the money to O'Hagen in exchange for his receipt.

'This is good,' Babushka repeated as she took the receipt from Joe and stuffed it into the bosom of her buttoned black dress.

'I give this to your mother.' Ignoring them both she re-arranged herself to sit back down on the step. They straightened themselves, stared at one another in confusion before O'Hagen recovered.

'Right, well, I've work to do,' he said letting himself back into the Police Station. 'Morning, to you both and,' he added, 'try not to get into any trouble, there's a bad element about.'

The comment got Joe's dander up but as he stepped towards O'Hagen he realised Babushka had a handful of his trousers firmly in her grasp. Joe blinked in the March sun. His head felt bad again and, succumbing to gravity, or fatigue, or commonsense, he slumped down beside her.

'You never learn? You are like your friend, Mick,' she said smiling wearily. She ruffled his hair. 'To retreat not glorious, but healthy.'

Joe knew she was right. He had to learn to control his responses, to discipline his body to his mind. Else he would be just like Mick. Push him too hard and he'd take the bait: hook, line and sinker. Wasn't that why they were here in the first place?

Thoughts swam in Joe's head like a shoal of river mullet.

'How does Nikolai even know we're here?' he asked, continuing his thinking aloud.

'He brings us here, your father and me. He takes your mother and Molly on to the hospital. Nikolai waits there, as I ask, until all is well with Mick Doyle. He brings them back here. Your mother stays. I send Molly home with him to do the breakfasts at the boarding house. Then your parents must go to work. I stay. I ask your father to send Nikolai past when he has a fare to the city. 8.30 am. Now you know.' Babushka was ready for home herself.

'Old Kaiser must be tired as a dog,' Joe said.

It seemed like everyone knew what the heck was happening except him. Molly had come to see him.

'Is Mick all right?' he asked, remembering he hadn't asked but that he wanted to know that first.

'Yes, Doctor Carroll also has busy night. Mick at hospital, then you at the station in South Brisbane, then back to Mick. He says all is clear with Mick. Oyoyoy! What can we do?' Babushka waved her hand over her shoulder towards Mt Cootha and the west.

'The doctor says Mick is sore, cracks the ribs,' she said poking Joe hard and painfully in his.

'But he has sense to cover his head,' she wagged her finger at him. 'You learn this. The doctor is more worried with you. They hit you in head. I am worried for you, but what can I do? Oyoyoy! What can any mother do.'

Joe relaxed a bit now he knew where everyone was and what was going on. Now he could begin to think about other things. It was Monday morning and he should have been at work at seven.

He felt the bandage wound around his head. He couldn't explain that away too readily. What would Jones do when he found out how it happened? He turned to Babushka.

'Your father has message to the Jones you are late because of accident,' Babushka answered before he could ask. 'Kaiser kick you. He has a sore hoof. You go to hospital. Doctor Carroll also sends note.'

Joe shook his head slowly until it hurt and he stopped and smiled broadly instead.

'Is there anything you didn't think of?' he laughed.

'I do not organise to keep foolish men out of trouble!' she answered solemnly, but her eyes twinkled. Joe almost felt like he was back in the land of the living. He heaved a deep sigh. It hurt. But there was one last thing he needed to know.

'Babushka,' Joe asked hesitantly, afraid of her reaction, but her socks had him so intrigued.

'Where did you get so much money?'

She glanced at him swiftly and for a moment he thought he'd get the sharp edge of her tongue. He probably deserved it.

'I am immigrant. This does not mean I am poor. Vanya and I work hard. Save our roubles. He does not drink and gamble like some. And my father is a man who has his grain in the barn long before the winter. When he died, rest his soul, I am his only child.' She leaned back with the air of one who has said enough.

'But I didn't know,' Joe said. 'You've got enough money in that bag to buy a house.'

'Maybe a few,' Babushka replied with a nod that almost passed for sly. 'I own the boarding house and Old Nik's shop already.' She tapped the side of her nose in a knowing way.

'You kept that secret,' Joe shook his head again and laughed. 'Do the Comrades know about the Capitalist in their midst?'

Suddenly Babushka was not amused. She rounded on him like a dog in the street.

'You are fool, Joseph Hill!' she breathed hard, her face matching the hardness of her voice. Joe was startled at the change in her. 'You are fool if you think having money makes Capitalist. Money is nothing. Not good, not bad. Money is like pages in a book. What is written on pages makes story. What people do with money makes good and bad. Never forget!' she hissed. Joe leaned away from her sudden attack. But she hadn't finished,

'You must keep secret my socks. No one knows this,' she said, grabbing his hand hard. He nodded and reddened, mouthing a promise, hand to heart.

Joe was genuinely afraid, for one moment, at her violence. He wondered if he had it in him to keep as silent as she wished.

As suddenly as she'd turned on him, Babushka was satisfied. At least she seemed to be. Her face fell back to its normal creases.

'Secrets are everywhere. Everyone keeps some. As you grow older you find this out,' she said almost wearily. 'The old carry many.' Then she turned again to Joe, as though sizing him up for something.

'But I am not the richest in this street,' she said, as though challenging him. Joe dared not look at her again. He didn't really want or need to know who was.

'The violin that old fool Nikolai plays for the dead wife? This fiddle is worth more than the whole street!' Joe couldn't control himself at this revelation. Every night just on dusk the whole district could hear Old Nik play his love song to Natalia.

'That old thing!' he blurted out. 'That's not worth a zack at the secondhands,' Joe said, adding, 'is it?'

'Eat what is cooked; listen to what is said!' Babushka said, her voice closed.

He didn't argue. They both sat, looking at the street.

'But perhaps,' Babushka said softly as she gazed ahead, 'the young also have secrets?' Joe reddened again. 'A secret is good for the goose is good for the gander … and the gander's friends?'

Joe glanced at her. Perhaps it was the morning sun or the weariness of the night but suddenly Babushka looked wizened and shrewd – her face like a squeezed lemon – not at all the cheery round-faced suffering soul. This was the real Babushka, exact and complete, not just the side of her Joe had seen before. This was the whole jigsaw puzzle.

They were both startled by a loud whistle. Nikolai sat atop his cab like Santa Claus in a top hat.

'You pay double to ride with me, Joe,' Old Nik called out, solemn as an undertaker.

'Why?' asked Joe as he bent to help Babushka up.

'Because,' Old Nik answered, his eyes twinkling under the white snow of his eyebrows, 'You are in the paper. *Youth Attacks Diggers In South Brisbane*. You pay danger money! The soldiers all want your blood!'

He laughed long and merrily as Joe helped Babushka into the cab.

'But every night this week you owe the Kaiser a rub down for his troubles! And some green pick too!'

Old Nikolai laughed again. Joe grimaced as a twinge of pain shot through him. Babushka, back to her old self, giggled at him as he climbed up beside her.

For the first time since he'd been belted, Joe really felt like finding out who'd done this to Mick and him, taking them up a nice dark alley and giving them a bloody good kicking.

But, he thought, and the thought comforted him as Old Nik started Kaiser clopping towards the river, Molly might think me a peace hero just as I am.

Chapter 15

Should I Ever Be A Soldier
Should I ever be a soldier,
'Neath the Red Flag I would fight;
Should the gun I ever shoulder,
It's to crush the tyrant's might.
Join the army of the toilers,
Men and women fall in line,
Wage slaves of the world! Arouse!
Do your duty for the cause,
For Land and Liberty.
Joel Emmanuel Hagglund

Blonde sawdust showered the sawyers as they drew the pine planks back, again and again, until they had slats sawn to the right thicknesses for box-ends. Jones & Son made any sort of boxes, as rough as guts or as finished as you like, for any sort of product: kerosene, butter, pineapples, grapes, milk, bananas or grog cases. Ted Hill wiped the sweat from his forehead with a red rag as he watched the wood being fed into the saw. He looked up to see the boss staring from his window on the top floor of the company office. Ted waved a little fairy wave. Jones noticed the movement and, breaking from his reverie, waved an absentminded hand before comprehending Ted Hill's sarcastic intention.

Alwyn Jones took little interest in the life of his company as it existed on the factory floor, or in the yard. He sat instead in his sales room on the top floor, slightly separate from the office and, in idle moments, (which Ted Hill thought many) he gazed across his domain, watching for anyone slacking, or trying to spot, 'Lesser Jones' or 'Jones the Lost', as the worker's and office staff called the 'Son' in, Jones & Son.

If he was feeling particularly vexed he'd go down to the floor on his side of the fence and berate Joe Hill and the other cabinetmaking apprentices for "going slow" on the order they'd been working on – desks for the Army. Tory platitudes dripped from his mouth like gravy from Sunday roast.

'Man of my word. A Matter of Honour. A labour of National Importance. Men of exemplary character. We of the Empire.' Joe always tried to be looking away when Jones made his speeches with his thumbs hooked in the pockets of his waistcoat and his clean-shaved face red as prime baked ham. He was a caricature, but caricatures found their genesis in truth.

'Jones the Hefty' left the actual workings of the plant to his foremen, Ted and the other three. He was too busy organising sales and materials (for which he paid canny prices) and chatting to customers who came to order "pieces" from the "other side". The "other side" being the Fine Furniture business separated from the bulk wood yard by an eight-foot high fence.

That always gave the workers a laugh. Both "sides" of the fence sat back to back along it at smokos and at lunchtimes, including the girls from the office and the whole Accounts Department. They'd sit and talk gossip … or politics, which was what it was at morning tea this morning.

As foreman, Ted had to bring hot water from the boiler for the tea for both sides, pouring it between two loose palings for the "t'othersiders" and he'd always have to be first left from smokos to make sure the steam was up for when they started work again. The only difference between the sides was Fine Furniture had milk poured in their teacups, if they wanted it, before they left the shed while everyone on t'otherside were expected to take their tea black as the boss's heart. Of course milk went through the fence too as required.

If he ever wanted anything from the office, or more likely, wanted to run any One Big Union business past the other side, Ted climbed up the boiler frame, looked over the fence and waved a hanky. White for "need to talk at smoko". Red for "urgent". Molly could see straight out the window of the Accounts Department and if it was red flag business she'd find some reason to go down as soon as she could. Jones never stopped her; she was a hard worker and … Jones appreciated her smile. But he never went so far as to put a gate in the fence either.

Ted finished wiping his hands and checked his company pocket watch. Steam was up. Still half an hour till smoko. He glanced around the yard for any problems.

Madorsky was struggling with the wire machine that secured the bundles of box parts in their separate orders. Ted decided not to yell cheek at him. That'd be dangerous. Especially with Madorsky, who didn't like the mick being taken. But Ted grinned at his workmate's agitation. He belted the wire feeder and tried to keep the slats together as he tied them. His hands were covered with scratches.

It's a beggar of a machine, Ted thought. I'll tell Jones to do something about it once and for all or it'll become an issue. The mongrel thing'll hurt someone bad one day.

He dragged a few offcuts back down to the boiler before he climbed the frame. A red handkerchief flittered from the bottom corner of the window. Molly never signalled him. It must be about Joe! Ted jumped down and ran to the smoko spot.

'Molly?' he asked the wall. 'What's on?'

'Babushka and Joe are here,' Molly said, her whisper urgent. 'I think one of Jones' snitches put a flea in his ear about what happened. He's mad as a cut snake. Read the Riot Act about political activities interfering with work. Joe's got a whopper of a black eye and a swollen lip that he can't hide. He's talking about showing him the door. You'd best be coming quick!' Ted was already on his way.

'Thanks, Moll,' he said as he strode off towards the gate. 'And you'd best get that handkerchief back in your pocket!' Molly laughed, but nervously, as she turned to run back upstairs.

'Hoy, Madorsky!' Ted bellowed above the noise of the yard. The man looked up. 'Leave that and look after the boiler for me,' he yelled.

'The Russian dropped the bundle he was working on and turned off his machine.

'Don't think!' Jones yelled at Babushka and Joe. 'Don't think for one minute that I don't know that it's you leading this "go slow" on the Army desks!'

'Got your own private army of narks have you!' Joe murmured indistinctly out the good side of his mouth. But Jones heard it. He could hear a personal insult at one hundred paces.

'I do have some loyal employees,' Jones rejoined, emphasizing the word "loyal" wilfully.

'Who turn up to work on time and don't sabotage the contracts I win for the War Effort.'

Joe Hill hung his head.

But Babushka stood her ground, her Gladstone bag clutched before her. She was crumpled as an unmade bed and tired as a fresh stabled plough horse, but Jones had fanned her anger.

'You go!' she told Joe. So Joe went, quick smart. Bit his tongue. Ted would be proud. Besides he hurt all over. His head ached, his lip was still tight with blood and his face throbbing after Jones's tirade. He couldn't be damned about the job or the Cause or … but then … there was Molly. Walking towards him, smiling, hand raised to touch his face, her fingers electric with cool sympathy.

'Poor lamb,' she said so soft and so low that Joe couldn't quite decide whether there wasn't a trace of sarcasm, 'does it hurt?'

'Looks worse than it is,' Joe answered awkwardly. He was happiest believing she meant it lovingly, he felt the blood rising. He wished he could stop this damn blushing. Now his lip would probably start to bleed again too. Molly took her hand down from his face. This was the big bit of all right he'd wished for all night.

'Your father's coming,' she told him.

'I hope he's quick,' Joe said. They could hear the heat rising in the voices behind the door in Jones' office and Ted taking the steps two at a time. He caught sight of Joe's face.

'Bloody hell, son!' he burst out. Ted examined the damage intently. In the clear light of day Joe looked so much worse than last night.

'The bastards! Wait till I …' he exclaimed, then, remembering the company, he looked shame-faced at Molly.

'Sorry about the language.' Molly smiled his manners away. Hadn't she thought the same thing indeed?

'They didn't touch you in the watch house did they?' Ted turned back to the job at hand. They could hear Babushka inside. It wouldn't be pretty in there and he needed as much information as he could get. Joe shook his head.

'What did they charge you with?'

'Nothing serious. I just got fined,' Joe stumbled, trying to remember what exactly the fines were for. 'Urquhart wanted me to do a deal to spy on you.' Ted's eyes widened in amazement, but he didn't interrupt.

'To spy on you and Mother and Artem and Uncle Bill and … everyone. I said no, or words to that effect. Then Babushka arrived and he stood no chance.'

Ted Hill shook his head in momentary wonderment.

'No charges, then?' he repeated. Joe shook his head.

'No charges … just a fine?'

Joe nodded.

'Babushka paid.'

'Well … well done!' Ted nodded. 'They wanted you and they didn't get you.' Joe began to blush at the praise though he still wasn't sure about charges.

'Still,' Ted finished as he grasped the handle to Jones' door. 'Maybe we could have done with a spy in their ranks.'

Jones had bitten off more than he could chew. Babushka spread her elbows as though she had her hands on her hips, which was difficult given she was holding the Gladstone bag, but she managed the effect.

'I am not British? This is true. I am Russian. And who is it, Little Man, fights on Eastern Front? Mother Russia!' Babushka paused. 'You small man.' She drew herself up to her full height of not very big. But big enough to overwhelm a room full of Jones'.

'Small man. Small brains. Small world. Small …' and here Babushka threw a withering look below Jones' belt, met his eye for an instant to revel in his dawning discomfit, then tossed back her head and laughed like a tickled child.

'I must say, Madam,' Jones began, his voice ugly, enunciating every word clearly, 'that I am not accustomed, to this type of gutter assault, by someone unknown to me, in my own office.'

Jones' eyes had shrunk into mean balls, his face purple and threatening to explode, showering whiskers and jowls all around the room. Irina stood smiling at the thought, as though she were looking forward to cleaning up the mess. Their interview was interrupted by a knock at the door. It inched open. Jones strode over and yanked, wrenching the doorknob from Ted's grip.

'What?' he yelled. He expected Joe or one of the more compliant employees. For a split second Jones thought that there might be some trouble in the yard. More likely someone had blabbered over the fence. Behind Ted Hill, Jones could see Molly disappearing into the Accounts Department. He knew it was her. That smile. They would have to come to an agreement, Molly and he, Jones shuddered lasciviously. Ted took the shudder as revulsion.

'This Russian filth!' Jones spat in Ted's nonplussed face. 'Is something to do with you, Hill?'

He knew there was no yard trouble and further he knew letting the younger Hill keep his job, for now, would provide some real leverage for later.

Ted had never seen Jones so genuinely angry. Babushka stood behind him, ready to rise up like over-boiled wrath. She wasn't helping Joe's case. He knew perfectly well Joe could get the boot, just for being late and as for the go slow, Jones only needed an excuse and it's "goodnight Joseph Hill". Ted thought quickly.

'Thank you, Irina,' he said. He sidestepped Jones, to stand beside her, taking her projecting arm. Babushka threw him a daggered look.

'Nyet!' she said pulling her elbow away. But Ted held hard.

'I think you've done enough for Joe now,' he insisted as she fought for possession of her arm.

'I …' she began again. But it was Ted's fight now and he needed to fight alone. She didn't know the rules here.

'You need some rest,' he cajoled. She opened her mouth to object but Ted pushed her firmly, quickly, towards the door. Jones stood aside. Ted spoke soft beside her.

'Leave this one to me.'

Babushka wrenched her arm from his grip. Ted tried one last shot, and hoped it didn't go too far.

'Vanya would say you've done enough.' Ted hoped she would understand his insistence.

'Goodbye, Irina,' he said finally, touching her hand. Ted closed the door behind her.

Irina stood outside blinking like a midday possum. She looked around Jones's ante-room, full of polished silky-oak furniture. Joe was nowhere to be seen.

Babushka sighed a world-weary sigh. Folding her yards of black skirt and shawl about her like a tired flying fox, she took the stairs down.

'This is not about that mad Russian woman. This is about your son. Not only,' Jones repeated, much more calmly now, 'does he turn up late but he is injured, as a direct result, I am informed, of his political activities.'

Ted knew he walked the edge of a crumbling cliff. This wasn't just about Joe. Stepping wrong might affect all the workers.

'Since when has saving your mate from taking a bashing from a mob of hooligans been a crime?' he asked quietly. Ted hoped Jones' details were sketchy.

'After a political meeting held by Bolsheviks and Socialists!' Jones countered.

'I thought this was a free country? Free to say what we think, how and when we like? I thought that's what we were fighting for?'

Jones drew himself up and extended his stomach a couple of inches.

'It is my duty as a citizen to ensure that my workers are not breaching any Laws of the country especially The War Precautions Act,' Jones said. 'That would amount to sedition and there is a war on.'

'Strange isn't it,' Ted Hill mused. 'We're fighting a war to ensure we can always say what we like, while at home we have Hughes passing laws that say we can't say what we like.' He let it sink in for a moment before adding, 'And "citizens",' Ted spat the word, 'like you who spy on the rest of us as though we have no right to speak at all.'

Jones was on the back foot. This was supposed to be about Joe. He couldn't let Hill turn it into a debate about politics.

'Your son, Joe …' he began, but Ted was waiting for it.

'Yes, Joe, who was beaten by a group of louts dressed in khaki uniforms. Did they tell you that they were your good old Army boys?' he needled.

It was obvious from the look on his face that this detail was news to Jones.

Ted almost felt sorry for the sad old buggar. Almost.

'That aside,' Jones began again.

'Aside?' Ted raised his voice. 'Yes, let's just push the inconvenient truths aside,' he said. 'You might think that we can't see what's going on. Maybe you can bluff an old woman,' Ted pushed on. 'And maybe you can confuse a young bloke who's had his bloody face pushed in, but I know perfectly well that you and your mates are in it with the Hughes mob. You make huge profits from the war while Hughes keeps us in line.' Ted could see the change in Jones as he spoke. Now was the moment.

'Joe was injured in a fight saving his mate,' Ted summarized. 'He was late to work because the police detained him wrongfully – without charge.'

It was obvious they hadn't told Jones that either from his look.

He knew he wasn't fighting fair but this was Joe's job at stake and he couldn't afford to have a black mark against his name either. Jones would use that later, when it suited him in some negotiation or other, and the whole staff could suffer.

'So let's just leave politics out of it and let Joe work off the three hours owing and leave it at that.' Ted tried not to let any note, either positive or negative, enter his voice. Jones did not bite back. But he said nothing.

'You know he's one of your best workers and those desks won't make themselves.' Jones's brow lined with effort.

'Four hours and no pay for the extra payback hour,' Ted suggested. He knew he jumped in too quick with this offer but he had to keep the ball rolling. Jones didn't think well under pressure.

'You know the doctor ordered him to stay in bed for at least twenty-four hours?' Ted asked. It was a complete porky but he didn't have anything else. Finally Jones spoke,

'Five hours extra, one every night this week. I pay for none of them, and I have his word on not going slow on the desk contract.' Ted Hill had his hand out to seal the deal almost before Jones closed his mouth. A bit of extra work would remind the boy to look before he leaped. They shook hands. But neither had finished,

'Starting tomorrow night,' Ted insisted, holding Jones's hand to be sure. Jones looked uncertain. 'I could ask the doctor for a letter and fight this in public instead if you like?' They had stopped shaking, but still held hands.

'No, of course,' Jones agreed. 'Next week will be fine.' He dropped Ted's hand suddenly as though it contained something rotten.

'You like it all too much,' Jones added enigmatically.

Ted raised one eyebrow. He was lost. It didn't happen often on the job.

'I like what too much?'

'The game. You like it so much you'll do anything to win. But you can't leave anything to chance. That's your weakness,' Jones answered. 'Sometimes things happen that you can't forsee. Then you've got trouble. And trouble is disorganised.'

Ted considered for a moment.

He was about to tell Jones he was a fool for revealing his hand when they were interrupted by a knock at the door and, almost simultaneously, the smoko bell clanging in the yard. Jones had recovered all of his authority.

'Enter!' he commanded in his high voice. Joe opened the door, a red handkerchief with which he'd just wiped blood from his lip grasped in one hand. Jones stared at him.

'Sorry, it was bleeding.' Joe's voice dribbled to silence before he noticed it was the handkerchief that Jones was staring at.

'I'm watching you!' he enunciated, pointing a threatening finger at Joe. 'You can get straight to work.'

Jones dismissed him with a flick of the hand, his voice hard.

Ted walked out, closing the door quickly behind them both.

Jones picked up his telephone and spoke to the operator.

'Bloody hell, mind out, Joe!' Ted was annoyed but managed to laugh. 'Show a red flag to the bull why don't you?' Joe joined in but kept the handkerchief tight to his face.

'What now?' he asked.

'You heard him, get to work, we'll talk this arvo. I'll send Molly over with a scone and tea,' Ted added. 'You must be hungry.'

'Babushka fed me porridge and prunes.'

'Those prunes'll make you run to work!' Ted clapped his son on the back. 'Or at least make you run faster when there's loyalists about. There's only two sorts of Socialists son: the quick and the dead.'

Ted began to walk down the stairs. Workers coming out from Accounts followed, Joe and Molly amongst them. The rest hurried past. Smoko was a quarter hour from the bell till the bell to be back in. Jones watched the time, and them, from the window.

'I didn't mean now, Dad,' Joe said. 'I meant what's happened, you know … in total?' Ted turned on the bottom step.

'In total you have five hours unpaid overtime starting tomorrow.'

'Five!' Joe repeated loud enough that everybody looked. 'But I was only late by three, at the most,' he whined.

'Five,' Ted repeated. It was agreed so it was finished. He hoped Madorsky had remembered to boil the tea.

'And no pay for any of them,' Ted ended.

'You … you agreed to that!' Joe stopped dead on the stairs two above his father. He was incredulous. Ted stepped back up the stairs with a warning look in his eyes.

'Shut up, boy! Do you want the whole bloody world gawking at our business?'

'Our business? I thought it was Union business. Why'd you agree to it?'

'Do you want your bloody job or not!' Ted hissed.

'But it's Union business – one in all in. We could have sat down, or walked out. You know he wouldn't have sacked me in the end,' Joe sputtered to a stop, waiting for an explanation. Ted breathed heavily. He felt bloody tired.

'It's personal, Joe. He'll use you to get at me,' he began, continuing as Joe tried to interrupt again. 'That's how they do it. Find out something personal and hold it against you. Then when you have a genuine industrial matter they drag up the private dirt.'

Joe shook his head.

'You always say, "Stick to your principles and the rest will fall in line" and I always have. I always try to decide what I believe and stick to it.' Joe stared at his father. Suddenly, somehow the rules had changed.

'Well that's leadership, Joe. Sometimes I have to see the big picture, even if it looks from the outside like I've thrown my principles to the devil!'

Ted's exasperation was beginning to show.

'That's not what this was about. If you can't see that this was a very minor battle in the big bloody war then you don't have the commonsense you'll need to get any-bloody-where. That smack in the head must have dented your bloody brain,' Ted swore as he walked off.

'So sometimes you just dump your principles is that it?' Joe almost sneered at his father's back. Ted swung around.

'Jesus, Joseph and Mary, Joe! I just told you! It's five hours bloody overtime or get the fucking boot and your whole apprenticeship's on the shit-cart! You decide!' Ted yelled throwing his hands in the air. He was already sorry before he'd finished. But he couldn't take it back.

'I've got to see about the tea,' he concluded and walked away. Joe stood dumb. He could feel the blood rise hot up his neck. He stepped down off the stairs and strode to the door.

'What?' Molly began.

'Bloody nothing!' Joe yelled as he strode toward the workshop. Molly picked up her red handkerchief from where it lay on the verandah and decided it probably wasn't the best time to give Joe Monty's letter.

Chapter 16

The Ragtime Army
We are the ragtime army
The A.N.Z.A.C.,
We cannot shoot
We won't salute
What bloody use are we?
And when we get to Berlin
The Kaiser he will say
Mein Got! Mein Got!
What a bloody rotten lot
To get six bob a day.
To the tune of 'Onward Christian Soldiers'.

Ted Hill climbed the ladder up the side of the frame of the boiler to ring the five-minute bell. Five minutes gave everybody using a machine time to finish what they were doing, clean-up and stand down – before he released the steam valve and all the machines stopped together.

The metal landing at the top of the boiler's ladder commanded an ever-changing view up and down the river's city reach. It was best in winter, the view, when the early morning fogs were infused with sunlight like liquid air, hung huge above the river water below it or, in the afternoons, when the shadows of the ships docked at the wharves along the southern bank, stretched across the riverway, making giants of the men working there, until the stars showed and the lanterns on both banks turned the river into a golden, shining, Earth-bound Milky Way. Sometimes he would climb up five minutes early just so he could sit and contemplate the ever-changing business of the city.

Ted Hill leaned against the boiler and scratched himself.

He knew he needed to apologise to Babushka for bundling her out of the morning's negotiations with Jones. A couple of fish would be just the ticket. He'd duck into the Anchor after work, to see if any of the fishermen had caught anything good enough to soothe her with.

Ted's reverie was cut short by a scream. Instinctively he began to climb down, before stopping himself. He swore, climbed back up the ladder and threw the safety valve wide open. Ted jumped down from the ladder six rungs up and was running before he hit the ground.

Madorsky had wired his hand into the last bundle of box slats of the day. They'd hammered the slats out from the centre of the bundle to release the pressure and free him by the time Ted arrived.

'What have you done to yourself, you mad Ruskie!' he yelled.

'Nobody calls me Ruskie!' Madorsky replied.

Ted was in no mood to apologise. He grabbed the Russian by his shirt and dragged him into the light, pulling Madorsky's hand upward as he did.

'Show us!' he demanded. The surface of the skin across the back of his hand was cut in a deep, thin, bone-white line.

'You're bloody lucky! That machine could take a hand clean off.'

Ted was relieved but annoyed that he'd forgotten to talk to Jones about it earlier. That bundler was a safety issue. Now he'd have to collar Jones tonight before he went home.

Madorsky'd be all right – thank God! His hand would be painful for a few days and stiff once the swelling started.

'If you knew that, Comrade,' Madorsky scowled as he wrapped a handkerchief around his wound. 'Why do I work on dangerous machine. What good is one-handed labourer to his family.'

Ted knew Madorsky's circumstances, a tribe of kids and his missus sick and all. Everyone tried to help the bloke out but, he was a hot-head, and some people don't try too hard to help themselves. Ted decided it best to retreat to safer territory.

'If the Wobblies ran the yard,' he began.

'If the Wobblies stop talking and do anything it will be a bloody wonder,' Madorsky sneered, obviously recovering quickly from the shock.

Ted couldn't be bothered fighting.

'I'm going to see Jones about it now. The rest of you should go home and … someone better ring the bell for knock-off.'

Molly ran towards the crowd.

'What is it?' she asked, then, seeing Madorsky's hand,

'You've hurt yourself.'

'I'm tip-top, Miss. Do not worry,' he answered.

'Take him home, Molly,' Ted said. 'He needs a proper bandage on that.'

'I'm not bloody child,' Madorsky snarled, his mood almost back to normal.

'I take care of myself and,' he added, 'I have wife!'

'Poor thing.' Molly's voice was almost inaudible, leaving it unclear whether she was talking about him or his missus.

Madorsky heard her though and reacted to the insult, storming out the gate.

'Well buggar you!' Molly yelled after him, emphasising the word in a most unladylike fashion. It had been a very long twenty-four hours and she, like all of them, was dog-tired.

'Last time I try to help!'

Madorsky stopped.

Joe intervened.

'No harm meant,' he offered.

Madorsky walked back towards Molly, purpose in his step.

Joe placed himself between them.

'Look,' Joe began. 'Let's just get home. I dunno about you, but I've had enough for one day.' He looked from each to each with his most appealing, bloody-lipped look.

'Well, I'm going to the hospital to see Mick,' Molly replied archly, staring defiantly at Madorsky, who said nothing – loudly.

'Yes! That sounds like a good idea, Moll!' Joe agreed. Then, appealing again to Madorsky,

'Come on. We can't let a mate down!'

Finally the Russian responded.

'What do you think I do half the night? I stick up for me mates!' Half-raising the clenched fist of his good hand, they saw skinned knuckles.

'Much thanks I get for helping you.'

'I didn't think you did it for the thanks,' Molly countered sourly – rubbing salt.

Joe was certain something was going to happen, but Madorsky surprised them both. Speaking very deliberately he responded,

'You take Golden-hair Boy and you do your Red-Cross-lady-visit-hospital. I have real work to do.'

'That's not fair,' Joe remonstrated gently.

'Not fair! By Christ, this is rich to come from you. Everyone knows you get special treatment because Daddy is Organiser.'

Madorsky waited for it to sting.

'I think this is first rule – Union is Strength. But not when the Organiser uses the Union to look after his own family. first Don't take me for fool. I see it. Everybody sees it.'

Joe wasn't about to back down… this was personal. He strode towards the Russian. Madorsky stared at him derisively.

Suddenly it was Molly trying to soothe what she'd provoked.

'Stop it the two of you!'

But she was too late. A fury burst in Madorsky. He launched himself at Joe, hitting him hard in the stomach.

'You're no better than the rest of us,' he snarled. 'Just because you know how to talk!'

Joe responded with his fists, but wasn't as practiced as his comrade.

'How's this?' Madorsky hit Joe again. 'Am I talking loud enough?'

Joe fell to the ground, Madorsky on him.

Molly began hitting them both with slaps and punches. Joe covered his head.

'For Christ's sake!' Ted Hill bellowed, dragging Madorsky off his son.

'What the bloody hell do you think you're playing at?'

Jones appeared on the footpath behind them.

Madorsky decided not to hit Ted, but wrenched himself away.

Joe struggled to his feet.

Molly stood, wild-eyed but silent, sobbing to gain her breath.

Jones smiled. A bemused smile.

'Well?' Ted demanded of Joe.

'It's your fault!' Joe shouted, challenging his father. 'They all say you did me a deal to keep my job.' His gaze fell to the ground in shame.

'Then they'd all be right,' Jones said, seizing the moment to cause maximum damage. Ted spun about.

Molly had taken a seat in the gutter.

'Are you all right, Miss Pearce?' Jones directed his attention to her, all concern.

'Perfectly,' Molly's breathing was calmer now. She refused his hand. Refused to acknowledge her part in provoking her own little war.

It was Joe who spoke first.

'I'm going to see Mick,' he said.

Putting word into action he stepped unsteadily off the footpath and onto the road. They watched him totter through the traffic like a wind-up toy.

Joe looked up at the Town Hall clock.

Knock-off at five. Knock-out at ten past!

24 hours ago he'd never been in a fair dinkum stoush. Now it seemed nearly normal.

Molly stared hard at Madorsky. The Russian stared back. There seemed no likelihood of apology or compromise. Finally, Madorsky decided.

'Stuff this for game of soldiers!' he spat.

Jones laughed aloud.

'Always, there is boss!' Madorsky addressed Jones. 'Revolution or no revolution – always boss.' He turned and slouched off.

Molly stood up, crumpled and adrift, watching as Madorsky broke into a trot, heading home. She breathed deeply as though she'd run a marathon.

Ted recovered too.

'Molly, I'll walk with you. I have to see Babushka.'

Molly mastered herself, brushed back her hair, picked up her hat.

'If you could call in and tell her I'll be home directly, I'd be grateful,' she answered, with as much dignity as she had left. 'I'm going up to the hospital.'

'As long as you're sure?' Ted remained unconvinced. Molly nodded.

'Afternoon, Mr Jones,' she added.

Jones inclined his head sidewards like a tame cockatoo. Molly took a deep breath before hopping over the gutter and weaving through the horses and cars after Joe.

'A bit of trouble in your camp it seems.' Jones smirked as he watched her receding figure.

'You'll need a new bloke on the bundler.' Ted smiled back. 'Why not try a non-Union member?' he suggested. 'Then we'll see about trouble.'

Jones shrugged his shoulders and tossed his head.

'Have it your way,' he answered.

A man sauntered out of the factory gate. Ted was sure he'd seen him before? At yesterday's rally?

Jones bundled him back inside.

'Looking for a job, mate?' Ted called after them, laughing at Jones's back.

He spat against the wall.

Chapter 17

The Sleeper Cutters' Camp
My sole address at present is a battlefield in France –
If it's ever going to alter there is only just a chance –
To dodge the "Jerry" rifles and the shrapnel flying around –
I've burrowed like a bunny to a funkhole in the ground.
The floor is just a puddle and the roof lets in the damp.
I wish I was in Aussie where the sleeper cutters camp.
The tea is foul and bitter like an ancient witch's brew –
The bread is sour and scanty and you ought to see the stew –
The "Lootenant" that is leading is a leery kind of coot –
We always call 'im "Mr" as plain "Bill" would never suit.
I'd sell my chance of Heaven for five minutes with the scamp
Where the red bull's chewing nut grass near the sleeper cutters camp.
If another war is starting I'll hang out with the "jibs"
Not much to be a hero with a bayonet 'tween your ribs –
Hard fighting for the Froggies pushing Huns across the Rhine
They can take Alsace and Flanders and Normandy for mine.
All I'm needing is a pozzie where ground is not too damp
'Neath azure skies of Aussie – just a sleeper cutters camp.
Dan Sheahan

She found him under the shade of a Moreton Bay fig tree outside the main doors of the hospital. He sat on a bench, staring at the ground between his feet. She moved to sit beside him but the bench slats were stained with ripe figs and a mush of undigested seeds. The flying foxes would be back to feast on them again tonight. She thought about brushing them off with her hat, but didn't and remained standing.

Limp with heat and tiredness, she waited. Joe neither moved nor acknowledged her.

'I don't like the smell of hospitals,' he finally said. 'Never have.'

Joe stood up, wiping the detritus from his trousers. 'Whenever I had to come up here to see Mother, or Uncle Bill, I'd stop outside for a minute, just to get myself ready. I hate the smell of carbolic and chloroform. She smells like it when she comes home. Especially since all the soldiers.' Joe nodded around the seats in the small garden.

Amputees, broken-limbed, and heavily-bandaged blokes stood, or sat around in invalid chairs or leaning on crutches or canes, some in uniform, some in civvies or pyjamas, sharing a smoke, or talking to loved ones, coughing, or just staring ahead into the bleak distance with their thousand yard stares.

Molly and Joe knew they were both looking at what they, and the rest of the world, didn't want to see – the lucky ones, the damaged, crippled, lame of heart and mind.

They looked until they were staring, then looked away, away from the living reasons for needing peace right now.

'What's happened, Joe?' Molly asked as she bowed her head. 'What's happened to Mick? And you and me?' Her lips trembled. 'It's like we're all being eaten by some huge beast. It's bigger than everything, bigger than all of us. It gnaws at us every moment, even in our dreams.'

She shuddered at the vision that assailed her.

'Everything we do, everyone we talk to, everywhere we look – the beast is.'

She fell silent. Joe looked at her as if seeing her for the first time. Shaking her head. Trying not to lose control.

'You're right,' Joe said, not knowing if he should touch her, even to comfort, though he knew that he so yearned, yearned until he ached, and never had he ached as much as now.

'I never saw it like a beast,' he answered, moving close to her side. 'But I saw it too, like a blanket. A black, suffocating blanket that covered the entire sky, stifling all the light, pushing down on me until I couldn't think, or move.'

Words failed him too. They stood alone together.

Molly swallowed her tears..

'Maybe that's what's wrong with Mick?' she suggested hopefully.

'And my father, and his,' Joe added.

'Maybe even the fellows who bashed you both?' Molly looked at Joe.

'It's a disease we all have,' he answered, in what he hoped sounded a convincing tone. 'War's a disease of the imagination. When you don't imagine anymore what it's like to be the other fellow. To live his life. To love what he loves. When men become enemies,' Joe said, 'it's because they force themselves to stop imagining they can love anyone, or anything, but their own. Come on, then,' he added quickly in case he was beginning to sound like a sermon. 'We'd best get in there.'

He took Molly's arm by the elbow.She felt so soft and alive. That faint perfume of her hair.

Joe stumbled on the bottom stair. Molly smiled.

'*You* need *me* holding *your* arm.' He steadied himself against her.

'Any time you like,' he mumbled, saying aloud what was on his mind.

'Sorry,' he added as they ascended the stairs, blushing, this time not because he felt self-conscious but because of the delicious pleasure of falling against her. Of having her smile for him.

Joe stopped his imagination there and dragged off his hat as they entered the ward.

Molly saw him first.

'There he is,' she whispered, elbowing Joe gently in the ribs. He winced.

'Thanks very much,' he grimaced.

'You're welcome, kind sir!' she laughed quietly. Every emotion was heightened, almost unhinged.

'It's good we're together for this. We'll be no good for Mick if we turn up like a pair of crows at a funeral,' Joe said.

Though they both looked for Mick, there was still the shock of finding him. He looked perfectly normal. No bandages, no blood, no nothing. His mouth hung open, as he clapped eyes on Joe, with a look of astonishment.

'Strike me lucky! What happened to you?' Mick asked before either of them had had a chance to speak. 'Were you kicked by Kaiser or something?'

'Pleased to see you too, Comrade!'

Joe laughed, half in relief at how well Mick looked, much better than he'd steeled himself to expect.

'And a good afternoon from me, my kind sir!' Molly curtsied and smiled. Mick smiled too, but he really wanted to know,

'What the hell happened?'

'All in the line of duty, old chap! Good oh, what!' Joe took up Molly's caper and bunged on an accent. Mick smiled again but still waited. It was Molly who replied.

''E'll never tell you,' she said continuing the play. ''E was quite me proper hero!' She fluttered her eyelashes and clasped her little hands in the proper music-hall style.

'Who, despite henormus hopposition copped a whizz-bang, ponk on the noggin, from one of them very hooli-gooli-gans what was so intent on kickin' you senseless, my good fellow.'

Mick's look suggested her story wasn't true. She nodded her head. Mick leaned quickly towards Joe, wanting the full story.

But stopped himself quickly, clutching at his side as a sharp, quick pain stabbed his ribcage. Joe looked more closely. Mick was bandaged around the chest and up over one shoulder. It was hard to see the bandage because of the hospital pyjamas.

'A few ribs broken,' Mick said as the pain passed and he breathed more freely again.

'You always give better than you get so the other bloke must be a bloody mess!' Mick smiled weakly at Joe.

'Thanks, cobber,' he said seriously.

Although he didn't seem hurt, Mick's voice already seemed tired.

'Mick,' Joe asked slyly, changing the subject again to lighten the air. 'If you had the choice between getting beaten up by a mob of hooligans on a dark night or kicked by a horse, which one would you take?'

'You mad beggar!' Mick smiled.

'No, Joe, you answer this one. If you had the chance would you rather get in a fight with Madorsky, or the bloke that hit you?'

Mick smiled again as Molly and Joe swapped glances. Neither spoke, Madorsky's words still hung between them.

'Well?' Mick pressed, missing the glance entirely.

'Madorsky's a mate. It wouldn't be right to fight a mate.' Joe looked helplessly to Molly. Mick shrugged a little and changed tack.

'How is he anyway?'

'Everyone's a bit tired after last night.'

'I bet they are,' Mick nodded.

'Yes,' Joe lied convincingly. 'He said to say g'day. Same from Ted and Babushka and Tomas and everyone at the yard.'

'Except the Jones's both Greater and Lesser,' Molly added for effect.

A silence fell then that they were too tired to try to cover up. Mick looked expectant, as though they were the evening's entertainment.

'We haven't asked what happened to you,' Joe said. 'All I know is I heard you call out. When I found you, they were kicking you on the ground. I got a few in, but after, Mother reckons I was more or less unconscious all evening – until they put me in the watch house anyway.'

Suddenly Mick took real notice.

'What were you doing in the watch house?' he asked quickly. 'You did nothing.'

'Well I did hit one bloke hard,' Joe said. 'So I suppose I was in the wrong.'

'But why were you in trouble for helping me?'

It was Mick's turn to be angry.

'They picked the fight. Five of them. Bloody cowards. I coulda done 'em all – one at a time.'

'Babushka's new lodger's a snitch,' Joe answered. 'And O'Hagen, the copper there, is too. What chance we got?' Molly gave him a surprised look, and concerned, but Joe didn't return it.

'I reckon he's been put there by the Police Commissioner or the Minister as a spy,' Joe said as matter-of-factly as he could. Mick and Molly were outraged.

'Think about it,' Joe continued, 'O'Hagen isn't Tomfool, but he isn't the sharpest knife in the drawer either. He'll do exactly what the other bloke, Winterson, says. He's the perfect spy.'

Mick and Molly were thinking hard.

'Anyway,' Joe concluded. 'I was fined for disrupting the peace and causing a public affray. I'm surprised they haven't got you up on charges yet!'

Mick was incensed.

'I was attacked! I didn't go out looking for a blue,' he remonstrated, adding a little coyly, 'for once.' Molly rolled her eyes.

'I reckon they just wanted a chance to remind us who's the law. That's how they work. They can always get you for something, so they do. So,' Joe changed tack, 'these blokes who jumped you. Did you see who they were?'

'Didn't have time,' Mick answered. 'I ran as fast as I could but the big, ugly bloke must have waited and jumped on me after I cleared the fence at Babushka's. I got away from him but the rest were waiting at the corner. Like you saw I suppose. The big mongrel hit me with something,'

'A fence paling.' Joe filled in the unknowable.

'From Babushka's fence!' Molly added indignantly.

'I went down like a bag of spuds. Pick me up out of the mud later.'

'I can tell you, if it makes you feel any better, that the ugly one was the one I hit ruddy hard,' Joe said. 'I'm not proud of the fact that I was violent, but given I was, I'm glad it was him!'

Molly smiled, but uncertainly.

'Well, there may be being times when you have to repel violence with a force of an equal and opposite nature,' she said quietly, but added, 'I'm just glad neither of you are seriously wounded. Not with us all leading the children in the Peace Army.'

Along the ward they could hear the clatter of the food trolley.

'Looks like someone's going to get fed any moment,' Molly said.

'If you had the choice between having roast beef, or fish, or tripe in white sauce what would it be?' Joe asked, his voice alive with cheek. Mick laughed.

'That's easy, none of them.' He crossed his arms across his chest.

'I want whatever's on the menu at the Anchor.'

Joe nodded across to Molly and they both began to take their leave. Goodbyes all round.

Molly bent to give Mick a kiss on the cheek. Joe turned away from the intimacy.

'Get well soon, mate,' he said. 'Has Uncle Bill told you when you're coming home?'

'Nah,' Mick answered. 'Tomorrow though I reckon.'

'But will you be able to work then?' Molly asked.

'If he can't the Union'll cover for him,' Joe answered. 'You know they always do.'

'Amen to that,' Mick agreed. 'But don't worry, I'll be right as rain.'

The dinner trolley was almost upon them.

From behind the dividing curtain, the soldier in the next bed asked,

'What's for din-din's then, luv? Corned beef and cabbage! A bloke wouldn't be dead for quids!'

'We'd better go,' Molly said as matter-of-factly at that. 'Babushka will be wanting a hand with dinner and I'm for being late already.'

She kissed Mick once more as Joe turned away with a wave.

Then they left him there, to make their way out together, silently, through the bandaged ward, the white-walled corridors of carbolic silence. Out to where the men and women who made up the world still strived together.

Chapter 18

Oh, the Colonel kicks the Major,
And the Major has a go.
He kicks the poor old Captain,
Who then kicks the NCO.
And as the kicks get harder,
They are passed on down to me.
And I am kicked to bleeding hell
To save democracy!
To the tune of 'MacNamara's Band'.

Saturday, 17th March 1917
Some days change the world.

They could hear him before they could see him. Artem's voice bellowing like a bull as he strode up Merivale Street towards them, a newspaper flailing in the hand above his head. Even Tomfool, wiping sleep from his eyes, was startled from his early morning daydreams. He looked around quickly then bolted down the street to meet the Russian.

'Tomas!' Babushka and Molly chorused from the front gate of *Erin*.

'You do this washing up, Tomas!' Babushka continued in a voice which brooked no contradiction. Caught, Tomfool stopped. Torn between instinct and obedience, he mastered himself, slowly turning back home.

'What's he saying?' Ted Hill asked. 'Can you make it out?'

Joe shrugged his shoulders.

'I can't quite hear,' Molly answered. 'Something about "evolution"?'

'That'd be a first! Segeyev yelling in the street about … revolution! He's saying revolution, Molly!' Ted Hill exclaimed. In one movement he spun on his heel and strode toward his comrade.

Joe and Molly shared wild-eyed glances before they too ran to meet the Russian. Tomfool saw his chance and turned in beside Ted, who slapped him on the back as they half-ran to Segeyev's side. Only Babushka stood, shoulders set, like a swimmer braced against an oncoming wave.

'My family,' she intoned. 'My people.'

Segeyev grabbed Ted Hill by the shoulders, his eyes shining, words gushing from him.

'It has begun, Comrade!' he laughed, dragging Ted Hill into a bear hug, kissing both his cheeks before throwing him to arm's length once more.

'The revolution is here! And in Mother Russia! The Tsar is gone. I leave on the first ship. I will join my brothers, wherever the need is greatest. Maybe to Ukraine. To be among my people once more. I cannot tell you,' he babbled. 'You come with me, Comrade,' he said before checking himself. 'No you must stay here! You must lead the revolution in Brisbane, in this country!'

Ted was dumbfounded but managed,

'We knew the comrades were causing trouble. But is the army onside? No one can stop them if the army's with them.'

'Yes, they will have the army! When the soldiers return you must organise them here. If you have them with you, no one will stop us here either.'

Molly and Joe had caught up and stood in the wash of Segeyev's wave-break. Joe wrested the special edition of *The Worker* from Segeyev's hand. Together they read beneath the headline:

Revolution in Russia.

Uprising in Petrograd. Women's Day Meetings Produce Strikes Throughout City. Tsar Abdicates. Country Crippled by War and Starvation. Comrades Demand Bread! Army joins ranks of Revolutionaries. Crowds gather outside Duma.

They turned from the paper, faces close enough to breathe each other's trembled breath.

'This is real, Joe! It's real for certain?' Molly said – incredulous.

'Yair, Moll. Yair,' was all Joe could manage through the lump in his throat and tears pricking his eyes.

Their Socialist dream was becoming reality. Sure for now it was all on the other side of the world, but Socialism was an idea whose time had come. From this beginning it would sound like a starter's gun around the world.

Molly kissed him and broke the kiss to hold his face in her hands. Laughing and crying, she sobbed,

'It's real, Joe! Real for certain! What we've been fighting for. 'Tis history and here we are living in it.'

She laughed and cried and kissed him again.

'Girl, you have work,' Babushka said. 'The world does not stop.'

She grabbed Tomas by the belt.

'You too,' she commanded. 'Washing up!'

'Come on Irina, let the young folk have their moment,' Ted laughed. 'We've had a bit of a win!'

Segeyev smiled broadly in agreement.

'Winning! Ha! All I see is suffering. Win or lose it is the poor, the women who suffer … and the fools,' she added grabbing Tomas' belt tighter.

'Winning? Oyoyoy! Men? Boys!' She frog-marched Tomfool off, his pants held so high he was on tiptoe and squeaked a little as he called,

'The revolution is coming! The revolution is coming!' as though it was the circus he was expecting in town.

'Pah!' Artem exclaimed. 'Leave her to the darkness, we have work to do.'

He pulled on Ted's arm, but Molly looked up the street after *Erin*-ward, already wondering.

'No, Artem,' Ted replied, breaking the Russian's grip.

'I've been thinking.' Segeyev glanced quickly at Ted Hill, surprised, but understanding whatever strategy had formed in his mind would be worth considering – but he wouldn't wait too long to hear it.

'Well?' he demanded. Joe waited too.

'I won't be joining you, but I won't be staying here either,' Ted began. 'I know these Australian blokes. When they're demobbed back home from the war, they're so happy to be alive they don't rock the boat. Give 'em a beer and a gutful of corned beef and some skirt to chase and they're sweet. But we need the army with us. If the army supports the revolution then who's to argue? We have to educate our blokes before they come home.'

He stopped. His brow was deeply creased, his hand to the side of his head as though in pain.

'I am going,' he said. 'I'll enlist today.'

'Yes! Yes! Comrade!' Segeyev nodded.

'You are right. In this country there is no starvation. Workers do not suffer as our Russian brothers do. The grain must be ripened by a different sun!'

Listening in disbelief, Joe found a voice for his shock.

'Dad? No! Tell me you're joking!'

Molly stared ashen-faced at Ted Hill.

'You can't leave us! What about the Wobblies' commitment to peace? What about Mum? Dad!' he demanded.

Ted Hill addressed his son.

'Joe, you have to look beyond our everyday squabbles to the sweep of history, to the whole of the world.'

Joe felt Molly's weight slump against him as though she was in danger of falling. He didn't know if he could support her. His world tottered too.

'Dad!' he implored, his voice almost child-like. 'What about me?'

'Son,' Ted said, his hand stretched out towards Joe. 'You have to understand. Nothing comes in this struggle without sacrifice. That's sacrifice from us all. You are not immune, nor am I, or your mother.'

Joe pulled away, his arm around Molly.

'This isn't true, Mr Hill?' she managed.

Ted Hill stopped.

'It is,' he said firmly. 'I'm going. Leave your mother to me,' he added for Joe's benefit. 'I'll tell her this evening.'

'So much for equality! You owe your wife a chance to have her thoughts heard!' Molly spat.

Even before the words had left her mouth she wanted to bite her tongue off, but she knew the emotion was real and he deserved it. Ted's answer was decided.

'Go to work,' he said to Joe. 'Jones is itching for an excuse to sack you and,' he added, 'tell him Miss Know-it-all here can fire the boiler from now on because I'm off to fight the war.'

'Well!' a voice slurred from the footpath behind them.

'How's that for a pretty picture? Me girl in the arms of me so-called best mate.' Molly swung, freeing herself from Joe's arm.

'Mick?' she said. 'It's not what you think! Mick!' she added in shock as she looked at him. 'What happened to your face?'

Mick Doyle swayed, considering her gravely. Both his eyes were near closed, purple bruises encasing them.

'Just a little Friday night fun with father,' he said. 'Who needs enemies when you've got family?' He shook his head sadly, adding,

'And friends.'

'Are you drunk?' Joe asked as he eyed his unsteady mate.

'Ah, Mr Best Friend,' Mick said. 'Surely I am! If you can't beat 'em … beat 'em again!' he added, swinging his fists wildly at Molly and Joe.

'You're just jealous of my new best friend, Mr O.P. Rum,' Mick giggled. 'At least he doesn't cheat on his best friend with his best friend's girl.'

'Mick, it's not what it seems,' Molly implored.

'It never is, Moll,' Mick answered. 'Do you know how many times you've said that lately?' But Molly was not for being made an excuse.

'There's a revolution in Russia, you blockhead!' she told Mick as he blinked, as far as his eyes allowed, in the early morning sun.

'Segeyev's going home and Ted Hill is deserting us all to enlist.'

It was Mick's turn to reel. He leaned against the nearest fence. Molly rushed to his side.

'Is that true?' Mick asked Ted. 'You're joining up?'

Ted nodded. Mick asked again, this time shifting his gaze to Segeyev. 'And you're going to Russia?'

'Yes, Mick Doyle. Our Russian brothers have begun the world revolution. I go to fight with them.'

Mick Doyle stood propped, Molly at his side, uncertain about touching him. His eyes moved from one to another.

'Come on, Mick,' Joe suggested. 'Let's get you home.'

'Home? Where the fuck's home!' Mick asked. 'It's all right for you. You got a home even if your old man's not in it.'

'Come on, Mick,' Joe said again, trying to grab his mate's arm and turn him back towards *Erin*.

'I got something to say,' Mick shouted.

Pulling himself away from Joe's grasp Mick turned to Ted Hill.

'I'm coming too!' he said. 'I'm enlisting.'

'You're drunk!' Molly decided. 'You don't know what you're saying. Go home with Joe and get some sleep.'

But Mick seemed sensible enough as he turned back on her.

'I can't take it any more, Molly,' he said. 'The old man bashing and thieving from me. I'm gunna kill someone if I stay here. At least if I go with Ted I'll get paid for it,' he slurred bitterly.

Joe spoke first.

'If you have to go away, then right-oh. But why not go up the coast for a job, Rocky maybe, or Cairns? Just don't go to the war. I won't have anyone left. What about peace?'

Tears welled in Mick's bloodied eyes.

'Look at me.' He whimpered like a whipped cur. 'There's no peace anywhere for me. Ted'll take care of me, won't you Ted?'

Mick asked without looking, turning instead to Molly.

'Listen to Joe,' she implored. 'Don't go, Mick. Listen to Joe. I need you. We all need you.'

She stopped, facing him.

'I can't do it anymore,' Mick moaned. 'Will you wait for me, Moll?' he whispered. 'Say you will.'

She threw herself at him, flailing fists at his damaged eyes.

Joe grabbed Molly's waist, trying to drag her away. But Mick lashed out, fists and boots, caught Joe unprepared.

'Don't you touch her. Don't you lay a finger on my girl.'

Ted and Segeyev dragged Mick away. Molly slumped against the fence.

'I'll wait for you, Mick!' she moaned. 'I will! I will! Don't die!'

Rounding the corner on her way home from her night shift, Kathleen O'Donahue saw figures grappling in the street. But it was Molly's voice she recognised.

'What in God's name?' she cried, lifting her skirts as she ran.

Our Joe Once More

Letter from Joseph Hill to Ted Hill

Merivale Street

South Brisbane

7 th August 1918

Dear Dad

I hope this finds you and that when it does you're out of harm's way. Hope you can read some of it too after the Censor's had his go.

A year and a half since you enlisted. I don't know how you do it. From what they tell me a meat mincer has nothing on what is happening to you all over there. I'll tell you something, there've been so many days since you've left when I've been afraid to wake up in the morning because of the new horrors that might have happened to you all as I slept. Yes, true, I haven't seen any Huns on the street, just the new recruits straight off the farms and factory floors all marching to Rule Britannia. It'll be a wonder if there's any Britannia left to rule after this lot.

Still, I've been bearing witness with Miss Thorpe and the Quaker ladies as the lads march down the road to be loaded like bags of wheat or tins of bully beef to feed the Capitalist war machine. Their folk scowl at our placards and spit at us. But without a word of a lie some of the blokes I've seen are even younger than I am. They're fresh-faced as sunflowers. Jack Hunter's 16 and Ted Malone, from over the back, turns 17 later this year. No doubt you've met them at your end. Look after them Ted, I know you'll try. But there's the thing – you can't can you?

It's much worse if a hospital ship's in. But the wounded's kin don't spit so much, which at least keeps my hanky dry! The music's not so flash either. The bands have stopped playing for hospital ships, truth to tell. I smile and help where I can. 'Well done, cobber!' I tell them and clap them on the shoulder. Am

I a hypocrite for doing that at the same time as I'm fighting against the war? Don't answer Ted, I know I am, but … then … I am. I can't help it, I feel so … obliged. I can't help but try for them, even though I know trying for them makes me part of their war machine – the part that tries to put the broken pieces back together. We are all part of it now. Why am I saying this to you? Though it seems endless, surely someday soon it must stop. No nation can go on like this forever and now that the United States is getting so many troops into France surely it can't be long?

No doubt you'll want to hear more gossip. Mother is well and sends her regards. She's working all hours in Repatriation so I spend a lot of time on my own. They miss Uncle Bill there she tells me often. I don't know if she's forgiven you but she always reads the letters you've sent to me as soon as I get them. The big news is sad but inevitable – Old Mr Doyle died. He was full as a boot and fell off the wharf. I can't bring myself to write that letter to Mick. Besides I don't know where he is. Moll should do it, but that's complicated.

Well, Molly? She's waiting for me to finish this letter so we can put the chairs out at the Russian Hall. Tonight is a fellow from Melbourne on Post-war Politics and the Labour Movement – right up your alley. I wish you were here. I wish you'd never left. I hope you come home safe. We all need you. Duck!

I'd better sign off now as it is too hard to concentrate. Someone (you guess who) is tickling the back of my neck with a long bit of grass!

Your loving son

Joseph (Joe) Hill

Ps. I am also talking briefly tonight about the need for socialist women to fill the post-war labour shortage. They're half the voters, not that many politicians seem to remember that now, and we have lost a generation of men my age. Every speech I make is reported in The Worker and The Daily Mail. The Brisbane Courier doesn't report, just runs muck on me. I hope you and Segeyev are proud!

Pps. Babushka's still at Old Nik about everything, but he's a survivor, like Tsar, his horse (not the other one, of course). Whatever their reasoning the Bolsheviks were wrong to murder the real Tsar, even more so his family. That one act has made the road to Socialism so much more difficult in all the other countries. It's all they talk of here.

Brisbane 1919

WAR is a racket. It always has been.

It is possibly the oldest, easily the most profitable, surely the most vicious. It is the only one international in scope. It is the only one in which the profits are reckoned in dollars and the losses in lives.

A racket is best described, I believe, as something that is not what it seems to the majority of the people. Only a small "inside" group knows what it is about. It is conducted for the benefit of the very few, at the expense of the very many. Out of war a few people make huge fortunes …

Out of war nations acquire additional territory, if they are victorious. They just take it. This newly acquired territory promptly is exploited by — the selfsame few who wrung dollars out of blood …

For a great many years, as a soldier, I had a suspicion that war was a racket; not until I retired to civil life did I fully realize it.

(Excerpt from 'War is a Racket' by Major General Smedley Butler (retired), 1935. At his death, Butler was the most decorated Marine in U.S. history. U.S. Marine Corps base 'Camp Smedley Butler' is named in his honour.)

Our Ted Hill

Mademoiselle from Armentieres
Mademoiselle from Armentieres, Parley-voo?
Mademoiselle from Armentieres, Parley-voo?
Mademoiselle from Armentieres,
She hasn't been kissed in forty years,
Hinky, dinky, parley-voo.
She led him up the rickety stairs, Parley-voo?
She led him up the rickety stairs, Parley-voo?
She led him up the rickety stairs,
To help her wash her underwears,
Hinky, dinky, parley-voo.
She's the hardest working girl in town, *(etc as above)*
But she makes her living upside down!
You might forget the gas and shells,
But you'll never forget the mademoiselles!
Just blow your nose, and dry your tears,
We'll all be back in a few short years.
Anon.

Letter from Ted Hill to Joseph Hill
November 1918
Well behind the Hindenburg Line!

Dear Joe,

Hope this letter finds you. A few more than normal seem to have gone astray lately. I trust you and your mother are well? We're sitting here on the border twiddling our thumbs, again, waiting for something to happen. The talk is all about peace. The Krauts are totally beggared and retreating but I reckon without the Americans and Monash, we'd be the ones going backwards. Those doughboys think they're good but Monash and the Australia Corps taught them a thing or two at Hamel!

This whole stoush was down to a points decision in March I can tell you, not that you'll read that in the Tory press. We've won the war for the flaming Empire but the buggars still won't let us go home. I'm well and truly ready. Homesick doesn't begin to tell the half of it. I miss you, and the boys in the Cause and at work, even old Jones seems all right from here – and your mother – can't wait to see her once more. We've been doing a bit of 'peaceful penetration' to good effect against Jerry in the last few months, but it's not the type of peaceful penetration I've been longing for. (Best not show your mother that bit!) But that reminds me, how is Molly? Have you heard from Mick? I've made enquiries but I've lost him. Hope the silly buggar's alive and keeping his head down. I know it was a blessing in some ways, but his old man dying might stir him up into all sorts of stupid heroics. I've seen it a thousand times. Bad news from home and next time we're in the thick of it with Fritz, 'Hello? There's some joker acting like he's got a death wish.' Which is all a bloke flaming well needs – lack of discipline's dangerous for everybody. They either die quick or are awarded a V.C.

Did I tell you I got a letter from Segeyev? He thinks he's the King's bloody britches and he might just be right. He and Trotsky and Lenin are all on the Central Organising Committee for the whole bloody country! Them and another dozen or so are the Russian government. Who'd have picked that eighteen months ago? You'd have to say he'd be a million to one but there he is: meetings in the Winter Palace and running bloody Ukraine. They've still got a fight on their hands with factions all over the joint and the Tsarist Loyalists holding out. He told me to come over straight away, there's a job waiting. It's not for me though. Now I'm here I'd never leave me mates. I wrote and told him I'd see him at the Internationale – me representing Australia of course! We'll learn a hell of a lot from them in Russia and get a lot of support too – financial and policy for when it's our turn for revolution.

I'm proud to say I know him but, like I've been saying in my letters, it's hard trying to sell Socialism here since the Russians pulled out of the East. Soon as they left Fritz sent all his crack troops over for a visit. I tell you it was a close race at the start of spring – half a nose in it.

Not that I helped too hard, as you can imagine.

'Over the top!' they'd say.

'Go to blazes!' my boys would answer. 'Not till we get some hot grub up here, or some duckboards or warm socks.' Or one of any of the things we soldiers need – and I can tell you that's not much to speak of. We even went on strike a few times over conditions. (The Pommy Generals shoot their blokes for striking – whose side are the bastards on? Between them, Fritz and this new Pneumatic Influenza outbreak … we'll all end up worm food.) Getting back to the point, organising the blokes for that sort of a show is easy enough, they know it's in their best interests, but talk a socialist state in Australia and they tell you the Russians are Socialists and they're traitors. I'm nearly ready to admit your mother was right. <u>Nearly</u>– and don't you tell her I said that – but only a mug would leave her side again.

Other news is that Bill Carroll turned up the other night. We loosened him up with a few squirts of some champagne I've been saving. (How I got it is a good story. Remind me to tell you when I'm home.) He reckons the top brass inform him the war's all but over. They're planning to send him back with the wounded next week. They want to get them out before the winter, or this 'flu, kills any more of them. It's killing hundreds of blokes, ours and Fritz's. But it's hardest on the wounded, as you can imagine. As if the poor sods aren't suffering enough. Fingers crossed I've not picked it up thus far. So it looks like it's first here, first home in this game. I envy the buggar – though I guess he'll be stuck with his patients somewhere out of town until they're well, so – maybe not. When I do see him it's his shout – the Captain tells me the champagne was worth a fortune.

I've written to Kathleen under separate cover. Is she still out at the Quarantine Station at Lytton or have they put her back at the hospital? I'll send it to Lytton – they'll know where she is. Hope she's still well. She's right in the firing line for picking it up. Best not to worry about it from here. Nothing I can do. Hope you are getting a good feed every now and then and keeping the house in order and keeping Jones on his toes and Staying Well? I'm sure you are but take care this 'flu is a proper whizz-bang.

Well, that's the news for now. I'd best sign off and see if I can have a bit of a camp before dinnertime. The bloody weather here is bloody, bloody, bloody –

give me a Brisbane storm any day, not this cat's piss dribbling that passes for rain in this neck of the woods.

Joe, I hope to get your return letter when I'm en route home, or even better, delivered, return to sender, to the front verandah at Merivale Street. Your mother can read it to me there while I have a long, cold beer.

Until then, Joe, look after Mother, (and Molly!) and say g'day to Babushka. For mine, I'll try not to catch the bloody 'flu – or anything else that whistles past! Keep the home fires burning. Be seeing you soon.

Yr loving Father

Ted Hill

Chapter 1

INFLUENZA IN MELBOURNE AND SYDNEY.
HOW TO GUARD AGAINST IT HERE.

The outbreak of Influenza In Melbourne and Sydney is a warning to residents in all other parts of the Commonwealth of the urgency of combating the epidemic, lest it develop virulence with the same appalling death rate that has been experienced in other parts of the world.
Inoculation is one precaution which every citizen should avail of, but other safeguards should also be adopted …

Advertisement, *The Brisbane Courier,* 1st February, 1919

And stars still all over the pale sky. At anchor the troopship *Manoora* eased her grey bulk from side to side like a chained elephant. An early March storm cracked the colourless dawn far to the north, too far to properly illuminate the islands in Moreton Bay, east and south of the river mouth. Ted Hill stood at the rail straining his eyes against the darkness to discern, through the gathering light, his first glimpse of home.

They'd smelt it since Fremantle. There the smell of eucalyptus in the heatwave nearly brought tears to every eye. It smelt like home and home smelt like peace. Peace at last. But until she was safe in his arms, nothing could be home.

When they arrived in the bay, the lights on the jetty at the Lytton Quarantine Station were clear and sharp, now they faded into the morning grey. All night the lights of the city itself faintly illuminated the western sky. It might as well have been a thousand miles away. The wait was almost as unbearable as the keeping of a terrible secret – that you'd killed many men no older than your own son. It was like waiting for the whistle to go over the top. A waiting that left your mind flayed. There was never going to be any sleep for anyone on board that night. Maybe there never would be again but, at least from now on they'd be lying awake at home.

Since the *Manoora* slid silently into anchor in the bay the murmuring of men, punctuated by a shout at a win in a game of cards or two-up and the orange glow of lit fags along the rails, filled the darkness. Men were waiting, waiting for the end, or the beginning depending how you saw it. The arrival of the river-pilot would be a great start. How much of war was just this … waiting.

The ship of men communed with their thoughts and the darkness.

Well before dawn young Mick Doyle, and some of the keener blokes, had drummed up some meat scraps from the galley to use as chum over the stern. Now they were trying to catch a couple of serious sharks they'd fed with it. Their ship's Captain James Mahoney, an avid fisherman himself, joined them in the early hours.

'Make way, make way! Let Jimbo the fisherman show you how it's done!' he commanded, elbowing them out of the way. As the morning wore on the cheers, curses and thumping splashes indicated either a strike at the bait, or a shark smashing the fishermen's latest cobbled together gear. Captain or no captain, no shark made it on deck.

A soldier, three down the rail from Ted, whistled through his teeth,

'Well, strike me roan, if there isn't a sheila on the beach, over at Lytton. A nurse from the look of it.'

'She's not on her Pat Malone either.' The entire rail gazed with suddenly avid interest toward the jetty.

'Go for it, mate!' another bloke added, peering through the gathering dawn.

'I'll tell you the second thing I'd do if I was over there. He paused. 'I'd tell her me name!' The rail smirked.

A set of German field glasses appeared from nowhere. The young lad who produced them took a good eyeful, turned to Ted.

'You want a look, Sarge? Better than leave in Paris that is!' Ted laughed, stubbed his cigarette and took the glasses. The banter continued around him,

'Strike, that's a bit of all right.'

'Jolly good sort.'

'And she's about to get jolly-rogered.'

'You're a married man, Corp. What would you want with a bit of crumpet?'

'I may be married, son, but I'm not bloody blind!'

'That's one helluva a friendly snog!'

'Hold on, she's not so keen! She's made a break for it!'

'But he's after her, round the boathouse!'

'I've got two bob on the bloke getting his wicked way!'

'You're on!'

'Ha, too late he's got her in a clinch again! Don't stop cobber! You're in your traces now.'

'Quite sure you're finished, Sarge?' the owner of the glasses asked hopefully. But Ted showed no signs of finishing, holding the glasses tight to his eyes until a few uniformed people appeared on the jetty and the lovers left the beach. The young private sneered his disappointment.

'Phah! Some people just got to spoil a man's entertainment.'

Ted handed them back to his subordinate as he walked off.

'Women,' Ted muttered. 'You'd throw rocks at 'em if they didn't have what you wanted.'

The young soldier stared after the bitter, receding voice.

'What's that all about?' he asked. 'The old man's got the bloody hump with something.'

More than an hour of intense shoreward interest later a smart little lighter tied up alongside the troopship. A small, officious looking Customs Officer climbed the rope ladder to be greeted by the captain. All the top monkeys and NCOs gathered for any news of an estimated time of arrival.

'Orders from the Government, sir,' he said, handing over a folder full of paperwork. 'You're under quarantine due to the Spanish Influenza.' Reading the looks on the faces surrounding him he added.

'Sorry, sir. This must be disappointing.'

'What! For how long?' the captain exploded.

'Seven days, sir, unless cases reported during that time, then seven days from last case leaving the ship. It's all in there. Any cases to be taken ashore to Lytton Quarantine Station.' He nodded at the folder.

'But we don't have any cases and we haven't had any for weeks,' the ship's doctor remonstrated. 'I can sign off on that.' The Custom's man shrugged.

'Well, are we going ashore, then?' the captain pressed.

'No, sorry sir it's full so you'll be transhipped to the grounds of the Dunwich Asylum on Stradbroke Island for a week.'

'But that's not the mainland!' the captain exploded. 'If I have a bloody mutiny on my hands it's your fault.'

The bitter disappointment written on the faces of the crew and gathered soldiers told the story.

'Well, it seems like we're not going anywhere,' he managed to mutter.

'Like flamin' hell we aren't!' said Ted Hill, organiser. 'Meeting. Aft deck. Five minutes.' Men jumped, running to muster the troops. The Custom's man looked genuinely shocked.

'You'll have an opportunity to speak to the meeting, Jim,' Ted continued. The captain tried to placate him.

'Ted, this is serious. No one's more disappointed than me but … this 'flu's killing tens of thousands overseas and now down South. You've read the papers.' But the remaining Army officers stared him down. Most were no friends of Ted's socialist tactics, but this time they knew which side their bread was buttered.

'Water off a duck's back, Jim.' Ted patted his shoulder. 'You know we haven't had a case for weeks, like the Doc says.' Turning to the Customs bloke, who was in the process of beating a hasty retreat, he added,

'Where do you think you're going, you flamin' ferret?' The man stood very still, expecting the worst. 'You can tell the meeting what you've just told us. Then they'll be fully informed.'

As most of the men were already on deck, in less than five minutes they were assembled aft or hanging from the rails above.

'Right!' said Ted. 'Thanks for coming, Comrades.' Some of the blokes groaned at the form of address. 'Especially the whingers,' Ted continued, acknowledging them.

'Now, we've just heard from this joker … what's your name, mate?' he asked as the Customs bloke coughed it up.

'Ernest here, some very important information from the Government which he'd like to share with us.'

Ernest looked anxiously at the Captain who nodded. Once given the go ahead he announced very clearly,

'The State Government has declared that, as a precaution against the spread of the deadly Spanish Influenza, this ship and all aboard her are to be placed in quarantine for seven days.' The crowd exploded in oaths and, 'They can go to hell's'. A movement inward tightened the circle around the speaker, which greatly unnerved him.

'Does that mean we aren't going ashore?' one bloke yelled. The Customs fellow nodded.

'Fuck that for a game of soldiers!' another answered. He grabbed at the crutch of his uniform and shook his wedding tackle.

'I've got urgent business to attend to!'

'Oi!' Ted Hill yelled. 'A bit of bloody shoosh! Righto then, Jim! Your go,' he continued. The ship's captain addressed the men.

'I've looked at the paperwork and this is a direct order from the Prime Minister to Customs and from the Premier to the Harbour Master. I'm as disappointed and as in need of a bit of comfort as the next man,' he said, the joke falling dead. 'But this Influenza is very bad. It's affecting the elderly and sick and the children. We don't want to get home only to bring even more death with us to our loved ones.' They respected Captain Jim Mahoney. The mood altered as he finished.

'If all we have to do is wait a bit longer.'

'Yeah all right, but seven days! We waited in Fremantle. Didn't get shore leave there. We've been on this bloody tub for flamin' weeks and now it's time to be home.'

'That's a good point,' Ted Hill agreed. 'Where's the Doc?' He searched the faces but found only an orderly from the sick bay.

'Have we got any flu cases on board?' he asked.

'No? Then only those who went ashore in Fremantle need stay in quarantine.' The meeting cheered, almost unanimously.

'But, Ted!' Jim began again. 'It's a direct order.'

'We didn't ever follow bloody ridiculous orders. Not over there and we'll be damned if we follow them here,' Ted finished.

'There'll be strife!' the Customs bloke predicted. Ted turned to him, peering down at him incredulously. Young Ernest had obviously been too old to go to war, but being old didn't mean he had the brains to have a bloody clue.

'Strife?' Ted answered slowly. 'We've been up to our balls in strife for years. You can tell the Honorable Premier to bring on the mustard gas and the Mills bombs. If he wants a stoush we're his men.' Then turning to the meeting he called,

'I move that the *Manoora* proceed to Brisbane!'

'I'll second that!' Mick Doyle yelled from the centre of the deck.

'Right, we vote. Those in favour say aye.' The ayes startled the seagulls from the surface of the bay.

The crew in the Customs lighter looked up.

'Nays? None? Good-oh then, Jimbo off we go.'

'You know it's bloody mutiny, Ted?'

'Well if it's a mutiny we'd better throw the Captain in the drink. That shark you've been teasing all night's looking for something a bit more substantial to chew!'

Jim Mahoney shook his head, looked across to his first mate, who nodded his.

'Well, you heard the man,' he finally said. 'Prepare to weigh anchor.'

'And Ernest,' added Ted as the Customs man started down the rope ladder, 'how about you telegraph the Premier and let him know he's got visitors.'

At fifteen minutes after noon on Friday 14th March, the *Manoora* docked at the South Brisbane wharves. From the top of the gangplank Captain James Mahoney saluted the first contingent to disembark. Down on the wharf, amongst the families and the regimental brass band, stood a contingent of parliamentarians, including the Commissioner for Public Health, the Deputy Premier and the Lord Mayor. They were all lined up, though they all looked a bit strange in their face masks. Jim Mahoney dipped his lid. There were no coppers or MPs to arrest anyone. They were all off doing duty on the State border to keep the Spanish 'flu out.

Ted looked hard but, as he expected, she wasn't there, only the Peace Army ladies were, still bearing bloody witness.

'Who's for a beer?' he yelled, and the rush was on.

Chapter 2

The Rebel Girl
There are women of many descriptions
In this queer world, as everyone knows,
Some are living in beautiful mansions,
And are wearing the finest of clothes.
There are blue-blooded queens and princesses,
Who have charms made of diamonds and pearl;
But the only and thoroughbred lady
Is the Rebel Girl.
Chorus
That's the Rebel Girl, That's the Rebel Girl.
To the working class she's a precious pearl.
She brings courage, pride and joy
To the fighting Rebel Boy
We've had girls before, but we need some more
In the Industrial Workers of the World.
For it's great to fight for freedom
With a Rebel Girl.
Joseph Hillstrom

With knock-off time happening the city over, just inside the factory gate Molly was gossiping with the other secretaries. As he passed, Joe Hill bent to kiss her on the top of the head, to a chorus of "Oohs!" and "Oo-waahs!" from her mates. The girls weren't too serious though, Joe and Molly's loose behaviour was the least this war had thrown up. Joe couldn't stay to chat but touched his hat with a smooth,

'Ladies!'

He dog-trotted off down the street. He was late for the train. His mother was due in from the Quarantine Station at Lytton. It had been a long six weeks, eating his dinners at Babushka's, not that that was of concern, given its obvious attractions. His parents' house had been very quiet with only him at home, but all that was about to change.

He had it planned: get home, have a quick wash at the tank stand, rip a spray of bougainvillia from the fence for a welcome home bouquet for Mother and then down to the station. After she arrived they could walk back via the wharves and he should be able to find out exactly when the *Manoora* was due. They reckoned the quarantine would hold the ship up – for how long was anybody's guess. A khaki clad soldier, who'd been lounging against the fence across the street pushed off and dropped the fag from the corner of his mouth. Joe didn't notice the bloke until he was almost on top of him. He blocked Joe's path and stuck out his hand to be shaken.

'G'day, cobber!' Mick said.

Joe looked up, shaken from his thoughts. It took a moment to register. The voice was changed, deeper and with even more of a drawl, but it was the face – brown and lean, and his tall, wiry physique that was changed so much.

'Mick? Mick! You coulda knocked me down with half a brick! Mick!' Joe babbled, grabbing the proffered hand, pulling his mate to him to embrace.

'Jesus, you're home mate, and in one piece. Thank Christ! Welcome home! Thank Christ! It's so good to see you, Mick. When did you get back? Were you on the *Manoora*? I have to get to the train. Is my old man here? We should have a beer.'

Words flowed like water from a storm drain. Mick held him with a steady hand and eye.

'Good to see you too, mate,' Mick replied, nodding slowly. But Joe knew from the look on his comrade's face that something was chewing him. Some things didn't change.

'You shoulda told me. You're me mate. You shoulda told me. I feel like a bloody dog finding out like this.'

Joe felt the prickling of blood creep up his neck. He knew. Mick knew. Joe knew he should have told him but … how can you. Mick was over in France. It was hell on earth over there. How could he tell his mate something so personal to add to his troubles. He'd made Molly swear to secrecy too – no 'Dear Mick' letter. Joe dropped his gaze and Mick's hand.

'I'm sorry,' he mumbled. 'I didn't … I couldn't.' His voice failed.

'How do you think I feel? Coming home after that … that … over there, only to find that me old man's dead nearly a year and no buggar bothered to tell me. Coming home to a home with a hole in it.'

To his undying shame, Joe Hill looked into his friend's pain-filled eyes and felt nothing but relief.

'It was … with the war … I just couldn't. It was such a terrible way to go, even for,' Joe searched for words, 'even for a bloke as enslaved by the drink.'

Only then, when Joe remembered the full horror he'd felt himself when he'd found out, his heart went out to Mick.

'How do you think I feel, Joe. How low? He was a bastard of a man, we all knew that, but he was my father and I should have been told, by you, instead of the new barmaid at the Anchor. She doesn't know me from Adam. It shouldn't have been her telling me what a shock it was when they pulled him from the river after he'd tipped off the wharf.' Joe felt the tears in his own eyes too, though he wept for his own frailties and betrayals.

'I couldn't, mate. I'm sorry. I was just trying to make it easier on you.'

'Well you fucked that up,' Mick replied, but he softened, taking the deep breath of a man who's lived with death and learned from its acquaintance how to get on with living.

'I'd like to go and see where you planted him,' he continued wiping his face with the back of his sleeve.

'Not right now,' he added, responding to the anxious look on Joe's dial.

'Now I'm going to surprise Molly. She is in there isn't she, Joe?'

Despite all the maturity war had conferred on him, Mick fiddled to fasten his top button and brush down his uniform. His nerves were shot.

Joe's face was on fire. He stared at his friend,

'Yeah,' he managed. 'I have to go!' Joe Hill turned. With not so much as a backward glance at the factory gate he ran, faster than he had run before. Surprised, Mick gazed after him for a moment.

'I'm at Babushka's!' he called at his friend's retreating back.

Joe neither turned nor waved.

Mick shook his head slowly then, stubbing his unlit cigarette under his boot heel, he crossed the road and strode towards the factory.

Joe smelt his father before he saw him, the waft of ciggie smoke, the same but different, leached into the backyard. The back door was always unlocked. Joe bounded into the kitchen to see Ted, still in uniform, sitting at the head of the far end of the table, fag dribbling from the corner of his lip, just as though he'd never left.

'Dad!' Joe yelled. 'You're home!' He wanted to rush to his father and hug him. Instead something about the man who sat at the head of the table made him stand, uncertain, feeling like the child he'd always felt in his presence. Joe sensed a change. Ted Hill looked up from where he rolled a .303 cartridge between his fingers.

'Word travels faster than shit down a sewer in this town,' he answered.

Ted's voice was lean as a starved dog and bitter as plug tobacco.

Joe stood on, awkward, searching for a sign on his father's face, not certain where next. It was changed too, the face, thin and sunken-cheeked, mapped with new creases, browned by the sun on the ship ride home, hair greying and thin, but with eyes that wouldn't meet his own. That was the change that most unnerved Joe. His father said real men always met each other's gaze. It was a matter of respect.

Finally Ted looked up, his pale blue eyes watery and weak somehow. Pushing his bentwood back from the table Ted stood and walked towards his son. When he drew close enough he threw his arms around Joe, gripping him like a drowning man.

'I've missed you, son,' Ted said to the air behind Joe's head. 'If only you knew. You and your … '

He fell silent, gripping even tighter. It was a moment before Joe realised that his father was weeping, sobbing into Joe's hair, his collar, crushing his arms to his side. Standing very still, he tried to be unconcerned.

Joe felt as though he'd been accosted by a mourner at a funeral – some man he didn't know. He tried not to blubber like a child. He tried not to blush. Something told him somebody had to stay calm. Finally his father broke his hold and checked himself. Turning away, he wiped his eyes on the inside of his sleeve.

'Oh, buggar me shitless,' he said. 'I'm sorry, boy.'

'Joe, Dad. It's Joe.'

Ted looked again at his son, as though seeing him for the first time.

'Yes,' he agreed slowly. 'Joe it is. I'm sorry, Joe for all … that.' He gesticulated with his arm.

'Just caught me out is all.' Joe smiled now.

'Fair enough, Dad,' he answered. Ted Hill turned to take his son's hand and meet his gaze.

'It's Ted, son. What's good for the goose.'

'Fair enough, Ted,' Joe answered as they shook hands to seal his homecoming.

'Now, what about a cuppa black and milch,' his father asked. Joe stood mystified.

'Cuppa tea, Joe?' his father asked. Joe looked up quickly at the mantelpiece for the time.

'We haven't got time Dad … Ted,' he corrected, 'Mum's on the train at South Brisbane. I said I'd … we'd, be there.' His father gripped the back of the bentwood with both his hands.

'You go, Joe,' he said quietly.

'But, she'll be so happy to see you.'

Joe stood mystified, quizzical, uncertain.

'Uncle Bill might be there too, you know he came back with a hospital ship late last year?'

'Go! Fuck ya, Joe!' Ted spat. Savage as a cornered dog with nowhere to run.

Joe stepped back. Ted's grip on the chair back loosened under his son's gaze.

'It's been a long time, Joe, and you know we didn't part on the best of terms.' Ted smiled wanly. 'These things take time. Besides,' he added apologetically. 'I don't want to look like a sook in public.'

Joe wanted to tell his father he'd seen a thousand men cry and there was no shame to it. In these war years things had changed. But Joe knew that, he too, needed time to get to know the man who was now Ted Hill. He turned and walked alone down the back stairs.

'Ted?' Kathleen called. Her voice querelous about the dark house.

'Dad? Ted?' Joe called into the house from the kitchen. The train had arrived late and evening was falling quickly.

Kathleen lit the kerosene lantern that stood at the centre of the table then moved to the stove. Joe lit a candle from the same match. The stove was cold, the fire unlit. Joe carried her Gladstone bag quietly, so's not to wake a sleeper, into the front bedroom. Depositing it there on the floor he returned with a shrug.

'He's not here,' he said.

'He won't be too far,' his mother replied to Joe's look of disappointment. 'Maybe he's saying hello to Old Nik or Babushka or one of the others.' But Joe thought she looked relieved.

'Mum,' he began, but for now, Kathleen O'Donahue sidestepped his questions.

'Let's get this fire going. Joe, can you do that for me?' she asked. 'I must get out of my travel clothes.' Joe nodded.

Pulling out the wood box he grabbed a handful of wood chips for kindling and opened the firebox door.

The grate was jammed full of a tightly rolled AIF uniform. He threw down the kindling and tried to pull the uniform out of the firebox. When he finally worked it free two medals clattered onto the kitchen floor.

As Joe bent to pick them up a wild banging, accompanied by a shout, echoed down the hallway.

'Open this door immediately or I'll break it down by force!'

Joe jumped. Motioning his mother back into her room, he walked to the door.

'Who is it?' he asked.

'Police!' came the answer.

'And Army Intelligence.' Joe knew both the voices.

Winterson stood next to O'Hagen, a supercillious look on both their faces.

'We have reason to believe treasonous activity has been taking place on this property and that seditious material is likely to be found here,' Winterson said.

'That's a ridiculous accusation. The war's over,' Kathleen countered over Joe's shoulder, 'in case you hadn't heard.'

O'Hagen ignored her comment, almost as though she wasn't there.

'We intend searching this property under the War Precautions Act. Please stand aside.' Joe bristled.

'It's just a wind-up, Ma. They must have heard Ted's home!' he said quietly to his mother.

'Do you gentlemen have a warrant to search?' he asked, direct and resistant, but he was wishing Ted Hill would arrive home anytime, but very soon.

Chapter 3

Keep The Home Fires Burning
('Till the Boys Come Home)
They were summoned from the hillside,
They were called in from the glen,
And the country found them ready
At the stirring call for men.
Let no tears add to their hardships
As the soldiers pass along,
And although your heart is breaking,
Make it sing this cheery song:
Keep the Home Fires Burning,
While your hearts are yearning.
Though your lads are far away
They dream of home.
There's a silver lining
Through the dark clouds shining,
Turn the dark cloud inside out
Till the boys come home.
Overseas there came a pleading,
'Help a nation in distress.'
And we gave our glorious laddies –
Honour bade us do no less,
For no gallant son of Britain
To a tyrant's yoke shall bend,
And no Englishman is silent
To the sacred call of 'Friend'.
Lena Gilbert Ford

Ted Hill did not return to his usual place of residence that night. Neither Joe nor his mother heard hide nor hair of him on Saturday, or Saturday night either.

It was true that they were both busy: Kathleen with washing, cleaning and shopping after her weeks away – catching up before her first night shift, and Joe with work and then a meeting after to organise Sunday's rally.

Joe'd asked them all at Jones' on Saturday morning. There'd been no sighting of Ted by anyone, anywhere.

Molly wasn't at work. Joe had no idea why. She didn't have the 'flu, he did know that much from Kathleen who'd looked at the lists. In a way, he was glad she wasn't there that morning. His head was mad-a-whirl with what to say to Mick, with his father's disappearance, and the rally. His mother repeated what she'd said the night before,

'Don't worry, Joe. He'll be back when he's ready.'

But she looked worried too, Joe thought and he worried then, even more.

By the following afternoon it was hot, even by March standards. Thunderheads threatened to crack the afternoon open, but stayed disorganised, grumbling in the distance.

It was late afternoon that Joe Hill stood between the two red flags on the rotunda, finishing his speech.

He could see Orlov, George Taylor, Madorsky and Zuzenko, all of the new leaders. Where were Molly and Kathleen and Ted and Tomas? Even Mick would have been a welcome sight about now! Joe had lost his passion, his speech was fuelled only by their absence. He knew he was convincing nobody.

'In conclusion ladies and gentlemen,' he called. 'We demand the Hughes government repeal the War Precautions Act. Whatever reason our coercive Commonwealth government gives for entering and searching a citizen's home without a warrant; whatever reason they give for holding a citizen without a charge; whatever reason this government may think they've had for their violations of our rights, that reason is ended. The war to end all wars is over.

'Write to the papers, talk to your neighbours, demand it in public of your member of parliament. Together let's end the war against free speech. Let's be rid once and for all of Billy "Warmonger" Hughes.'

The crowd gave Joe a round of applause and a few, 'Hear, hear's' from behind their face masks as Mrs Griffiths took the Chair to conduct the final sing-a-long with the Railways Brass Band who'd waited so patiently to play.

Joe Hill stood down, shaking the hand of the new President of the Children's Peace Army.

'Your turn next week, Arthur,' he nodded. Patting the lad on the shoulder, he received a nervous grin in reply.

That's me just three years ago, Joe thought. How much has changed since then.

Joe cast an eye again around the disappointing crowd. The crowds were so small now the war was over. It was as though everyone simply wanted to wipe the war and all it entailed from the slate as though it have never been. And there was still no sign of anyone important.

Molly wasn't on the organising committee but, he knew, she knew it was on, and Kathleen did too, he'd told her. He craned his neck to search the back row but couldn't see his mother anywhere. Wherever his father was, she, at least, promised to be there.

Blow the lot of them, he thought. They make my head hurt.

Distracting himself, Joe organised,

'Here, Arthur! You take the Peace Army banner. I'll take the flags back to the Union rooms.'

Joe turned, his arms full of red flag. Walking through the gate out of the Domain was a figure he recognised: by the walk, the height, the red hair, the floppy hat.

'Molly?' he half-called.

The young woman was hand-in-hand with a man in uniform. She did not hear him but walked on, laughing.

Orlov stood beside him.

'No need to roll the flags, Joe.'

'Nyet,' added Zuzenko, taking the second flagstaff. 'We fly them a little longer yet as we walk home.'

Orlov led off toward the gates.

Beyond the Domain fence Joe saw the young couple run to jump the tram. They kissed. A third man joined them, gangling and tall. Laughter split his face as he shrieked,

'The world's as sweet as honey, Micky Doyle!'

The tram was already moving on.

'Come!' called Orlov. 'We go!'

Dazed, Joe staggered down the rotunda steps. By the time they reached the street the tram was gone.

Many of the crowd who lived across the bridge, headed northward along William Street. As the red flags were still flying, some of the mob behind them started to sing.

Joe was thankful for the crowd and the noise. No one tried to talk to him, though he couldn't have spoken if they did.

His mind refused to function.

Molly walking, laughing, kissing, Mick.

How could that be when it was only last week they'd talked about his career in politics, how she would help him.

He felt like a horse had kicked him in the guts. He felt like vomiting.

Joe was jostled along like flotsam in the swirling flood of the crowd. As they passed Stephens Lane men, quite a few in Army uniform, ran towards them.

Joe stopped, staring at the surge of faces who yelled things he couldn't hear above the hubbub from his own mob. The people behind him looked too, as they drew nearer. The faces of the men in the lane were set and, as they rushed closer, Joe could hear them.

'Kill the Bolshies! Kill the traitors!'

A rage rose up in Joe, an anger such as he had never known. He turned to face the onslaught. Planting the flagstaff he drew himself up beneath his flag.

'Fuck you!'

He screamed defiance at the hundred filling the lane. It was all he could manage not to drop his flag and run at them, snarling like a mad dog.

'With me!' he yelled to his people, but cooler heads prevailed.

'We pick the battles we can win.' George Taylor spoke Ted Hill's words. Joe wished his father was here. Joe wished many things.

'Get those women and children out of the way!' Orlov shouted to the Peace Army. Like sweets spilled from a paper bag they scarpered, the older dragging or carrying the younger, the women helping to organise their retreat.

'We slow them. Give children and women time. Then we run!' Orlov ordered the fifty or so men, assembled around the twin flags.

'We should fight them. They're cowards,' Joe countered, his face flaming with rage.

'We do not win,' said Zuzenko. 'So we are beaten, for what, Comrade?'

'It's our duty!' Joe yelled.

'Our duty is to win,' Orlov replied. 'Do not worry, this is not Russia, they do not shoot us.'

Adjusting his glasses he yelled at the leaders of the pack now spilling from the lane onto the street, arriving in an ugly waft of beer and vitriol.

'Lovely evening for a stroll!' he greeted them – even and calm.

'Russian scum like you shouldn't be allowed on the street,' said a man in an officer's uniform, who seemed their self-appointed leader. His face was lopsided so he appeared to leer, even without the hatred that filled his eyes.

'You should be sent back home with your coward Comrades.'

Joe could feel Madorsky and Zuzenko straining at the leash. Orlov held them back

The men continued to pour out of the lane onto the street trying to circle the marchers and back them over to the riverside.

As one the comrades moved back, but to the north, trying to keep the run to the bridge open, letting their attackers fill the street to the south behind.

'You Communists should all be flogged,' the officer taunted.

'Then we'll put 'em on the next ship to Bolshie land, hey Cap'n Markson?'

Joe had nothing to lose.

'If you want a stoush, I'm ready,' he spat.

Orlov gripped his shirt sleeve tight, drawing him up the street. Markson turned his sights on Joe.

'You're Australian. You'd be well advised to stick with your own kind, boy, and give these trouble-makers the flick.'

'Why? Because they did the right thing?'

But the Captain wasn't for turning.

'They deserted. Left us to do the fighting for them. They're cowards,' he declared with vicious finality. The crowd glared its agreement, moving in.

'They can go back where they come from, and you traitors can go with 'em.'

Orlov couldn't hold Zuzenko anymore. He fronted their ranks with his chest. He was a big man and no one was up for taking the first swing. The men around the flags tried to make a final push for the bridge only quarter of a block away. The attackers ran north to try and cut them off. Scuffles broke out.

A thin blue line of coppers appeared, trying to force their way between the antagonists. Orlov stepped backward, as if pushed, and slumped, his glasses askew. Staggering to regain his balance his hand came up from his side, covered in blood. Taylor grabbed him, holding him upright as he sagged.

'Stabbed?' he said, his face a mixture of pain and bewilderment. 'Stabbed! In Australia!'

It was so quick, none of them saw a thing.

Zuzenko and Madorsky bellowed.

Whistles sounded the attack. The soldiers surged. The coppers whaled in with batons. In disarray the attacking ranks loosened. The Russians fought free, half-jogging in a tight knot towards the bridge.

The captain's voice bellowed above the din.

'It's the Russians we want! Sergeants assemble your men! We'll deal with the bastards once and for all.'

A single gunshot cracked the evening like a lightning strike.

Silence fell across the soldiers, startled by the sound they knew so well, but had never before heard in the streets of their city. The sound of civil war.

The comrades ran across the bridge half-carrying the bleeding Orlov. Even in his wounded state Orlov had his wits about him. He stopped them to regroup, holding his bloodied shirt hard to his side.

'Find your father, Joe. Tell him they're coming.'

Joe stood uncertainly. Orlov sagged again.

George Taylor took command.

'Run Joe! Two of you help Orlov to the Anchor. They'll take care of him there. The rest of you take all the papers from the meeting rooms. Empty the building. Warn everyone, then go home and stay there! We won't win this one.'

Joe ran, the two red flags streaming over his shoulder behind him. Blood on his hands. His heart pounding. He needed his father and his mother. He needed Molly and he needed Mick – even Tomfool. He needed them now and he had no idea where they were.

Joe had never felt so alone.

Past the wharves and pubs empty of drinkers; beside the trams of sportsmen making their ways home; through the streets of worker's cottages, men and women in their yards and on verandahs, Joe ran. One word, Revolution, thundered like his heart.

Jettisoning the flagstaffs in his backyard, Joe took the stairs two at a time. He could hear voices in the kitchen. One a man's. Thank God! Ted's home!

His mother screamed,

'The war's over and he's my husband!'

Joe flew, gasping for breath, into the kitchen to be met by the resounding slap of flesh on flesh. His mother stood before the stove, her hand still tensed, anguish flooding her face. Uncle Bill's cheek was already reddening. The three of them stared wildly each to each. Joe's shoulders heaved with exertion.

'They're going to kill the Russians!' he exploded. Kathleen O'Donahue finally registered her son. Saw blood on his shirt. She screamed, hands covering her face. Joe was dumbstruck. She was his rock, always calm. But even with the war over there were no certainties. Everything was changed.

Joe looked to Uncle Bill who moved to comfort her. But Kathleen howled,

'Get out! Get out! Get out!'

She waved her arms in windmills as if swiping at wasps.

'Get out!' She fell into a chair. Joe did not move. But Uncle Bill strode to him.

'What did you say?' he demanded. Joe had recovered breath enough to speak.

'The army. They're coming to deal with the Russians. They stabbed Orlov. Not too bad,' Joe added in response to Bill's look. 'I think he'll be all right. Zuzenko took him to the Anchor.'

'Steady, Joe. The army? The government's sending the army?'

'No, not the proper army. The returned men. There's a proper Captain leading them though. He said,' Joe took a deep breath. 'He said that they were going to "deal with the Russians once and for all".'

Joe looked at Uncle Bill then to his mother. Her face was grey. Joe noticed the grey in her hair matched her eyes – the strangest of realisations at such a moment.

He tore himself back to Uncle Bill. Controlling the rage that threatened to grow in him again, Joe continued,

'They're organising their men now at the city end of the bridge. They're coming to deal with the Russians. That's what he said. Orlov said to tell Ted. But, I don't know where he is.' Joe felt close to tears of helplessness.

'He's sleeping on the floor at Jones' office,' his mother said. Her voice devoid of all emotion. It sounded to Joe as grey as her face.

'You know where he is? Why didn't you say?'

'Oh, Joe,' she said almost to herself. Then she looked at Bill. Her eyes dull as a dying patient's.

'I thought you were gone,' she said.

'I'll find him, Joe. Don't worry. I'll tell the others,' Bill muttered. 'Stay here. Make your mother a strong cup of tea.'

'Go to hell,' Kathleen O'Donahue continued in a monotone. 'Go quickly.'

Chapter 4

… strange things happen in Queensland from time to time.
W. A. Watt, Acting Prime Minister of Australia, 1919

Not the drum of distant thunder; not the mighty voice of thousands of men singing *Keep the Home Fires Burning* as they marched, relentless and purposeful, closer and closer, across the bridge; not the explosions of shouting and the helter-skelter of running feet up the roads; not the frantic barking of every dog in every street of South Brisbane; nor the silence that fell before the first smash of glass and the cheers as the moving mass of men turned onto Grey Street; no sound entered into Joe Hill's mind as he sat on the back stairs contemplating the ruins of a life which two days ago was ripe with promise. It was his mother's voice that finally registered.

'We're going to Babushka's!' she shook his shoulder. 'Joe, we have to go now. She isn't safe there alone.'

'You go then. You and Molly. What a fine couple you make.' A bitter rage overwhelmed him. It was true. Everywhere he looked his world was torn to shreds. But no matter how depressed that made him feel, one fact overwhelmed it all, the fact that he knew there was no one to blame but himself. He may have been wronged but not before he himself had wronged a friend. And the worst betrayal was his. How could he be casting stones?

'Oh, Joe,' said his mother. 'If only you could understand what happens sometimes between women and men.'

'If I can't understand,' Joe spat, 'then let's not discuss it!' His mother's hand touched the top of his head and smoothed his hair. Joe pulled away, turning to face her,

'Go to hell!' he swore.

'But Babushka needs you. God knows what they'll do,' his mother implored him.

'Then let God bloody-well care!' Joe yelled at her.

The toe of his mother's ankle boot caught him hard in the armpit. He flew like a well-kicked ball down two stairs. His head cracked against the rail. As he turned he heard his mother's indrawn "oh" of breath. He felt blood run across his cheek. It felt good. He stood and turned to ascend the stairs. The door slammed shut above him, the bolt shot tight. His whole body slammed against the door. He beat against that door that he had never before seen locked in his life. Skin tore from his knuckles. It scared him how good the pain felt. Tears of rage, impotence, regret, streamed on his cheeks and, could he have seen her, on his mother's. Joe beat on until he heard the front door slam and whatever it was he intended to do was left undone.

It was the sound of a contingent of horses clattering full gallop up Hope Street that finally raised Joe from the back stairs. Running to the front of the house he saw the backs of the mounted police, on their thoroughbred-cross horses. Joe guessed they were intent on reaching Russell Street before the marching mob.

Joe walked into the street and followed them aimlessy. He was unable to think a thought through to any conclusion, as though he was floating some way above his body, watching Joe Hill do things, his eyes were fixed in a thousand yard stare.

But barely twenty paces up the street he stopped, returning to the house. Leaning a ladder against the sill of his bedroom window he crawled through. When next he left the house, the back door hung wide and the half bottle of Christmas rum his mother kept in the kitchen cupboard sat empty on the table. As he ran towards the tumult of oaths, orders and the whickering of horses, his breath was on fire. He was ready. Nothing could stand in his way. Joe Hill had nothing to lose.

The scene from the corner of Hope Street was as Joe had dreamed his Revolution would be.

'But it's supposed to be us Socialists down there,' he mumbled as he stumbled out into the middle of the street for a better view.

'Somebody should tell those beggars!' he yelled drunkenly at the crowd. Halfway down the block on the city side the mob formed a ragged line across the street, the heaving mass of them behind, hurling abuse and rocks, arming themselves with wooden pickets torn from front yard fences. He could see some officers brandished service revolvers.

'Burn their place down!' someone yelled.

There must be thousands of them, Joe guessed. At the upper end of Russell Street sixteen Mounted Police appeared from thin air to spread themselves in two ranks, full across the roadway.

'I've read you the Riot Act it's time to disperse. You've had your fun. Now you'll be getting home for your tea and not disturbing the Sabbath,' Sergeant O'Hagen suggested reasonably from astride his horse.

'I didn't know you could ride, O'Hagen,' Joe addressed the air behind the horses. 'You're not even in the mounted police are you? Let me up there on one of those horses and I'll crack some heads!' he suggested to the backs of the troopers. If they heard him above the din, they ignored him. The angry mob continued to flood higher and higher up the street, urging each other on. Joe walked towards them. Occasionally one threw a rock to smash a window of one of the cottages on the street, for the noise and wanton pleasure of it. No one tried to stop them. No one dared.

'Not till we've finished what we come to do!' Winterson yelled above the din. 'Out of the way O'Hagen, we've no quarrel with you!'

'I am lawfully instructed, in the name of the King, to request that you disperse,' O'Hagen insisted again.

'We are the King's men,' the captain responded. 'Been working for him for years and it's the King's business we're about – getting rid of the enemy at home.' The front ranks of his men began to move more quickly up the street.

'Steady lads!' the captain called, but his command only checked them slightly. Joe began to dog trot towards them.

'This is a lawful instruction,' O'Hagen began again. 'I have officers in the streets already to protect the life and property of citizens.'

'Citizens be damned! Hang the Communists!' rang out from the front ranks. There was no holding them. The leaders rushed towards the mounted troops, intent on bringing the horses down.

Surprised by the sudden onset of the mob O'Hagen yelled,

'Detachment, charge! Regroup on the other side! At them!'

At a jump the horses charged, accelerating the few short yards to the crowd in a matter of strides. The men at the centre of the roadway scattered like tossed grain. Some of them cleared out of the horses' way, others were mown down as they ran – rolled and trampled beneath the thundering hooves. Joe could hear the crack of bone, the oaths and screams of the wounded.

Some men at the edges of the mob stopped to drag their comrades from the horses' path, cursing the coppers as dogs. But the rest surged forward with an almighty roar towards the objective.

Joe saw them come. He knew he could stand. He knew he could take them one by one but ... he turned and ran. At last there was one clear thought in his head. She would be at Babushka's. His place was there.

The front door was shut but he had no time. He belted it hard, and again, and again, with the flat of his hand. As he'd run, they'd run behind him. Now they were regrouped and rushed on towards the meeting hall just two doors beyond *Erin*. A contingent of coppers formed up at the Glenelg Street intersection. Two ranks, fifty in all, with bayonets, fixed as their faces, marched down Merivale Street to meet the rioters, leaving a third thin blue line of twenty at the Glenelg corner.

Looks like all the coppers left in Brisbane, Joe thought. Don't like your odds, lads, if you fail to hold the line? He slammed the door harder, imploring,

'It's me! Joe! For God's sake, let me in!'

The coppers' dependable marching left, right, left was a counterpoint to the soldiers who'd broken ranks after the cavalry charge and sloshed up the street in a drunken, seething wave. Bricks flew. Windows smashed. A mob howling – incensed now as much with the police as the Russians. Men trained in hand to hand combat and being shot at for a living, came on. The coppers' faces showed white, sweating with the strain. The heat grew, steam in a kettle. The captain's voice bellowed above the din,

'Advance together! Form ranks, damn you!'

Joe half-ran back down the steep stairs, compelled for the first time he could ever remember to join the coppers.

'Joe! Come back!' Molly threw open the door. Joe looked up. Mick was behind her. Babushka and his mother.

The rioters smashed against the police, like a wave against a breakwater, with a pile-driving thud. He was so close Joe could hear the crack of rifle butt on flesh. The screams and oaths of those the bayonets slashed and stabbed. The smell of blood. And there was Winterson screaming,

'That's enough boys! You made your point! Steady on!'

'Be careful what you wish for!' Joe bellowed back.

Winterson turned to Joe's voice and was hit in the temple by half a brick. He crumpled like a slaughtered beast.

Mick vaulted down the stairs.

'You in, Comrade?' he screamed. 'Or just selling tickets?'

The mob came on. The coppers now at Babushka's gate. Joe tore the centre paling from it as he ran. Mick stooped for a dropped rifle, thrusting it, stabbing the first soldier he met. Shots cracked and hissed up the street. Joe raised his weapon above his head to bash the head of a soldier as Mick threw his rifle back to use the butt against his attacker. The bayonet point pierced Joe's left shoulder. Puncturing deep. He half-called in surprise as he fell, blood weeping through his shirt.

Joe dragged himself from the roadway to prop against the fence three houses down from *Erin*. The mêlée ground past him as he tried to staunch his wound. Now they fought before their objective, the Union hall. The police reinforcements at Glenelg edged forward.

'The horses! Behind! Behind!' the captain screamed. A roar burst from the rear of the mob as O'Hagen charged. But this time they were ready. The horses lost their momentum amongst the tight-packed push of men. Joe staggered to his feet, his left arm lifeless. He made his way along the fences until he fell through *Erin's* gate.

'Joe!' Kathleen screamed. Tearing the shirt from her son's body she pulled Molly's apron from her. Tearing the material from beneath the waistband she folded a pad to staunch Joe's wound, tying it in place with the apron strings. Joe felt woozy. Relieved he was half drunk, feeling no pain. Exhilarated. Mad. Dead.

'Shoot the horses!' a voice roared from the thickest of the press.

'Shoot the red flag!' another ordered. Joe recognised the second voice. He looked up.

'Ted?'

Shots fired. O'Hagen's horse screamed as it was hit. Windows smashed in the upstairs rooms of the Russian meeting hall. The red flag skittered and flipped as bullets tore it to shreds. A dull cheer rose from the ranks. The air oppressive with heat. Becalmed by the men packed about it O'Hagen's horse reared, throwing him to the ground. Several men whaled into him with boots and palings.

'Stop!' bellowed the captain, Canute to the tide. But he managed to pull O'Hagen away, dragging him to the edge of the fray.

'Take him, Doc!' he ordered. Bill Carroll tried to drag the Sergeant to Babushka's yard, but O'Hagen was on his feet again just as quickly and calling for his horse.

Dr Carroll yelled through *Erin's* gate,

'I'll bring them all here, Sister. You know what to do!'

He exchanged a professional glance with Sister O'Donahue before he was gone. She turned.

'Irina, quick! Bring sheets and water,' she called. But Babushka was already on the stairs with arms full.

'Molly, hold this man's head still.'

'No!' Molly answered, eyes aflame. 'Winterson's one of them! They'd be for killing us all!'

Kathleen O'Donahue was not for debate.

'Grow up, woman!' she commanded. 'The man's wounded. Do unto others or do nothing at all!'

Molly hesitated for a moment before she quailed beneath Kathleen O'Donahue's steel humanity. Still reluctant, she knelt by Winterson's head.

'Mother?' he moaned.

'Yes, hush. I'm here,' Molly replied, wiping the blood from his eyes.

Babushka screamed. Dropping the linen to sprawl across the bottom steps she stared across the street.

'Nyet! Nyet!' she screamed. Like a small, dishevelled hen she rushed through the gate straight into the fray. Molly tried to rise, to follow her, to help.

'Hold still, woman!' Kathleen ordered again. She pulled Molly back. 'Let Irina take care of it.'

More men were being delivered to Babushka's yard by the minute. It looked like a field hospital triage in the midst of a push. Men propped against the fence. Others lay moaning.

'Irina is a strong woman. Be quick, Nurse.' Molly held Winterson's head clamped still between her knees. But they both listened for Babushka's voice, wail and babbling through the throng,

'Not this thing. Never! I had a husband. I too had sons. Leave him. Leave him.' Her scarf ripped from her. From her uncovered head long grey hair fell, undone. She could see them smashing the windows of Nikolai Droshky's house, her house where he lived, running from the door with anything of value.

Babushka reached the far side of the street as one of the three soldier's gathered around him hit Nik Droshky a walloping backhander. The old man fell to the gutter. A second put in the boot, as he lay. The third ripped the wooden violin case from his hands.

'Here, I'll have that. Might be worth a quid or two, or be full of cash. These Jews are all rich bastards.'

Babushka threw herself on top of Old Nik copping a boot in the back as she did.

'You bring shame!' she wailed. 'The Tsar is dead! You do the same!'

'Yes, he is. Killed by Boshies like you!'

Babushka struggled up, pulling Old Nik after her. Blood streamed from his nose.

'You are wrong. He is Christian! Nikolai Droshky is Christian,' Babushka said.

'Well he's Russian. You're all the bloody same.'

'It is you who are all the same!' Babushka spat back, defiant, unafraid. 'Soldiers all the same.'

'Shut your mouth, you fat cow or I'll shut it for you!'

'Ha!' Babushka spat. 'Soldiers? You sheep! Tsar's sheep, Kaiser sheep, King's sheep.'

'See I told you they were all traitors. What would you know about it anyway you old witch!'

'Tsar's men kill my husband, my sons. They shoot them because they strike for a safe mine and bread without horseshit in it.'

Tears streamed on her face but Babushka was exalted in her pain.

'You are the same,' she wailed. 'Look!' she threw her arm in the direction of the looting of Droshky's house.

'They burn my house in Russia. I have nothing. You burn his house. Your mothers are ashamed of their sons. You bring them shame. They have sons. I have sons. I had sons! I had sons! Never again.'

She finished in a river of tears. But unafraid.

'I take that,' she said snatching the violin case from the soldier's yielding hands. 'And I, Irina Davidovna Kerenskaya, the Jew, take Nikolai Droshky, the Christian, to my home and there,' she spat. 'There we will be Russians together.'

She took Old Nik's hand like a child's. Ducking as they entered the mêlée once more she led him across the street, past Molly and Kathleen.

'Babushka, are you all right? ' Molly asked as they climbed the stairs past them.

'She is a strong woman,' Kathleen answered. 'We have our job cut out here. Rip some more sheets for bandages.

Irina climbed up the stairs and into the kitchen. She placed his violin gently on the table.

'It is time for your meal,' she said. She brought him borsht and bread as the battle raged. He wiped the blood from his nose,

'We still have some grain left for winter, don't we, my Irina?' Babushka nodded.

'There is no way to cry, but to cry,' she murmured as their glances met, 'no way to love, but to love, my Nikolai.'

A drop of cold rain hit Kathleen's arm.

'Rain! Just what we need.' She continued cleaning bloodied wounds of policemen and rioters alike.

'We'll have to move them under the verandah!' she called to Molly. 'Get some men here to do it!'

'I can't!' Molly remonstrated. 'They'll take no notice of me.'

'Just tell them!' Kathleen ordered. 'Don't take no for an answer.'

Molly walked uncertainly to the gate.

Joe wasn't there. She looked around quickly but could see nothing of him, nor Mick. No time to fret. The rain was spitting in earnest. She picked a young, strong-looking fellow.

'You!' she ordered. 'Get three others in here now. We need to move the wounded.'

To her amazement he jumped.

'Righto, Miss!' he called. 'Jacko! Get Billy and young Roberts over here on the double.'

'Kill the Communists!' a drunken voice screamed. 'Kill 'em all!'

'Ted?' Joe raised himself from the footpath outside the Russian Union Hall. It was his father's voice. Surely? Steadying himself for a moment on the gatepost he staggered back into the fray.

'Ted?' Joe could see his father now. In full uniform, with medals. Joe pushed forward. The combatants seemed to clear a path for him. The storm rained heavier with sudden cold. Ted caught sight of his son and waved his service revolver.

'Like me get-up?' Ted Hill slurred. 'Going to a funeral,' he added.

'You're drunk!' They stood, unsteadily surveying each other.

'A man'd have to be mad or drunk to live like this,' Ted answered waving his pistol across the spread of the riot. He looked at his son, his gaze direct but unfocussed.

'You're hurt,' he said.

'Lucky I'm drunk too then,' Joe answered, 'or I wouldn't be upright at all.'

'Who did that to you, Joe? I'll shoot the bastard.'

'It was an accident. Mick didn't mean to …'

Saying it aloud made Joe's shoulder pain more than his heart. Maybe we're even now Mick and me? Joe thought.

Ted Hill seemed to look straight through him. Finally he spoke,

'S'pose you know your mother's been playing doctors and nurses?' Joe hung his head but not before he'd seen his father's face. Ted spun around like a wild-west gunfighter, quick and unexpected, firing a shot at the red flag blowing from the front of the Russian's headquarters. It whipped with a hit.

'Kill the Communists!' he bellowed.

'But Dad, you're one of us,' Joe nearly whimpered.

They stood together in the rain. Joe's arm limp at his side. His mother, his father, Uncle Bill, Molly, Molly, Molly, Mick …

Joe swayed with the drink, his face awash with the rain, his father, the stranger, only a few feet away.

Ted Hill stared at his son.

'You want to know what I learned from the war, Joe?' Ted asked. 'Two things. The flags are all the same. All the flag wavers reckon they're on the side of freedom but stand in their way and they'll shoot you like a dog. The only thing kept me going was mates. And then I come home to this … buggar-up.' Ted wiped the water from his brow, his face, with a sweep of his hand. He leered a madman's grin.

'And I learned when death comes looking for you, Joe, look the bastard fair in the eye and … laugh!' He raised the pistol barrel to his temple.

'Shoot the fucking Communists!' he screamed, cocking his revolver. In one movement Joe threw himself at his father, knocking the pistol upward. Ted staggered back. Joe's shoulder seared with pain, blood reddening his bandages, his right hand contended for the revolver. The father was stronger than the son, a working man and soldier, he controlled the trigger. He fired. O'Hagen's horse screamed and finally fell.

'We're all wounded, Joe,' Ted panted. 'And the wounded die when there's nothing left *to be* for!'

'No!' Joe hissed in exertion, his face white in the storm's green light. Letting go of his father's wrist. He drew back his fist and punched him hard in the face.

Ted Hill staggered in surprise. Joe struck his father again.

'No!' he repeated, 'I won't let you.'

Joe hit out again, again, and again.

Ted threw his arms up to cover his face. A second pistol shot cracked. Ted Hill exhaled a deathly moan. His thigh, just above the knee spouted blood. His body crumpled to the ground.

Joe fell with his father.

'No,' Joe whimpered. 'I won't let you.'

A copper hauled Joe up by his wounded arm. He teetered on the edge of unconsciousness.

'Joseph Hill,' said a voice. 'I am arresting you under the provisions of the War Precautions Act and regulations for flying a prohibited symbol, namely a red flag, and for causing an affray.'

Joe struggled against the pain as the rain gave way to hail. Blood streamed from his shoulder. He was white, numb, his mind fading. Turning to face the constable who held him, he found his voice.

'Fuck you and fuck the War Precautions Act!' he said, before he fell into bloody unconsciousness.

Chapter 5

It's The Same The Whole World Over
She was poor but she was honest,
Victim of a rich man's game.
First he loved her, then he left her,
And she lost her honest name.
Chorus
It's the same the whole world over,
It's the poor what gets the blame,
It's the rich what gets the pleasure,
Ain't it all a bleeding shame.
See him at the fine theatre,
In the front row with the best,
While the girl that he has ruined,
Entertains a sordid guest.
When they dragged her from the river,
Water from her clothes they wrung,
And they thought that she had downdéd,
Till her corpse got up and sung … Chorus
Anon. Music hall favourite.

Joe shook his head to wake his Molly-filled mind – her red hair a netted mass across his face, the smell of it, its gossamer touch, the taste of her lips. The memory of that night behind the big water tank in the back yard at Babushka's those few days ago seemed now the unlikeliest of fantasies. He must be remembering it wrong. But he remembered right enough Molly on the tram and Mick, Tomfool.

The actual pain that floated into his consciousness was all too real. As the morphine faded, his dream was shot through with a heavy ache deep within his shoulder. He was sure too of the memory of his father, surviving the war to be shot like a mad dog in the streets of South Brisbane? But no, the whispered assurances at the hospital as the Matron dressed his wound that his father was alive, that he'd be well again given time and care. But it was another voice, Zuzenko's, Joe heard now.

'Those of you who were sleeping did not hear. After storm last night gangs came back and burned, smashed and looted shops and houses of our Russian comrades. Police do nothing. It is pogrom. Now it is started we will be persecuted here as long as we stay. We must go home, back to Russia. We help the revolution there.'

Another voice, George Taylor's, continued,

'We know if these mongrels have their way we're all off to the rusty nail. So, I reckon if we're going down, we give three things a push.' He glanced around, making sure they were all with him.

'First, beat the drum for the red flag as a symbol of an internationalist world. Second, the repeal of the Act and third, as Zuzenko just said, repatriation of Russians back to Russia.'

Joe leaned heavily against the wall behind Taylor, opened his eyes and attempted to focus on the world. Morning light sliced into the room from tall, barred windows. Joe had been here before. Fourteen others stood or sat around the small cell. Joe recognised all of them. Most, like Taylor, Madorsky, Orlov and Zuzenko, he knew very well. George caught his eye.

'You in, son?' Joe nodded, but his response was cut short as a heavy door was flung open, clanging like a bell when it hit the cell bars.

'C'mon you lot!' a voice called. The Bailiff stood behind the opened door, flanked by a couple of uniformed plods.

'You're all going up together.'

'You take the irons,' Zuzenko said shaking his shackled hands before him.

'We are innocent men.'

'You were armed and took part in a violent demonstration. Dangerous prisoners stay handcuffed in Court.'

'We are innocent men,' Zuzenko remonstrated again. 'Until you prove otherwise.'

'You're filth and murderers! Like all Bolsheviks. Thank your stars I'm not the judge. I'd hang the lot of ye!' the Bailiff spat. 'Now, out!'

Fifteen men shuffled together, leg and handcuff irons clinking like a Capitalist's pocket, through the door and up into the dock. All were bandaged in some wise or another. Joe's arm was bound tight to his chest, his shirt sleeve hung limp as he climbed the stairs. As they shuffled in to sit on the form running the length of the dock Joe looked about. The Court and gallery were packed with spectators, many on the Court floor were in military uniform, but there were many more with red handkerchiefs poking from pockets, red shirts and blouses, socks and scarves, and in the gallery, Mrs Griffiths leading a bevy of women with vivid corsages of red poinsettia emblazoning their chests.

There was a buzz of talk and calls as the prisoners appeared, almost a party atmosphere, despite the gravity of the affair. Joe caught sight of his mother and Babushka and Tomas and … her. He turned quickly away from them with a forced smile which showed more like a grimace of pain on his lips. His father and Mick were nowhere to be seen.

At their appearance one of the women from the gallery started into *The Red Flag* which, with the first strains, caught the crowd like bushfire, echoing lustily around the Court. The Bailiff entered from a door behind the bench, his face as red as the poinsettias.

'Silence in Court!' he bellowed, then again. The singing stopped but a rumbling hubbub continued.

'All rise!' the Bailiff called to the accompaniment of a clatter and scrape of chairs. 'This Court is now in session. Police Magistrate, James Acheson presiding.'

The magistrate sat. The courtroom followed. The clerk recited the *Lord's Prayer*.

'Shouldn't we tell him we're all God-fearing atheists?' George Taylor sniggered. The accused smiled. Waiting for complete silence before he spoke, Acheson addressed the room.

'Before proceeding to the matters set down before me I say to those who have turned my court into a cacophony of seditious street-song that my courtroom will not be turned into a three-ring circus of Socialist sympathisers. Any further displays of a political nature in this court will result in a charge of contempt against the perpetrators. I trust I have made myself clear.'

And we *will* embrace that eventuality if it presents itself, he thought, with all due legal enthusiasm.

Acheson looked down.

'First case!'

'Someone got up the wrong side of the bed this morning,' Taylor whispered.

'Humph!' grunted Zuzenko. 'We do not have justice from this … Justice!'

The Clerk of the Court read the first charge,

'That on the 23rd day of March, 1919, Joseph Hill, Apprentice Cabinetmaker, of 13 Merivale Street, South Brisbane, did carry aloft a red flag in William Street and on the Queen Victoria Bridge in contravention of the War Precautions Act of 1916 and attendant Regulations.'

'How do you plead. Guilty or Not Guilty?'

'Neither, Your Honor,' Joe said. 'I committed no crime to be either guilty or not guilty of. I simply expressed my political opinion as is the right of every citizen in a free country.'

Joe closed his eyes. His shoulder ached with the blood pulsing through his body. He must keep calm. Only the Cause mattered now. He realised that for once he wasn't showing off for Molly's attentions. He no longer cared what she thought. The realisation filled him with a clear-headed resolve to do the one thing that mattered.

But this judge was not for bandying words. He gripped the edge of the bench top as he leaned forward.

'Be advised, boy, that I have endured enough political claptrap from your choral comrades without any from you. You face a charge brought by the State. Guilty or not guilty.'

'I thought that's why we fought this war, to have a State that ensured a political fair go?' Joe challenged. 'It's what I fight for always.'

James Acheson almost leapt from the bench, leaning across the towards the dock.

'It was the State who afforded you protection yesterday! Fifty of my best constables are wounded because of you! I can assure you, boy, that is far more protection than you would get in your belovéd Russia. They'd hang you from the nearest lamp-post. If the State hadn't protected you yesterday we'd be in the Coroner's Court today not discussing the rights and wrongs of the British Empire!'

Face red with the effort, Acheson turned to the Clerk's table.

'Record a plea of Not Guilty!' he spat. 'Prosecution? Now!'

'Yes, your Honor.'

Joe hadn't noticed with the judge's performance that O'Hagen had stepped up.

'If it please your Honor I call my first witness, Major Harold Winterson.'

'Good, good! Now for sure we get fair go,' Zuzenko growled, glaring at O'Hagen. Taylor laughed.

'Now, now! Whatever makes you think he's not on the square, old son.' He laughed again. Zuzenko remained unamused.

'Silence in court!' Acheson glowered at the prisoners in the dock.

The Bailiff went to the door, called Winterson's name and waited. After a minute without response he called again. Still nothing. A woman's voice drifted down from the gallery.

'He does not pay his rent on Friday. I move him out. His goods and chattels at South Brisbane Police Station.'

Judge Acheson gazed up, over the top of his glasses.

'Who said that?'

'I do sir,' Babushka said quietly.

'Stand up, woman,' he growled. 'So I can see you!'

'I stand already,' Babushka cooed sadly. 'Would Your Honor like me stand on chair?' The court laughed. Babushka played the crowd.

'Well, that being as it may,' Acheson blustered on. 'Do you mean to tell me, my good woman, that you have evicted a returned man, a Major no less, because his rent was three days late?'

'Yes, sir. It's the law. Maybe he's looking for his books at the Station makes him late.'

'But damn it, woman, he was busy. With me. We had to quell a riot.'

'Not on Friday he wasn't. Was he?' Acheson reddened, unused to such attacks – and in his own court. 'Was he?' she repeated.

'She's the best little capitalist I know,' Taylor smirked and half-waved to Babushka. 'If they were all as fair dinkum and fearless as her we wouldn't need a revolution.' Zuzenko humphed,

'She is fair because she has suffered. How will we teach the generation who do not suffer what "fair" means, Comrade?'

Joe Hill glanced up at the gallery. His mother was averting her eyes and smothering a laugh with her handkerchief. Molly chuckled aloud. She caught Joe's eye and stopped.

'Could you not give the man the benefit of his service to King and Country before you throw him out on the street?'

'Is this Friday?' Babushka asked to an accompaniment of titters from the court. 'If government declare end of war on Friday and on Monday soldier shoot other soldier dead is it not murder?'

'This is not at all like that. Not at all a proper analogy!' Acheson was riled.

'It is the law,' Babushka retorted.

'Then the law is an ass!' Acheson yelled, forgetful of his position.

'If the law is an ass then judges must bray,' Babushka agreed solemnly. 'This is saying also in my country.' She retook her seat. The courtroom exploded in laughter, though some curses directed at Babushka were discernible through the din.

Acheson sat back to compose himself, berating himself for his undisciplined intercourse with the woman, letting the room calm before he banged his gavel again.

'Silence! It seems we must assume that Major Winterson may be delayed by domestic matters.'

Babushka had a final go,

'The chicken who puts his foot in the soup suffers the consequences.'

Acheson scowled hard at Babushka and those who laughed loudest.

'Enough!' he said, his voice both challenge and demand. 'Would the prosecution like to request an adjournment?' he asked.

'Why bother waiting?' It was an uniformed man from the body of the court below who spoke.

'I was there. I saw the lot of those Bolshevik traitors.'

Acheson raised his eyebrows, questioning the prosecutor.

'I'm sure Captain Markson will perform his duty very well as an eye witness.' O'Hagen nodded imperceptibly to Markson, or Acheson, or both. 'If you'd care to take the witness box, Sir.'

'I do not see him yesterday,' Zuzenko whispered. 'You see him?'

'No,' Joe answered quietly.

'Anybody see him?' George Taylor asked. Heads shook down the line.

'He wasn't there, Your Honor. No one who was there saw him,' Taylor complained as Markson mounted the witness stand. The judge's patience was overtaxed.

'One more unsolicited remark from the dock, or from anywhere in court for that matter,' Acheson warned, casting his eyes across the floor and around the gallery, 'will attract a charge of contempt.'

Silence fell.

'Administer the oath then. It's almost time for morning tea.'

Markson took the stand and the oath before O'Hagen had his go. 'Where were you on the afternoon and evening of 23rd March? Did you see Joe Hill? Did he carry the flag? Was he part of the affray?' Markson had all the right answers.

'"Tell them Joe Hill's guilty!"' a voice yelled from the gallery. Every eye turned to look. Tomfool yelled again, jumping up and down on the spot.

'That's him, Joe. That's the copper that Winterson told, "Tell them Joe Hill's guilty. We got the bastard at last." That's him, Joe! And that's the other bloke too!'

Tomas gesticulated wildly at O'Hagen and Markson. The court erupted with catcalls at Tomas 'the idiot' and counter-demands that he 'be heard'.

'I've been robbed!' Tomas yelled to his audience.

'Tomas!' Molly pulled him down by the shirt tail.

'Molly, take him out – quick, love,' Kathleen muttered. 'I'll watch for Joseph. Quick now.'

Acheson was livid.

'Bailiff, I want that youth charged with contempt.'

'Don't be ridiculous,' Mrs Griffiths called down. 'He's not of sound mind.'

'No! He don't mean it. He's a few bob short of a quid, that's all, your Honor,' Taylor added, in exasperation. Even the returned nationalists joined the court of public opinion arguing against punitive extremes. Molly looked on the verge of saying something feisty but Kathleen pushed her firmly away. Molly caught Joe's eye again. Defiant, despairing, loving: as she led Tomfool away. Kathleen nodded to Joe. His shoulder pained.

Acheson belted his gavel like a Morse code operator, countermanding his order to the Bailiff to arrest Tomas. Somebody had been talking all right. Joe began his defence before Acheson had a chance to speak.

'I demand a mis-trial,' he said. 'I believe the witness on the stand,' he turned to point at Markson only to find he'd left the stand and, as Joe surveyed the room for him, it seemed he'd left courtroom entirely. Joe finished nonetheless.

'I believe Captain Markson has been improperly coached by the police prosecutor.' Joe closed his eyes and sat heavily.

'You have no evidence for such an outrageous accusation!' O'Hagen yelled. 'This court shan't take no notice of a …' he floundered, searching for the word. 'An imbecile!'

Joe's eyes flew open. Raising himself he leaned against the dock rail. Pointing with the fingers of his good hand he stared O'Hagen down, enunciating every word,

'Don't you ever call Tomas that again. He is a good friend of mine.' O'Hagen's cheeks coloured as yells and catcalls filled the court.

'And my friends know more about honour than you, or all of this … charade,' Joe finished with a flourish of his arm to encompass the whole near-riotous room. For a moment, he meant it. My friends may betray me, but they are mine and mine alone to forgive – or not.

'For Gawsake, shut up yer row!' the Bailiff bellowed, finally silencing the din before Acheson could be heard again.

'No! We will not hear these allegations. They are extraneous to the case at hand.'

'Extraneous! To you maybe, but this is my life you're judging,' Joe insisted loudly. 'I demand a mis-trial!'

Acheson ignored him, turning to O'Hagen instead.

'Do you have any further witnesses?' O'Hagen shook his head.

'Tell him you want to cross-examine Markson,' George Taylor said quietly. 'It's your right to do it.' Joe could feel blood beginning to seep warmly down his chest.

'I want to question Markson. It is my right to cross-examine.'

'You have missed your opportunity.'

This remark was too much for Mrs Griffiths. She called down loudly from the gallery,

'This is the worst case of procedural unfairness I've ever seen. None of the accused are represented by legal counsel and when they try to conduct their own defence they are denied.'

Acheson turned toward the Bailiff, who'd seen easier days at work, but Mrs Griffiths beat him to it.

'Don't you worry about that! I'm going! Come on ladies,' she said, raising her sisters-in-arms to their feet. 'We are off to see the Premier. He'll know how the courts are operating by day's end or my name's not Jeanie Griffiths – if you need my name for the paperwork,' she added over her shoulder. En masse the Socialist ladies left the gallery.

Joe felt clammy and cold, his face pale. He could see a small patch of blood beginning to spread across his shirt-front. Their heart's blood dyed its every fold. It reminded him of Segeyev. It reminded him of what he was doing here. It reminded him of 1917, when everything was simple.

'I want a lawyer to defend me,' Joe managed. Closing his eyes again to see only Molly and Mick in the darkness, laughing their way onto the tram.

'You don't need a lawyer!' Acheson bellowed. 'It is all very simple.' He waved O'Hagen on.

'Were you in William Street, Brisbane at approximately 6.10pm yesterday afternoon?' Joe felt very tired, he knew he was beaten, but he had trained many years for this, or worse.

'Yes,' he answered.

'Did you fly a red flag on that occasion?'

'Yes,' Joe answered, closing his eyes once more. 'In contravention of your War Precautions Act.'

'There, your Honor, I rest my case.' O'Hagen smiled. A smile not triumphant, but of a job proper done. Joe felt no malice towards him. He was a fool in a fool's job enforcing foolish laws.

'Then,' said Acheson. 'By your own admission you are guilty of the offence as charged.' He smiled.

'I told you you'd no need of representation. This is an open and shut case. Now,' he said benignly, 'as to the matter of sentence.' He looked around the court, reveling in the thrill of sending the entire rabble a long overdue judicial rebuke to their collective behaviour.

'You have quite a long list of misdemeanours of a similar nature which have escalated over time to result in yesterday's unforgivable display of provocation to violence in company with actual violence.'

He looked over his glasses to address the room, rather than the defendant.

'In this instance I have only one choice, that is to sentence you to five months incarceration, followed by a further month on the count of contempt of court to be served subsequently.'

Before the court's indrawn breath was allowed to explode from lips either outraged or satisfied, Joe Hill spoke, and they listened.

'You've dispensed with even the slightest sham of justice. I accept that. But will you not even let a condemned man speak before he's taken down?'

James Acheson demurred.

'If you must, but make it brief.'

Bending down he tapped his associate on the shoulder.

'See that the kettle's on will you, Mr McKenzie. I'm in dire need of a good cup of tea.'

Joe heard but did not mind the indifference, nor did he care what the crowd thought. He spoke this truth for himself.

'I was cautioned as a child never to show a red rag to a bull, but I had no idea a piece of ordinary red cloth could raise the same antipathy in the human as in the beast. You ask if I carried the red flag and I have said I have and I will carry it again. Because the red flag is a symbol of an ideal – to uplift the human race to its betterment. This flag stands for what can be achieved by us Socialists for the common good of the citizens of the world.'

Joe stopped, sore in heart and mind and, though he had spoken softly, they listened to his testament. They gave him a fair go.

'I am now, and have always been, a Socialist,' he said. 'Because Socialism means to act together, working to all share in the riches for which we all toil, to all share that for which so many have died. To be free means to be free from a system which uses us: our sweat, our skills, our brains, to make its millions while leaving us with next to nothing. This is why I am a Socialist, because to people who believe in one another, not to be, makes no sense at all.

'Where people believe in one another, they fly the red flag. People all over Britain fly the red flag and are free to do so. I can only ask why those at Home can fly the flag when it is banned here? This flag is now the flag of the Russian state and I fully understand why our Russian friends wish to be allowed to flee your persecutions and return to their motherland.'

Acheson leaned back in his chair.

'Mr Hill, will there be much more of this?'

Joe ignored him.

'That is why I am here. That is what I believe. You can sneer at me, you can put me in gaol, you can try to break my heart … but law or no law, I'll be here just the same and I'll be here carrying the red flag.'

A young woman's voice called down from the balcony,

'I'm sorry, Joe.'

Molly back again.

He did not listen to her. Joseph Hill was beyond all need for encouragement now.

'Take him down. Take him down,' Acheson burbled. 'I think we have time for another before morning tea.'

A constable helped Joe down the steps and back into the holding cell. He lay on a blanket on the floor and slept, waking only briefly when the door clanged fourteen more times throughout the morning.

Chapter 6

It is better to be in chains with friends, than to be in a garden with strangers.

Persian proverb

As top dog of the on-duty turnkeys, Jack Heffernan always unlocked the exercise yard gate as the clock on the South Brisbane Town Hall chimed nine. Not one second before. Jack ran his shift like clockwork. Joe didn't mind him though, despite despising the job the bloke did: gaoler for a so-called Socialist government that accepted the gaoling of its own for defying a law that oppressed the very people who fought to put it there. But he would always remember the man's refusal to cross their picket line when the government ordered them to make brooms for threepence a day.

'Buggar that for a game of soldiers,' George Taylor, leader of their strike delegation, told Jack Heffernan. 'The union rate is threepence a broom-head, not threepence a day. We won't add to the suffering of our broom-making Comrades on the outside by undercutting their pay, especially on behalf of a mob of mongrel politicians who keep us locked up for fun.'

'They won't like it,' Jack warned.

'You just tell 'em we're on strike. Equal work for equal pay or they can go to hell.' Jack never crossed the picket line despite them ordering him to do so. No brooms ever got made by The Brisbane Fifteen in Boggo Road nick.

'It's the same the whole world over,' Joe murmured through shivering lips as he followed the rest of them into the yard.

'But it needn't be,' he added, reassuring himself as he did every morning.

The July sun was warm but the westerly wind whipping over the exercise yard wall drained it of any effect. They made for the western wall and stood in a line against it like deserters facing a firing squad. But their backs were warm against the sun-soaked bricks and they were in the lee, out of the breeze. They had two good wool blankets each, but last night was a three blanket night. It was amazing that none of them had contracted the Spanish 'flu. Half the gaolers had had it and one died. The wall felt like heaven. Jack followed them in and handed a carefully folded newspaper to George Taylor.

'Leave it with Thomson when you're done,' he said nodding at a younger guard. 'I've been called up to the Superintendent's office for a chat.'

'Nothing trouble?' Zuzenko asked.

'No, she'll be jake,' Jack Heffernan replied. 'Routine monthly report on you lot!'

'We're model prisoners,' Joe smirked.

'Shouldn't be here,' Jack replied.

'What was that?' Joe asked loudly, his smirk developing into a laugh.

'I said, "You got big ears," you jackass. Don't push your luck,' he continued conspiratorially. 'The walls have ears.'

'Thanks, Jack. Then I'll talk to the wall while it thaws me out,' Joe laughed.

Heffernan paused on his way out of the yard to speak to Thomson.

'I'm reliably informed you've got a visitor,' Heffernan called over his shoulder to Joe.

'Come on, Hill. I'll take you over myself.'

'Mummy calls. Go quick,' Madorsky growled. Joe turned.

'Put a sock in your ugly mug.' Madorsky was off the wall in a second, his mood bitter as the wind. But Zuzenko was quicker.

'Nyet!' he said, his hand on Madorsky's chest, holding him back. 'Go,' he continued to Joe.

Joe turned, but unwillingly, tired of Madorsky singling him out. They all knew Hughes' dogs had sent his wife and children to Melbourne from where they'd be deported back to Russia. They all knew they had no money save what the Socialists could gather for them. But all the Russian families here were the same, whether the head of the family was in gaol or not: businesses ransacked, breadwinners fired from their jobs, lives destroyed. They were all Government scapegoats for the damage the war had done to everyone but … it wasn't Joe's fault that Madorsky had shit on the liver.

'We'll talk later,' he said as he followed Heffernan out the yard gate.

'You'd be wise to pull your head in with that one, son,' Jack Heffernan offered.

'Why's he always onto me?' Joe asked. 'As if I can do anything about what's happening.'

Heffernan shrugged his shoulders.

'He'd do better to take a leaf out of Zuzenko's book,' he answered. '"Suffering is good for the soul!"' he intoned in a fair impression of Zuzenko's voice. Joe had to smile as they stopped outside the visiting room.

'Fifteen minutes only,' Heffernan said to the officer. 'No need to handcuff him if he keeps his hands on the table.' The officer raised his eyebrows at such a concession but nodded a, Yes Sir, as he opened the door.

Kathleen O'Donahue removed the white cloth mask from her face. She stood as Joe entered and leaned towards him for a kiss. He recoiled. Not because he thought she'd infect him. He'd always appreciated her visits before, especially at the beginning, but today he found her presence almost suffocating. Maybe Madorsky was right and it was his jibe that rankled. Or maybe it was Joe. His time was almost up and his future was mud. It was weighing on his mind.

Joe sat opposite her, placing both hands palm down on the table before him.

'How are you?' she asked. He wondered how many times she'd asked that same inane question since she'd been visiting. Three times a week, four weeks a month for five months. And sixty times he'd answered inanely. This time he said nothing.

'Your father sends his best,' she continued, undaunted. 'It looks like he might be able to come home in a few weeks.'

'Where's home?' Joe asked.

'With me, you know where his home is,' she answered, perplexed as she studied his face. 'Where else would he go?'

'Anywhere to get away from you.' Joe felt the pain of his utterance even as he spoke. It hurt his mouth, his tongue, his breath … but it was said. Kathleen was ready though if that's how it was to be.

'Really? Well you're a fine one to say such a thing, Joseph Hill. The pot calling the kettle black!' she spat back beneath her breath. The officer looked at her.

'Yes, quite a pair, aren't we?' Joe agreed, staring at her. But Kathleen met his gaze. The clock on the visiting room wall ticked through the silence.

'Mr Gandhi is causing the British some grief I read,' she said.

'Good,' Joe answered. 'The sooner India is for the Indians the better. Who'd want anything to do with the British and their wars?'

'Well, not Mrs Gandhi for one,' Kathleen answered. Her comment was so disconnected from the conversation Joe gazed at her in puzzlement.

'I brought you this from Molly,' she said. Pulling a letter from her handbag, she held it aloft. The officer took it from her, opened the envelope, unfolded the letter and handed it to Joe.

'They read them if they come through the mail,' she muttered.

'Then they'll know more about her than I will,' Joe said.

'You read the letter, Joseph Hill. That young lady is pouring her heart and soul out to you and you can't even be bothered to read it,' Kathleen railed.

The officer in attendance smirked and she shot him a foul look. He pointed at the clock and smirked again.

'It's not as though you don't have enough time on your hands!' Kathleen admonished her son. 'Just open the door a bit, Joe. The whole world doesn't revolve around you.'

But her son had changed these last few months. No longer the blushing boy, his look was hard and vacant.

'We've got world revolution to organise, Comrade,' Joe answered. 'Takes up a fair bit of our time.'

He sat back almost insolently and put his hands above his head. The officer moved towards him.

'Hands down!' he snapped.

Joe slapped his hands down on the table before him.

'Your father's leg is much better now,' Kathleen tried again.

'I'm glad to hear that Uncle Bill hasn't managed to kill him yet,' Joe sneered, his voice thick with sarcasm. 'Now he's inconveniently come home alive from the war and found you two at it like rabbits.'

'What's got into you, Joe? I'll not be spoken to like that!' Kathleen cried, her body shaking with anger.

'I know I've made some unfortunate choices, but that does not give you the right to use such a disrespectful tone.'

The officer at the door laughed aloud at her.

Joe leaned back a little, surprised that her outburst had so little effect on him.

'Just telling you what they are saying about your choices,' Joe answered, emphasising the words nastily.

'In the very words they're using. You'll have to live with that. I hope you are happy.'

'Happy my foot,' Kathleen sneered in return. 'You know they save a special place in Hell for cowards who stay at home to steal the sweethearts of brave soldiers away from them,' she spat. 'You know what they're saying about you? Micky Doyle is calling you every name under the sun in every pub from South Brisbane to Sandgate. "Joe Hill doesn't believe in Pacifism or Socialism, he just used the Movement to have his way with my girl." Your name's mud!'

Though he knew it was true, it was hard to hear, especially from his mother. Joe fell silent as Kathleen tried to regain her composure. Finally he spoke.

'Well, it looks like I do know something about what happens between men and women after all, Mother.'

Kathleen O'Donahue gazed wearily at her son as he continued. 'Who says we have nothing in common? Dad enlisting, you and Lt Carroll and me and Molly and Mick. How many bad choices do we need? And we're just a few small people, how many more must there be around this old world.'

Joe paused, thinking. He met his mother's gaze.

'Quite the model Socialist family aren't we?' he asked, trying to force a smile.

'Oh, Joe,' she said. 'I'm sorry … for everything.'

'This is war, Mother,' he replied with ineffable self-pity. 'It never ends.'

Laying her hands palm downward on the table, Kathleen O'Donahue pushed them toward his until their fingers touched. They both fell silent then, sitting like that until Heffernan returned calling,

'Time!'

The officer smirked over to them, as Kathleen gave Joe a quick peck on the cheek. Forcing Joe's hands behind his back, the screw screwed the handcuffs locked and picked up Molly's letter from the table. But Kathleen was too quick.

'That'll be my son's letter,' she said plucking it from his grasp. 'And you'll not be reading it therefore,' she said. Smiling sweetly she handed it to Jack Heffernan.

'If you could be so kind, Mr Heffernan, as to see my son has his property placed safely about his person.' Heffernan gave it back to the officer to fold and place in Joe's pocket. Kathleen smiled broadly at Heffernan, saying confidentially,

'It's a letter from his sweetheart. She would have mailed it but … they read them you know.'

She turned to wink at the now scowling guard.

'Goodbye, Joe!' she finished. 'Not long now.'

Heffernan was in a good mood, dropping back to walk beside Joe after the first gate.

'Letters always stir a bloke up, don't they Hill?'

'I don't know. I don't read them, sir,' Joe answered truthfully.

'Hmmm,' Heffernan said shrewdly, 'Well, whatever she says, Hill, keep it for the privacy of your cell. Don't let your … comrades,' he coughed slightly at the word, 'have any part of it. Especially the Russians,' he added confidentially. 'They're a bad lot. Criminal class, not real working men like the rest of you. Let 'em have their version of socialism in Russia and we'll have ours here, eh? The sooner we get rid of them the better.' He nudged Joe in the ribs. 'And stay clear of that Madorsky. He's a mad dog.'

'He hates me for some reason,' Joe agreed.

'No imagination,' Heffernan said, as the officer opened the yard gate. 'Hate is achieved through the wilful suspension of the imaginative faculty.' Joe looked askance at his gaoler.

'You can never really hate somebody if you can imagine what it's like to walk a mile in their shoes,' Heffernan explained. 'That's how wars start,' he winked as the officer opened the yard.

The gate clanged behind him with the jangle-music of keys he'd grown to hate in so short a time. Heffernan called out,

'Five minutes left with the paper, tell them.'

Joe waved a righto. As he approached he could hear Taylor reading an article aloud. Taking his place against the wall he listened.

'Mr Gandhi stated that he believed, "that non-violence is infinitely superior to violence, forgiveness is more manly than punishment. Forgiveness," according to this Gandhi, "adorns a soldier". The Indian agent provocateur then continued in the same vein saying, "Let me not be misunderstood. Strength does not come from physical capacity. It comes from an indomitable will." After some interjections, though admittedly with overwhelming support from the crowd assembled to hear him speak, Gandhi most humbly asserted that he was not a visionary. "I claim," he said, "to be a practical idealist. The religion of non-violence is not meant merely for the holy people and saints. It is meant for the common people as well.'

'Hear, hear!' Joe muttered, his mind on what his mother said Mick had been saying about him. That he didn't believe in Pacifism. Mick knows I do. He's said so a thousand times.

'This Gandhi is for cowards and queer-boys!' Madorsky pushed himself from the wall.

'Forgiveness is weak. There is no place in Socialism for this. We have turned our souls to steel. This is our oath. We show no mercy to the bourgeois. Does Ryan show us mercy? Does Hughes? No! We take what is ours by force.'

'Well I'm sick of fighting,' Taylor said. 'I want peace. We'll win the war with words. Take the parliament and enact a Socialist state.'

Madorsky was incensed.

'No talk. You read what the Tsarist troops do to the Bolseviki? They will cling to the reins of power until we cut their hands away from them. Have you forgotten why we are here Comrade?'

'I haven't forgotten why I'm here,' Joe said. 'I'm here for peace. We've already won the war. It's over. Why start another one.'

'You are coward and thief already. You would like a new war to profit from.' Madorsky moved menacingly towards Joe. Zuzenko was not close enough. A couple of blokes tried to stop him but he brushed them aside.

This time Joe was not for backstepping. He knew what Madorsky meant. Hadn't he just heard it from his mother?

'What is your problem, mate? It's you Russians causing the trouble if the truth be told,' he countered.

'You are problem. You steal from the working class – steal Mick's woman, Ted Hill steals workers rights, the mother works when all other women cannot – you take what you want. You are not one of us, Comrade! We don't have choices.'

Before Joe or anyone could say more, Madorsky was at him. Joe shaped for a fight, but then … dropped his hands to his side. Quick as a snake Madorsky spun him to the wall. Joe tried to protect his head but Madorsky smashed his face into the bricks. He felt his cheek fracture and the warmth of his blood as he covered his head. Joe could hear his own voice,

'Do not resist.'

And he fell true.

As he lay, Joe heard his ribs crack to Madorsky's boot and the Russian's disembodied voice thudding with the blows,

'You're not … one of us … bourgeoise dog!'

It was all so quick. Joe's head settled to the concrete of the yard. It was bitterly cold, as cold as a Comrade's kiss.

Chapter 7

The Soldier is Home
Weary is he, and sick of the sorrow of war,
Hating the shriek of loud music, the beat of the drum;
Is this the shadow called glory men sell themselves for?
The pangs in his heart they have paled him, and stricken him dumb!
Oh! yes, the soldier is home!
Still does he think of one morning, the march and the sun!
A smoke, and a scream, and the dark, and next to his mind
Comes the time of his torment, when all the red fighting was done!
And he mourned for the good legs he left in the desert behind.
Oh! yes, the soldier is home!
He was caught with the valour of music, the glory of kings,
The diplomat's delicate lying, the cheers of a crowd,
And now does he hate the dull tempest, the shrill vapourings —
He who was proud, and no beggar now waits for his shroud!
Oh! yes, the soldier is home!
Now shall he sit in the dark, his world shall be fearfully small —
He shall sit with old people, and pray and praise God for fine weather;
Only at times shall he move for a glimpse away over the wall,
Where the men and the women who make up the world
are striving together!
Oh! yes, the soldier is home!
Simple, salt tears, full often will redden his eyes;
No one shall hear what he hears, or see what he sees;
He shall be mocked by a flower, and the flush of the skies!
He shall behold the kissing of sweethearts — close by him, here,
under the trees —
Oh! yes, the soldier is home!
John Shaw Neilson

Like a well-trained dog the driverless iceman's horse picked its way along the late September street, hauling the ice-cart to the next house along the familiar route. It was an unwelcoming morning, a grey-black blanket of heavy cloud with a sneaking, wheeze-breathed breeze. The sky was only now growing light. A hessian bag draped over his shoulder protected the iceman a little from the weather and the freezing of the block of ice he balanced there. The greasy wool pullover and oiled leather gloves, warmed him little more. He would normally have been alone on the streets when the Town Hall clock chimed five but he could see people moving up from the 'Gabba and across from South Brisbane. Not many, just a few but … he paused at a picket gate wondering … before it struck him. Today must be the release – a day early. He smiled then, turning back to the gate latch. At least that meant there'd be no journalists stirring up strife. The *Herald* mob would still be drunk in bed!

'Ice!' the big man called softly, almost apologetically, just letting the householders know he wasn't a robber.

Kathleen O'Donahue struggled to push the wheelchair up Boggo Road. It wasn't steep but Ted Hill was no featherweight, even with the weight he'd lost, and she'd already pushed him from the Mater. Besides she still hadn't fully recovered from the influenza. Molly offered to take a turn but finally it was Tomfool who took to the handles, pushing like a draught horse in harness. Molly appreciated the handover, it stopped Tomfool swinging his arms around like a windmill to warm himself. He was excited and walking anywhere near him was downright dangerous. Molly took Kathleen's arm and they walked a pace behind. She had no doubt Ted would call if he needed them. He'd become good at that since his confinement.

'Will Mick be there?' Kathleen asked quietly. Molly looked down at her boots, nodding without a word. 'Why?' Kathleen asked, but it was as though she already knew. Mick too had to make his peace.

'Couldn't you have asked him not to make a scene?' Molly shrugged her shoulders and pulled her shawl closer with her free hand. Kathleen sighed.

'Well, we'll see then,' she concluded, straightening her shoulders.

'Almost there,' Ted encouraged Tomfool as he pushed hard, puffing by now up the last of the steeper slope to the gaol.

At the end of the entry lane that led to the small door in the main iron gate they could see the huddles of families and red-splashed well-wishers from the Movement. Behind them more trailed in. One of the Russians produced a squeeze box and sang folksongs, mournful with suffering and hope. It sounded like a funeral to their untrained ears.

'Dawn chorus of the Socialist magpies,' Ted groaned, but he was smiling, as far as he ever smiled these days, grimly as though it hurt. Kathleen squeezed Molly's arm. Surely the world was better, the war an echo, though casualties still died at her hospital from wounds and influenza and Ted's leg was gone since Bill Carroll had botched setting the break and the gangrene set in. Kathleen wondered for a moment what Joe would think of his father now. The half of the man he had known. A man who could no longer do as he had or be as he was – broken and bitter.

'Kathleen! You take this,' a voice called. She turned. Babushka clutched a large wicker basket and her Gladstone bag. Sat on the driver's seat of Nik Droshky's hansom cab, Babushka looked for all the world like a dishevelled swamp pheasant. Kathleen took the basket as Babushka scrambled down.

'Where are they?' she demanded, reclaiming the basket.

'Not released yet,' Kathleen smiled at the older woman's impatience.

'We wait.' With some squirm and wriggling Babushka managed to work her kitchen apron completely around her waist until it hung across her bottom. Smoothing it under her, she sat on the gutter stones, Gladstone bag between her ankles, basket filling her lap. She patted the spot beside her. Nikolai sat down.

'I was beautiful once,' she said, chasing a loose hair from her face.

'You are beautiful always,' he said, stroking her cheek as he would his horse's soft muzzle.

'I am happy I put the roof over your head Nikolai Droshky,' Babushka smiled.

'We were both fools to stay apart,' he answered. 'Now we know better.' Babushka smiled like a young lover and leaned towards him for a moment before catching herself. She looked up quickly towards the gate, shaking her fist.

'Oyoyoy! Why do you take so long?'

Kathleen turned, blushing, away from them, taking the handles of Ted's wheelchair from Tomas and fussing with the brake.

Molly scanned the crowd, nodding to those she knew. If Mick was here she couldn't see him. She breathed easier but still turned to look back down the street to the stragglers. He'd said he was coming to see Joe but she could never be sure with Mick these days.

At the first stroke of six from the Town Hall clock Jack Heffernan unlocked the Judas gate. As the prisoners stepped through from the guardhouse sally port he clapped each on the back.

'Good luck to ye,' he said earnestly. 'Ye'll need it with the sharks still about.' Many of them shook his hand.

Joe came second to last. He glanced around and saw his people. He nodded but hung back, unwilling, or perhaps unsure, about breaking solidarity. His hand moved unconsciously to touch the still-red welt on his sunken cheek. He watched Madorsky like a hawk, a look returned by the Russian until he saw one of his mates and shouldered his way through the crowd to embrace him.

'Come, Comrade,' Madorsky called loud across the crowd, 'enough of time spent in cage with rats. It is time to return to our true friends.' The two strode down the hill together. Only then did Joe breathe freely and Zuzenko give his comrades his full attention.

'Joe! It's me, Joe!' Tomfool yelled, pulling at the shoulder of Molly's cardigan. 'It's Joe Hill. It's our Joe coming home at last!' Still Joe held back, but half-waved. He had looked forward to this day, but now it came with Molly and … where was Mick? Joe cast around, needing to see his mate, not wanting to. The moment Heffernan closed the door Ted Hill called for three cheers for the true workers republic of The Brisbane Fifteen. Unexpectedly from inside the prison the inmates answered with cheers and pannikins rattled against the bars. A quick rendition of *The Red Flag* and the solemnities were over. The released prisoners dispersed into the crowd or shook Ted's hand or Kathleen's.

Joe still stood still.

'Take me over, Kathleen,' Ted Hill urged, 'or give me the crutches.' Kathleen pushed. Molly held Tomfool's arm as he rushed forward.

'Not yet, Tomas. Not yet.' Tomfool rubbed his hair in confusion.

'Molly! Molly!' he repeated. 'Why Molly? It's our Joe! I love him, Tomas, and I can't change that.'

Molly trembled at his words but held Tomas hard.

His eyes full, Ted Hill thrust his hand out to be shaken.

'Hello, Joe,' he managed. 'How are you?' They shook hands, awkwardly, Joe confronted by the blunt reality of his father's missing leg, but also by the memory of their last meeting and all that had happened since his return. True, his mother had visited him in gaol, but it was different between them.

'Right as rain,' he answered. Kathleen hugged her son.

'What would you like for breakfast?' she asked.

'They fed us early,' Joe said. 'I've eaten.' He looked over her shoulder to where Molly waited. She scanned his features for a sign. Breaking Kathleen's embrace, he stared down at his feet. Finally it was Ted Hill who spoke,

'Well, we can't stay here forever. Would you mind giving us a push. I'm breaking out of prison myself today. They've let me come home.'

'Sorry, Ted,' Joe answered, soft but firmly. 'I won't be coming with you. I've decided I'll be striking out on my own for a while.' Old Nik and Babushka joined Joe's parents, standing quiet. It was Kathleen who broke the silence.

'Are you sure, Joseph?' There was a plea in her voice but it sounded hopeless. Joe shook his head

'No, but that's what I'm doing. My apprenticeship's gone now I've got a criminal record, so I thought I could get some labouring on the railways out west.' He gesticulated vaguely.

'You need food, now!' Babushka interrupted. 'I bring you food, Joe. You eat!' She placed the basket at Joe's feet, flicking open the cloth that covered piroshki and cabbage soup and still-warm bread and pickled herring and cheese and sausage enough for an army and, in the corner, a bottle of vodka.

'We celebrate our Joe come back to us.'

'Yes, good to see you out, Joe. I see they've given you a bit of a touch-up in prison.'

None of them had noticed Mick until he was standing beside them. He held out his hand. Joe stared at him but did not take it. Mick dropped his paw, wiping it against the leg of his trousers.

'Sorry, my hands aren't clean,' he said, returning Joe's gaze. 'But then yours aren't exactly either.' His eyes shifted to Molly. 'You see the thing is Molly, that our Joe was right all along. He said war is hell, that it murders and maims and that the profiteers stay home and make merry while the fools are in the front line. He was right. Look at us. When I left I had something – a father, a girl, a future – but now I been robbed of it all.' Mick drew a service revolver from his trouser pocket. Cocking it he pointed it straight at Joe's head.

'It's a gun!' Tomfool whispered, pulling excitedly at Molly's arm. She stood transfixed, not breathing.

'You always were the clever one, Joe. But you're not one of us. You got ideas, speeches, books, friends, family, choices – typical bourgeoisie. The working class got no choices, just solidarity, and fists.'

Joe stared hard at his friend, into eyes that he had seen full of hatred so many times on the streets of their childhood. As they were now. But now there was something more, something Joe had never seen and it made him afraid. His eyes showed it, but he did not flinch, nor blink.

'Steady son,' Ted Hill said. 'Give me that revolver.' Mick ignored him. The crowd of men who had seen such confrontations often in the trenches moved closer, unafraid, watching intently, silently surrounding the family.

'Every day for two years I've stared down the barrel of one of these. Every whistle, screech, whizz-bang and I coulda been dead and every time I thought of you Joe, fighting with me not to go and me hating the old man so much I went anyway. I thought of you and Molly and even bloody Tom and I wasn't so fucking afraid.' He paused and looked from each to each, his eyes tear-brimmed. 'Someone shoulda told me. No, you shoulda, Joe. You shoulda told me how things stood. With me dad. With her. I thought we were mates?' Mick's hand shook on the grip of his pistol. He held it in both hands to brace his aim.

Joe met his friend's gaze. Maybe this was his punishment. His world, the whole world, collided in him and left him in tatters. Perhaps he deserved to die.

Go on, he thought. *Just do it.*

'Will this make it end?' he asked them all.

No one moved.

But Mick.

His finger squeezed the trigger.

The hammer fell.

Joe winced at the click of hammer on empty chamber.

And took another breath.

Molly gasped, gripping Tomas with white knuckles.

'You were right Joe. There'll never be any good in wars for people like me.' Mick shook the empty pistol for emphasis then threw it hard out onto Boggo Road.

'Fuck this for a game of soldiers!' he said. 'You gotta rely on your mates, even though you know some of them are bastards! She's yours, Joe. You can have her! But look out,' he sneered, 'she's changeable.'

Turning, Mick shouldered through the crowd – a man who's said goodbye in his mind. It was Molly who cried out,

'Where are you going?' Calling after him.

Mick stopped without turning.

'Something you learn in the trenches, Molly my love, is that the future is a gamble. You kill and you expect to be killed. But every now and then you stop and find yourself still alive and there still is a future. I'm going to do my gambling on that as far away from you as I can bloody-well get! Don't bother writing.' He strode off, jumping the fence and crossing the railway lines towards the 'Gabba.

'And what would be the point o'that, Patrick Doyle, you've never written back!' Molly yelled at him. 'Not ever!'

'Mick!' Joe finally yelled, too late – always too late.

'Leave him, son,' Ted Hill said. 'He needs time.' Tomfool scuttled out onto the road to scoop up the gun.

'Fuck this for a game of soldiers, Joe,' he laughed shaking the pistol above his head like a toy. Old Nik took the weapon from him, placing it with the food in Babushka's basket.

'We need to go,' Kathleen decided suddenly, wheeling the wheelchair round. The crowd breathed again, laughed off the tension. The squeeze-box started up.

'I take you home again, Kathleen,' Old Nik said, holding up his hand against their remonstrations. 'It is too far to walk. We strap the chair on behind.'

'Nyet, nyet! We eat! Joe!' Babushka was determined. It was Old Nik who turned her,

'We eat under your roof now Irina Davidovna Kerenskaya.' Babushka gazed at him, blinked, then looked to Joe. He smiled sadly as one who has imagined the worst, though it didn't happen.

'I'll be seeing you some time, Babushka. Thanks for everything.' There were tears welling in her eyes as Joe kissed her cheeks, hugging her.

'He is like the son to me. You have son, I have son. What can we do? Oyoyoy! What will we do with this … this … everything. Be good boy, Joe. Dress warm. Be good. Be kind.'

Kathleen bent to fold the tea towel closed and pick up Babushka's basket. Joe's urge to kiss her passed and he turned away, standing amongst the other comrades and their families. Waiting for … who knew what?

Ted's shoulder's slumped, resigned, knowing nothing he could say would change the way things stood.

'Son … Joe,' he said. 'I'll always be proud of you. And when you're right again, your mother and I have your room ready at home.' Joe gazed away, somewhere above them, but he nodded his head imperceptibly. It was enough.

Old Nik strapped the wheelchair behind his cab and with Kathleen, half-lifted Ted Hill in before hoisting Babushka and her bag onto the driver's seat. Joe did not move to help. Nor did anyone else. It was as though they were all detached, as though they were all watching the pictures in a cinema.

'Tomas! Molly! You too,' Babushka ordered, but Molly countered.

'Could he walk home with me, Grandmother? It would be a kindness.'

Babushka relented,

'Oyoyoy! These young people. Was I ever young, Nikolai Droshky?'

'Never a chick, always the old hen,' Old Nik answered, twinkle-eyed. 'Come my dumpling!' He released the brake and flicked the reins. Kaiser leaned into the load. Babushka smiled coquettishly, wiping tears from her eyes.

'Men … Oyoyoy! … Boys!' His parents waved, tentative. Joe merely nodded again before they were gone. But his heart was bitter-torn. He breathed deep and again.

What now, Joe? he thought, looking anywhere but at her. Molly waited, watching his every move. Waiting for a moment to tell her heart, however it may be received. But it was Tomfool, too excited in the moment, who broke their self-pitying up. He capered through the crowd, pockets turned out.

'I've been robbed! Help! I've been robbed!' he called, imploring them over his shoulder. Even now Joe couldn't but nearly smile.

'Not with this mob, Tomas, they know your game. They invented it.' Molly called, her voice tinkling like broken glass on a tiled pub floor.

'I've been robbed!' Tomfool continued, flittering like a small bird with a snake at its nest. The squeeze-box player struck up a boisterous tune, though still full of Russian melancholy, as accompaniment to Tomas' capering.

'Come on,' Molly urged. 'Please, Joe.' Joe looked down into her eyes for the longest moment before he stepped towards the crowd.

'Yes he's been robbed, ladies and gentlemen.'

Tomfool hooted with delight.

'And so have I. I've been robbed by this stinking war. I've been robbed of my friends, my job, my trust, my love, my future. My life, your lives, our lives are shattered like a broken looking glass. How can I, how can we, ever re-build what we have lost? If we try to put the pieces back together all we will ever see is the place where it's been broken. We'll never see anything whole again. We've been robbed ladies and gentlemen. Yes, we've been robbed.'

Joe slipped, falling on dew wet paving stones. The music stopped. But he continued, appealing from the gutter.

'We've lost the battle Comrades, but we must win this bastard war.'

Whether the tears on his cheeks were of self-pity, or pity for humankind, Joe no longer knew, nor cared.

Then two hands appeared, one on either side.

'She'll be right, Joseph Hill. She'll be right as rain!' Tomfool's face shone with compassion.

'You are one of us Joe, and you will be, as long as you keep believing,' she said from the other side. 'Like I believe in you.'

'But I'm dead, Moll. They've killed us all and we let them.'

She smiled.

'You said it yourself, Joe. The world is broken but there's no-one to fix it up but us. We'll lead the Capitalists and war profiteers a pretty dance now peace is come. Won't you dance with me, Joe?'

He clasped her outstretched fingers.

Raising himself up he faced her, one hand to her hand, the other to her waist. Molly pressed a folded piece of paper to his palm.

And then there was music again, as if by magic, that old, sad dance for two. Joe saw a desperate fear in Molly's eyes, a fierce supplication and he too prayed as he held her to him and they whirled into a new dance … round and around and around. Spinning faster and faster they forgot the heart's inexorable betrayals, the world's great illness and despair. They set aside the unutterable grief of humanity's acceptable wars. They held hard to each other to stop themselves from spinning out of control, from losing all they believed, from forgetting all that was, and could be, right with the world. They saw all the old faces flash around them, as Tomas Madorsky, that beautiful, best-loved boy, laughed and laughed with inexplicable joy.

Over the city, and across the whole world, the sun rose red through breaking cloud, pouring across the blood-red river like molten glass, shining like an enduring ideal, ripe for the refashioning.

Whatever Happens On This Hill

If I die here, my work is done,
I was wearied, lay me low,
Where bright flowers woo the sun,
Where the balmy breezes blow.

For I have striven, hard and long,
To fight this world's unequal fight,
Always to resist the wrong,
Always to maintain the right.

Always with a brave, stout heart.
Giving, taking, blow for blow,
Comrades, I have played my part,
If I am wearied, lay me low.

Montague Miller
Eureka Stockade, Ballarat
2nd December, 1854

Addendum for Joseph Hill

But as we live for humankind,
Then Comrades all, let's take this oath:
To strive together, hard and long,
To fight this world's unequal fight –
Resist the things we know are wrong,
And with one purpose make them right.

Author's note

Shoot The Red Flag is a work of fiction. Please don't read it as history – it is not and attempts to do so will only end in great distress for the reader. The liberties taken with dates, events and opinions are an attempt to portray an impressionistic mosaic of voices and happenings from which to garner a feel for the politically turbulent years in Brisbane, capital of the state of Queensland, Australia, during and immediately after the First World War.

Despite my claim that this is not a work of history, the names of some of the characters are identical with those of real historical characters. Where I have taken the liberty of appropriating names I have studied primary sources and attempted, as far as my artistic limitations allow, not to misrepresent the personality of that person in my interpretation of them as a fictional character. As I subscribe to the adage not to speak ill of the dead, I hope I have not caused them to speak ill of themselves nor out of character.

Though the novel is not a history a nodding acquaintance with some historical facts may help the reader situate themselves in the novel's world. After a trip to the front lines in 1916, Australian Prime Minister, William (Billy) Hughes, promised the Allies more Australian soldiers for the war effort. When he returned home he met implacable resistance from his own political party to his idea of forcibly conscripting men to the Australian military services. As a consequence Hughes split the Labor Party and, with his parliamentary backers, formed a new Labor government.

Hughes then held the first of two Conscription referenda – one in 1916; the second in 1917. The first was narrowly defeated, the second defeated by a wider margin. The Conscription campaigns were bitter affairs which invoked class, religious, ethnic and political sectarianism as weapons of propaganda for each side. These referenda nearly tore the young Commonwealth and its Constitution apart. It also gave tacit approval to the scapegoating of various ethnic groups, such as the Russians, by Australians at large and by Queenslanders in particular.

Per capita Queensland had the largest minorities of both Irish-Catholics and Russians in Australia. Both groups were inclined to support: socialism (in one form or another); the Irish Uprising of Easter 1916; the Russian Revolutions of 1917 (especially the Bolshevik October Revolution); anti-Empire activity and; the anti-Conscription campaigns. By 1918 Queensland was known as the "arch-home of everything anti-Empire and anti-Australian".

Great fears of other kinds also abounded. The Russian Revolutions of March and October 1917 shocked the world in a way hard to imagine now. It was a real fear for very many that the whole of Western Europe would fall to Communism as a matter of course.

The Spanish Influenza travelled world-wide with returning soldiers causing the world's first pandemic and millions of deaths. The first Queensland case was registered in June 1919 though the police had been manning quarantine stations at all borders for some time trying to prevent its spread. Numbers of cases and deaths were already published in southern papers.

To top all that, Queensland had a Socialist government at the time and the general body politic of the Left was filled with a plethora of anti-war groups and associations such as the OBU (One Big Union) Propaganda League, the Brisbane Industrial Council (BIC), the Women's Peace Army, the Children's Peace Army, the Industrial Workers of the World (Wobblies), and *The Worker* newspaper among many others.

Queensland had elected the first Socialist government in the world. Revolutionary Artem Segeyev, like many socialists and communists ousted from Russia during the 1905 uprising and Jewish pogrom, travelled to Brisbane in 1911 because he fervently believed world revolution would begin there. He eventually took over and ran the Union of Russian Workers. On his return to Russia he became one of the members of the USSR's founding Comintern beside Lenin, Trotsky and Stalin. He is remembered in Russia as a great organiser of workers especially industrial workers to the Communist cause. He died in an "accident" along with another Australian unionist on an experimental monorail in 1922, just as Stalin's star was rising and accidental deaths of his politically powerful "friends" began in earnest.

Mark Svendsen
Zilzie, 2020

Glossary of Slang Terms

ANZAC – Australian and New Zealand Army Corps. Troops first served at Gallipoli campaign 1915.

Arvo – afternoon

Billy (just off the fire) – a billy is a small metal bucket used to boil water over an open fire. Usually used for making tea

Black devils – informants for the government

Bloke – any male person

Blue/s – a fight or fights

By and by (in the) – the future

Capo – capitalist, Tory

Clinch – an embrace, friendly or otherwise

Clot – a fool, a dill

Cobber – good mate or friend (usually a male)

Cockatoo – a lookout, especially for those engaged in illegal activities

Conchies – conscientious objectors who, for moral or religious reasons, refused to support State sanctioned killing

Coppers – police

Coot – any male person. A leery coot is a man not to be trusted

Dead cert – a complete certainty

Deadset – fair dinkum, on the level, true and truthful

Digger – Australian serviceman so named because of being continually ordered to dig trenches during WWI

Dill – a fool

Donnybrook – an all in brawl

Dopey bastard (you) – a term of endearment applied to a fool

Dosey plod – slow-witted policeman

Drum (the) – the best information or instructions available

Fag – a cigarette

Fair dinkum – without a word of a lie. Or if applied to a person, of truthful values

Fair go – an unimpeded opportunity to do or say something

Fib, fibbed – a lie, to have lied. Usually a "little white lie" of no importance

Flamin' galah – a loud-mouthed fool. The word flaming was often used as a 'polite'"F" word. A galah is a type of parrot with a loud, incessant and aggravating screech

Give 'em curry – heat up or enliven some other person/s through action or words

Gob – the mouth, as in "a smack in the gob" or "gobsmacked". Interchangeable with the word "mug" as in mugshot

Good oil – a well considered opinion usually offered as advice

Gyp (I've got the) – to be upset by someone or something to the point of taking action against it

Half a brick (you coulda knocked me down with) – an ironic expression of surprise. Derived from street gang fights. Meaning: I was so surprised you wouldn't even need to bash my head with the full brick usually required to knock me down in a fight

Hit them for six – a cricketing term meaning to hit the ball out of the ground on the full

Hump (I've got the) – feeling of disenchantment

Jingo or jingoist – supporter of the war

Joker/s – any person or persons. Usually male and usually used in the negative: "Some joker's stolen me bloody hat!"

Keen as mustard – to be very willing. A joke based on a very popular brand of mustard made under the company name *Keen's Mustard*

Lairise – act like hooligans or "lairs". Lairs usually more flash (well-dressed and well spoken) than hooligans

Leg it – run away

Mob – a group of people, often a family. Same word describes a flock of sheep

Mooch (a) – an aimless hanging around. To chill out. Mooching – chilling, hanging as in, 'They were mooching about on the street corner.'

My foot – an expression expressing doubt in the truthfulness of a statement. "I just got back from a quick trip to the moon." "You went to the moon? My foot."

Nancy-boys – homosexuals

Nark – police informant

Or by the divil – Literally "Or by the Devil". An oath sworn in the name of the Devil usually used as a threat meaning the oath-taker will cause the "right thing" to occur

Out West – any isolated rural area inland from the eastern Australian seaboard

Paddy wagon – literally a wagon for holding prisoners, particularly the Irish

Peter (the) – gaol

Porky pie – rhyming slang for a lie

Put in the boot – kick an opponent when they are on the ground

Quids – folding paper money either Australian or British pound or multiple shilling notes

Red-raggers – Socialists or anyone who flew the red flag

Scab – one who crosses a picket line to return to work breaking a Union strike. Therefore a scab's bum is the lowest of the low.

Sheila – a woman

Shirker – one who "shirks" his duty to sign up as a volunteer and go to war

Shoosh – quiet or Quiet!

Six o'clock swill – pub closing time on Sundays was 6pm. Caused a drinking spree similar to, though more desperate than that which happens when last drinks is called

Skarpered – ran away

Skite – to exaggerate one's abilities, deeds or words

Smoko – morning and/or afternoon tea when one can break for a cigarette or "a smoke"

Sook (a) – a cry baby

Squatter (a) – any landowner with a substantial country landholding usually for grazing cattle or sheep

Stoush – a fight

Strike me roan – expression of amazement

The Struggle or the Movement or the Cause – the Socialist movement's struggle to ensure Socialist rule in society

Thousand-yard stare – blank facial expression symptomatic of shell-shock

Thunderbox – small, detached building to house an outdoor toilet

Touch-up – a beating either physical or psychological

Two-bob's worth – had your fair share or your say. Two bob is a two shilling coin which became twenty cents when decimal currency was introduced to Australia

Two up – a game played by tossing two coins into the air and betting on the heads or tails outcome. Very popular in Australia especially on Anzac Day (25th April)

Upped stumps – the person who "ups stumps" has finished a job or left a place, or both. When cricketers leave the field of play, or the game is finished, the "stumps" (cylindrical wooden stakes) are pulled up from the cricket pitch and removed from the field. Hence the expression

Wagging – playing truant from school

Wobblies – members of Industrial Workers of the World (IWW)

Zack (a) – a sixpence

Cast

Joseph *Joe* **Hill** – *President of the Children's Peace Army 1917. Friend of Molly Pearce and Mick Doyle. Socialist and Pacifist. Apprentice French polisher at Jones & Son*

Kathleen O'Donoghue – *Mother of Joe, wife of Ted Hill. Nursing sister and 'practical' Socialist. Keeps her family name as pretense that she is unmarried as married nurses will lose their employment*

Edward *Ted* **Hill** – *Father of Joe Hill. Husband of Kathleen O'Donoghue. Union organiser. Foreman at Jones & Son*

William *Bill* **Carroll** – *Local doctor. Close friend of Hills. Socialist*

Molly Pearce – *Secretary of Children's Peace Army 1917. Girlfriend of Mick Doyle. Socialist. Works in accounts office Jones & Son*

Patrick *Mick* **Doyle** – *Member of Children's Peace Army. Boyfriend of Molly Pearce. Friend of Joe Hill. Socialist. Wharf labourer*

Artem Segeyev – *Russian Bolshevik. President: Union Russian Workers 1917*

O'Hagen, *Sergeant* – *Local copper. Socialist tendencies but tries to be as impartial as possible*

Irina Babushka Davidovna Kerenskaya – *Russian boarding house owner. Widow. Humanist. Grandmother to Tomfool and all strays. Friend to Nikolai Droshky*

Nikolai *Old Nik* **Droshky** – *Cab driver. Russian widower. Old Believer. Socialist. Ex-schoolmaster. Friend to Babushka*

Harold *Harry* **Winterson** – *Wounded returned serviceman. Police informant*

Madorsky – *Member: Union of Russian Workers. Enforcer. Machine operator Jones & Son. Enforcer.*

Orlov – *Russian Bolshevik. President: Union of Russian Workers 1919*

Zuzenko – *Member: Union of Russian Workers. Enforcer.*